ANNE TIBBETS

SCREAMS FROM THE VOID

This is a **FLAME TREE PRESS** book

Text copyright © 2021 Anne Tibbets

FLAME TREE PRESS
6 Melbray Mews, London, SW6 3NS, UK
flametreepress.com

US sales, distribution and warehouse:
Simon & Schuster
simonandschuster.biz

UK distribution and warehouse:
Marston Book Services Ltd
marston.co.uk

Thanks to the Flame Tree Press team, including:
Taylor Bentley, Frances Bodiam, Federica Ciaravella, Don D'Auria,
Chris Herbert, Josie Karani, Molly Rosevear, Will Rough, Mike Spender,
Cat Taylor, Maria Tissot, Nick Wells, Gillian Whitaker.

The cover is created by Flame Tree Studio with
thanks to Nik Keevil and Shutterstock.com.
The font families used are Avenir and Bembo.

Flame Tree Press is an imprint of Flame Tree Publishing Ltd

flametreepublishing.com

A copy of the CIP data for this book is available from the British Library
and the Library of Congress.

3 5 7 9 8 6 4 2

HB ISBN: 978-1-78758-573-7
US PB ISBN: 978-1-78758-571-3
UK PB ISBN: 978-1-78758-572-0
ebook ISBN: 978-1-78758-574-4

Printed and bound in USA by Integrated Books International

ANNE TIBBETS

SCREAMS FROM THE VOID

FLAME TREE PRESS
London & New York

CHAPTER ONE

United Space Corps Vessel *Demeter*
30.8.2231 AD
0900 hours

Ensign Kris Cunningham blinks at the screen on the flight deck not once, but twice.

It's too ludicrous to be true. But there it is, a blip on the monitor as bright as a comet, and coming straight at them.

"Captain?" Kris forces her eyelids closed, then reopens them.

Still there.

Fuck.

The captain leans back in his command chair and stretches. His hands graze the ceiling of the battered flight deck. Kris suppresses a sigh. He must have fallen asleep again. He does that. Especially when the botany team is on a planet's surface and they're left in orbit, waiting for hours. "What?" the captain mumbles, smacking his lips.

"There's a foreign mass approaching, sir," Kris says.

"Hmm." He sits up in his chair and takes his feet off the dash. His boots hit the floor with a clunk. "What's the trajectory?"

Kris can hear the annoyance in his voice and hesitates. He's referring to the asteroids that circulate through this sector. He's probably just as sick of them as are the rest of the crew. Normally they'd power up the lasers and blast the asteroid out of existence before it even gets close, but this is something else.

Something worse.

Kris blinks at the monitor again and considers how best to correct him. She looks to the pilot, who sits on the captain's right, as if she can provide silent guidance.

She doesn't.

No surprise there.

Instead, the pilot readies the controls for the lasers with a flick of three overhead switches. They snap like bones and glow blood red. "Ready," the pilot says, cracking her neck by contorting it to one side and rolling her shoulders.

Kris shifts at her console.

"What are the coordinates?" the pilot asks, and Kris's frown deepens.

Uncertainty silences her. The familiar buzz of the laser controls resonates in her ears, and for lack of anything better to do she checks the monitor again. Maybe she read the alert incorrectly.

Nope. Still blipping.

The little fucker.

"Come on, Ensign, where is it?" the captain barks. "We're waiting!"

"The g-grille panel, sir." Kris's eyes dart over her shoulder, indicating the grilles that serve as ventilation between decks.

The captain turns toward her, disbelief on his face. His mustache twitches. "Come again?"

Kris clears her throat. She'd give anything not to be the one sitting at the navigations station. A kidney. A toe. Maybe even an eye. If she screws up again, she'll be on kitchen duty for the rest of the mission and that's not why she's here. She has big plans for her career in the United Space Corps and she doesn't want it to be over before it's even begun. "It's one hundred meters away and closing, sir," she finally says.

The pilot scoffs. "Are you serious?"

"Yes, ma'am. No joke."

"From *inside* the ship?" the captain clarifies.

Kris nods. "Yes, sir."

"What's the classification?" The captain turns to the monitor on his left so Kris can screen-share the data. He rubs his sleeve on the display to remove the dust. "Do we have visual? Come on, Ensign, don't just sit there."

Kris fights her growing anxiety and sends the data to the captain's screen, and then to the pilot's, just to be on the safe side. She's got to be reading it wrong, surely. She's missing something. She's sure of it. Maybe they can make sense of what it is, because it certainly doesn't make sense to her.

"Goddamnit." The captain squints at his monitor. "What the hell is that?"

"Can't get a visual. There aren't any cameras in the shafts," the pilot says quickly.

"It's classified as a 'foreign biological'," Kris reads, her stomach rolling over.

This is bad news, no matter what. Foreign biologicals carry toxins, viruses, and various dangers currently unknown and uncured by man. It's happened to other vessels in the Corps – wiped clean by some alien bug. And now, it's happening to them. Even if they catch whatever the biological is, the damage could already be done.

Kris envisions weeks of quarantine and medicated showers, correspondence home to worried loved ones and the embarrassment of the debriefing at headquarters, plus the impending headlines on Earth announcing their failure to take the necessary precautions – this is, if they survive.

She shudders. A thin layer of sweat bleeds through her sun-deprived skin and she fights the rise of bile in the back of her throat.

They're so fucked.

"Could it be a glitch?" the pilot asks, pulling Kris back to reality. "Maybe the internal sensors are malfunctioning?"

There's an idea. "Should I call maintenance?" she offers, but the captain shakes his head.

"I doubt it's a glitch. How far away is it?"

She checks the monitor and blinks. Whatever it is, it's really booking. "Fifty meters, sir." Kris sends an updated readout to both their screens.

"I don't get it." The pilot shakes her head at her monitor.

Kris's tongue thickens. "It appears there's something crawling up the ventilation shaft."

"No *shit*." The pilot unlatches her restraints. "What I meant was, I don't get how it got on the ship to begin with. We're in orbit."

"Right now I'm more concerned with what the hell it is," the captain says.

Kris forces her eyes back to the nav monitor. "Unidentified, sir." She wipes droplets of sweat from her forehead. It leaves a greasy smudge on the sleeve of her uniform.

Great.

"It's not in any of the databases?" the captain challenges her.

Kris shakes her head, checking again for the third time. "No, sir. It just says 'unknown'."

The captain slams his fist against his console. "Then how the hell are we supposed to know what to do with it?"

Swinging her leg over the joystick, the pilot labors out of her chair. She steps into the small space behind her station and looms over the access shaft, tapping the ladder with the tip of her boot. "I don't see anything."

"The grille, ma'am," Kris corrects her. "On your left."

The pilot gives her a glare that could skin a cat, then bends to her knees and wraps her fingers around the metal grate to the left of the shaft, giving it a tug. "Screwed in," she grunts.

The captain fumbles around his console and hands the pilot a screwdriver. She places it directly over the first screw, flicks the switch and lets the magnets do their job.

"Hurry up," the captain grumbles at her. "And let's hope the damned thing is docile."

"That's more than likely," the pilot sighs. "An aggressive species would have attacked by now or made itself known sooner. My guess is we picked it up on Gliese 163c."

"What makes you say that?"

The pilot shrugs at the captain. "Most advanced ecosystem we've encountered this whole trip. Wouldn't surprise me if we missed biologicals. It seemed odd to me we didn't see any to begin with."

"That was two planets ago!" the captain says.

"Twenty-five meters, and closing," Kris says. She wipes more sweat onto her sleeve. "Should I alert the crew?"

"No." The captain unlatches his restraints and stands to assist the pilot.

"Let's not cause a panic while the team is away. Not until we figure out what it is."

The pilot places the first loose screw into the pocket of her flight suit. "I still don't see how it could have gotten aboard, though. We were so careful."

The captain runs his hands through his hair. "Maybe while we loaded the specimens, it snuck on? Although, I'm not sure how that could've happened given that the airlock is so small. This is insane. Where's Sorrel when you need him?"

"Want me to call him up?" Kris suggests. It makes sense to ask the payload supervisor to come. Maybe he has an idea what to do with it. Besides, that will bring one more senior officer to the flight deck, and then Kris will get dismissed – she hopes.

The captain nods. "Yeah. Call him."

With relief, Kris presses her finger to the ship's intercom control on the dash of the navigations console. The button jams. She wiggles it with her thumb and it finally catches. "Sorrel, report to the flight deck, please." She adds that last word by accident and cringes when the captain raises an eyebrow at her.

The pilot drops the second screw onto the floor and bends over to retrieve it. "Son of a bitch."

"Would you quit clowning around and hurry up?" the captain barks at her.

"I'm trying!"

The captain turns his attention to Kris. "Did we miss any documented biologicals on Gliese 163c?"

She types on her monitor, pulling up the information. "No biologicals listed except for plant life, sir."

"You know, maybe it wasn't Gliese," the pilot points out. "It could have been on any number of the planets, and just been lurking about the ship all this time."

"There's a comforting thought," Kris says.

The intercom squeals to life. Sorrel's craggy voice sounds from the dented speakers above Kris's station. "I just started eating. What's up?"

The captain reaches over Kris's shoulder and presses the intercom button. "Just get your ass up here."

"Yes, sir," Sorrel responds, sounding dejected.

"If this is a previously undocumented species, Captain," the pilot says, full of excitement, "we'll make the Universal News Feed."

"Save your celebration for after we have it contained," he grumbles.

Kris agrees. Another blip on the nav monitor catches her attention. "Ten meters."

The pilot has the last screw out and pockets it. She pulls the heavy iron grate up and quickly hands it to the captain. Getting on her hands and knees, she peers down into the shaft. "I need a torch," she says.

The captain hands her the flashlight from his utility belt. "See anything?"

"I think so. It looks…furry."

"Careful," the captain says. "Could be aggressive."

"Oh man." Kris reaches across her console to raise the alert level to yellow. She does so without asking for the captain's approval, but he doesn't seem to notice. He's looking over the pilot's shoulder into the shaft. The vent grate rests on his hip.

"What are we going to do with it once it gets here?" Kris hates the fear in her voice. She unlatches her restraints so she can move about the flight deck, hoping to find some sort of weapon, but damned if all the laser rifles aren't locked in the armory two decks down.

"Let's herd it to the airlock and release it out the bay doors," the captain says.

"That's assuming it wants to be herded." Kris wrenches the fire extinguisher off the wall.

"You're just going to release it into outer space?" The pilot peers down the shaft and then back up to the captain. "Better if we kill it. Then we can take fluids, tissue samples, and a detailed scan afterwards."

"I say we use the bay doors," the captain says. "Better it emits whatever toxins it's carrying out into space than in here. If it's not too late already." As if Kris hadn't just said it a moment ago, he asks, "What the hell are we going to do with it? Is there anything in here we could restrain it with?"

"We could push it back down the grate," Kris suggests. "Force it onto the other floors. If it gets loose in here with the controls, the whole ship could be floating dead in space by the time we catch it."

The captain scans the flight deck for something useful. "Good point."

Kris barely has time to register the compliment before the pilot shrieks, "There it is!"

"How big is it?" The others ignore Kris's question as they peer down into the shaft.

"What class is that?" the captain asks. He shifts the metal grate on his hip.

"Looks like a mammal," the pilot says. "The fur is silver. Four legs, maybe six. Two eyes. No, four. Two on each side of its head. It's about as big as a dog. Look at the size of that mouth! Hold on, it's stopped."

"Good. It's probably scared." The captain relaxes his posture. "Ensign, call Sorrel again and see if he can't bring some sort of container we can keep it in."

Kris nods and backs up toward her console, too petrified to speak.

The pilot leans away from the shaft. "Get ready. It's moving again." She holds the flashlight in her hands like a club.

In a flash of gray fur the creature erupts from the shaft and lands on the flight deck floor, on all six of its muscular, hairy legs.

Kris stifles a scream and backs up into the navigations console as far as she can, pressing her spine against the controls.

The creature's four unblinking eyes scan the flight deck and the officers, allowing them time to watch the animal. The pilot's description is accurate.

It has six padded paws and a large mouth. Its bulbous head and slender body sit motionless atop the vent shaft as it watches them. It's not tall, and only comes up to just under the captain's knees.

There's a ripple across the beast's shaggy fur as if the animal has a chill, and the hair changes color to match the flight deck controls in one fluid motion. With the creature's coat matching the environment so closely, it becomes virtually invisible.

"Holy fuck," Kris whispers.

"Don't move," the captain says softly, and his voice causes the beast's eyes to turn toward him. He labors to quietly lift the vent grate up off his hip. "Maybe we can knock it out?"

In an instant, the creature lowers itself close to the floor, and then windlessly lifts into the air. Before anyone can move, it launches at the captain's chest, legs extended.

"What the—" he starts to say. Dropping the grate in his hands with a clatter, the captain yelps and attempts to step aside, but he's too slow.

Massive talons the size of scissor blades emerge from the creature's paws mid-flight and pierce straight into the captain's torso, cascading a mist of blood in all directions. Shock and pain cross the captain's face as his skin fades to ashen white. The beast opens its colossal mouth and clamps its jaws onto the captain's throat. With a sharp twist it rips the flesh wide open, splattering the pilot and Kris with a wave of bloody meat.

The pilot screams.

Kris releases the safety on the fire extinguisher and fires once, but the foam doesn't slow the creature in the slightest.

The captain's eyes roll back into his head. His body collapses backward onto the main controls and he splays out, slapping numerous controls when he lands. The dash blazes alive with warning lights.

With both arms at full swing, Kris heaves the extinguisher, thrashing the creature off the captain's limp body. Both it and the extinguisher crash into the pilot's chair.

In the meantime, the pilot makes a mad dash for the ladder.

Kris watches with mounting horror as the creature recovers from the extinguisher's blow. It twists around as if it had never been struck at all. Maneuvering without a whisper, it spins and leaps back into the air. Claws extended, it pounces on the pilot's back with a growl.

She's three rungs down when the beast plunges its talons into her back. Barbs as strong as vises shred her body to ribbons, pressing and slicing into her flesh like hot steel.

Kris shrieks.

The creature reaches through the pilot's spinal cord and pulls back her beating heart. Blood and tissue spew across the entire flight deck and controls, burning Kris's face like acid rain. With her back pressed firmly against the navigations console, and nowhere to run, Kris can do nothing but scream. "No! Oh god! *No!*"

The creature drops the pilot's shredded body, then turns to face her. For a brief moment, it considers her, turning its head from side to side as if waiting for something. It's all Kris can do not to die from fear.

Just as she feels the slightest hope that it will turn away, the animal bounds forward with a silent leap, separating her head from her sweat-covered body with one slice of its front razor-like hooks.

CHAPTER TWO

Planet Gliese 581g
30.8.2231 AD
0915 hours

Technical Sergeant Pollux stares at the crevasse and mentally calculates her odds.

Not bad. But not great either.

Seems close enough, but she's low on oxygen and if she gets too excited she runs the risk of using too much, and there's nothing worse, in her mind, than breathing her own backwash. Besides which, with the gravity-assist boots she's not sure she's buoyant enough to clear it.

Corporal Gayla has gone the long way, taking the winding path down the side of the mound, and holding a specimen sample in front of her like it's radioactive. Science Ensign Avram is nipping at her heels. Their oxygen tanks bob on their backs, pushing them closer to the plateau where they've parked the freight pod.

Pollux scans the fading horizon. The orange light from this system's sun is almost gone. This particular planet's axis isn't symmetrical and whiplashes like a slingshot. They have a good hour before they're swallowed by darkness but for some reason Pollux feels anxious to get back to the ship, and the path seems like such a pussy move.

If she clears the ravine, she could beat them to the freighter and still have time enough to start the engines. It might save them a whole ten minutes.

Less backwash.

"Sarge," Ensign Avram speaks over the com. "Tell me something. Are you feeling lucky, punk?"

Pollux turns her body away from the ravine. "Excuse me?"

Avram's stopped on the path and has craned his body to watch her. "It's a line from…you've never heard it? Never mind. Sorry, ma'am."

She glares back at him but doubts he can see her expression. The helmet's visual field is only three-quarters and he's barely in her line of sight.

She hears her breath increase before she feels it. The sound echoes off the inside of her helmet and reverberates in her ears. Jump or not, she's burning through too much oxygen either way.

"Pollux? See something we missed, eh?" It's Gayla.

"No," she answers, still debating.

There's no way they missed anything on this rock. They've spent the last week exploring what the Planetary Commission has deemed a possibly habitable planet, but the oxygen levels are too low to sustain human life, and the plants on the surface confirm that. They're small, low-level organisms. Mostly bacteria and a few patches of algae. But no greenery, and that limits the atmospheric oxygen.

The planet needs more time to evolve – another hundred thousand years, at least. The Commission won't be happy with this but that's not Pollux's problem. She just wants off this rock.

She scratches the inside of her elbow but can't quite reach the itch underneath the confines of her suit. Frustrated, she eyes the ravine again.

What is that? A meter? Two?

She taps the suit's processor on her arm, trying to calculate the distance, but as usual, it's off-line.

Piece of shit.

"Pollux?" It's Gayla again. The worrywart.

"I'm fine!"

"What are you doing?"

Pollux takes a few steps back, hoping to gain some momentum. Step one, two….

Jump!

Bending her knees, she pushes forward and feels her boots lift off the ground.

"My processor is online, gimme a minute, eh?" Gayla says over the com.

"Sarge!" Avram bellows.

Too late. Pollux is in flight.

She's halfway across the ravine before she realizes she's going to come up short. Reaching out her hands, she grasps thin air. There are no roots to grip. No branches. Nothing but rock, and the other side of the ravine is at least two arm lengths away.

She feels her boots heat as they recalibrate on her way down, trying to cushion her fall. They don't finish in time. A wall of rock zips by her visual field. Red warning lights flash on her com. She tries to slow her descent, spiraling her arms, but it's useless. She knows the ground is coming but can't gauge the distance.

She bends her knees and hits solid rock. Trying to roll out of the fall, she feels rather than hears a control panel on her hip crunch as she rotates onto her side and tumbles a few meters.

Better the control panel than her pelvis, she guesses.

Still….

"Ouch."

"Inconceivable!" Avram shouts.

"Oh my god. Pollux, are you okay?" Gayla sounds like she's crying.

Lying in a pile of rubble, Pollux stares straight into the orange sky, but she still manages to roll her eyes. "That sucked."

Gayla appears in Pollux's visual field. "Is anything broken?"

Pollux shakes her head and feels it swimming. Something's wrong. The orange sky has gone blurry, and she can't make out Gayla's freckled face anymore. Plus, the itch from her elbow has spread down to her fingertips and she's sweating from head to toe. Dribbles of perspiration cascade down her face. It's salty and stings her lips. "Too hot," she says. It feels like her head has grown a mile wide and her temples press against the sides of her helmet. "Too…hot…."

The orange fades. Is it whiplash already? Too early for that.

Blackness takes its place.

★　　★　　★

When she comes to, she hears more than sees what's happening.

She's being dragged. Someone is doing a piss-poor job of carrying her feet. Someone else with boney fingers drags her from under her arms.

Pollux tries to swat their hands away. She'll be damned if she's carried anywhere. She's the chief science officer! Who the hell do they think—?

★ ★ ★

Her eyes flutter open.

She's inside the freighter.

Someone shouts.

She wants to shush them. Every syllable makes her head grow a meter wider. It's pressing on the inside of her helmet like a goiter.

Why aren't they moving?

What is she doing on the floor?

Her mouth isn't working.

God, the itch. Her arm is on fire.

She shoves her hands on the floor, attempts to sit up. Someone pushes her down. If she ever finds out who that motherfucker is she's going to bash their head in.

She hears the docking sequence sensors ring in her ear. The computer, for some reason, has its emergency protocols in play and they're burning up as they exit the planet's atmosphere. They must be.

It's so fucking hot.

★ ★ ★

Demeter
30.8.2231 AD
0930 hours

The circuit boards of the control panel dangle from red wires like corpses on the gallows. If there were a breeze, they would waft from side to side, but since the greenhouse has the stagnant air of a sauna, the circuits only hang, suffocating. All Mechanics Ensign Raina can do is tuck a tuft of wayward hair behind her ear, wipe the sweat from her palm onto the pants of her uniform, and rebuild the lifeless boards, piece by piece.

Above, her boss looms, which is difficult for him to pull off since he's only five and a half feet tall. Still, he's a good half-foot taller than she is, so he manages. Sergeant Osric's beaded upper lip purses as he judges her every breath. "Why are you so fucking slow?"

Raina doesn't answer. Truthfully, no matter what she says, it'll only set him off. It takes great effort to swallow her reply. She concentrates on the control panel and fixes a short, but the warning lights above flash yellow and draw her attention. Again. She can't help it and opens her mouth. "Why are we on yellow alert?"

Osric snaps his fingers in her face. "Focus, will you?"

She bites the inside of her cheek to keep from saying something rude. "I just thought maybe we should find out why we're on yellow alert?"

"Why?" he asks. "So the captain can pontificate for an hour about asteroid field safety? Fuck that. Just do your job. Wait, hold on a second. What are you doing there?"

Her hands float in position over the pieces of control panel. One look at Osric's face and she knows what's coming.

Good god, here we go again. Meltdown in three, two....

"Did you just—?" In a fit of disgust, he grips his bald head with both his palms and runs them across his scalp, scrunching his skin like rolls of leather. "That's not a regulation repair. Again! What the hell are you *thinking*?"

She follows his gaze back to her handiwork. Almost immediately she realizes her mistake.

She'd been 'thinking' that the current control panel in the greenhouse is an antiquated pile of shit, and that this new design, *her* design, is far superior. Like most of the electronics aboard the *Demeter,* the panel needs an upgrade. But given that she's only a first-year ensign, nothing more than a trainee, and on her very first mission with the Corps, she doesn't have much of a leg to stand on. She realizes her mistake is not in making the upgrade, but in not proposing it to Osric for his approval first, thus, making the decision his.

Stupid. Should have known better.

She grimaces but forces herself to reply. "If we bypass the safety protocol we can raise the greenhouse humidity level." She tries to keep her tone even as she watches Osric's face for a sign of comprehension. There isn't any. "Tech Sergeant Pollux wants to raise the humidity to ninety per cent but the current protocols won't go that high." She opens her mouth to continue but thinks better of it. Instead, she tucks another strand of hair behind her ear and waits for the inevitable.

Osric doesn't disappoint. He curses under his breath and kicks the greenhouse wall. His boots leave a scuff on the wall panel. "It isn't up to *you*," he begins, turning his customary shade of purple, "a fucking mechanics *ensign,* and a piss-poor Academy flunky besides, to decide what percentage of humidity is necessary in the greenhouse."

"But Pollux said—"

"Did she *ask* for the humidity to be raised to ninety per cent? Did she put in a work order?"

Raina sighs deeply and regrets it. The humidity has given Osric an even more pungent stench. Some cross between body odor, sweat, and rocket fuel. It leaves a rancid taste in her mouth. "No, she asked, but didn't put in a work order," she admits.

"No, what?"

Raina inhales slowly to still her surging frustration. "No, *sir.*"

Typical Osric – serving up ridicule with a side of humiliation.

She looks away, unable to tolerate his expression any moment longer. Out of the corner of her eye she sees him smirk and her annoyance pulses. She'd like nothing better than to tell him to fuck off, but he's still her superior, and the last thing she needs is another mark against her already poor military record. No matter how much she despises him, she just has to shut up and take it – even if he is the second worst human being in the universe.

It's a sad twist of fate that the first worst human in the universe is also aboard the *Demeter*. But she'd rather not think about him just now.

"Then don't touch the humidity level," Osric sighs, tossing his arms out for effect. "Safety protocols are installed for a *reason*. Now, reconfigure this back the way it was. I swear, when we're back on Earth, I hope I never have to lay eyes on your sorry-ass mug again."

"Yes, *sir*," Raina snaps. The feeling is mutual.

"Hurry up," he says, leaning against the wall beside the panel and folding his doughy arms across his chest. "They're almost back."

She doesn't respond. Instead, she clenches her teeth and sets about undoing an hour's worth of work, cutting wires, stripping off the connector caps, and adjusting her position on the floor. Her legs have gone stiff.

Two weeks, she reminds herself. *One year and eleven-and-a half months down. Two weeks left.*

It takes an effort not to yank the wires out of the wall in irritation, but despite her best efforts her eyes go back to the flashing yellow alert above. She'd almost forgotten.

Shouldn't they call the captain and find out what's wrong? Why hasn't there been an announcement over the ship's intercom?

It pains her to admit it, but Osric is right about one thing – it's not her job to worry about it. She sets back to work, listening to Osric's raspy breaths over her shoulder. She wishes she could slap a strip of duct tape over his mouth. Either that or drill holes in his nose so he would actually breathe through it.

Her hands shake and she clenches them into fists. Forcing herself to pay attention, she blocks out Osric's heavy breathing and loses herself in the control panel reconfiguration. There's a certain comfort forgetting all else and only seeing wires. They don't talk back. They don't do anything other than what they're supposed to do. As she focuses, the yellow alert slips from her mind.

"Team ascending," a voice reverberates over the intercom.

Raina snaps her head back, yanked from the caverns of her mind.

"Mechanics to airlock, stat!" the speaker squeals. It's Corporal Gayla. She sounds rushed for some reason.

"See?" Osric yaps, pointing his finger at Raina's face. "I swear, it's like you enjoy failure. Now, get your ass to the space prep chamber and prepare the airlock."

"I know," Raina sighs.

A sneer crawls across his lips. It's almost like he enjoys it when she dishes it back. "Watch your tone, *Ensign*. I'll write you up for insubordination," he warns her. "Again."

She shakes her head.

"Don't give me that look," he adds. "I've had it up to here with you. I really have. I've seen your kind before – spineless whiners that get off on playing the helpless victim. 'Oh, poor me, I'm abused. Give me a promotion.' *Bullshit*. If you didn't like getting slapped around, you wouldn't have put up with it. I'm only giving you what you want, so don't you scowl at me. I see you for what you really are."

She swallows her rage. He doesn't know what the hell he's talking about, but she can't correct him. It's enough to give her goose bumps in a hundred degrees. "Yes, *sir*." Getting up from her position on the floor, it's all she can do not to shove a pair of wire cutters down his throat.

"Aren't you forgetting something?" he asks, pointing at the unfinished control panel, still dangling in pieces.

She squints at him, speaking through clenched teeth. "You just told me to get up to space prep. Would you have me leave the payload team in the airlock?"

He frowns.

She's right.

"Go away," he says. "I'll clean up your mess, like always."

She gathers up her tools and exits the greenhouse.

Motherfucking jerk.

Two. Weeks. Left.

Then she'll never have to listen to that pint-size Napoleon again, or any of the other assholes on this ship.

CHAPTER THREE

Demeter
30.8.2231 AD
0935 hours

Outside the greenhouse, in the dim hallway of lower deck, away from Osric's stench and the oppressive humidity, Raina waits for the door to seal closed, then releases the death grip in her right hand.

No sense in strangling her screwdriver. It's not its fault Osric is such a jackass.

She takes a deep breath and lets it out her mouth, then latches the screwdriver into her tool belt.

It'd be one thing if he was right about her, but he's not. Not completely. Maybe she did play the victim, but it's not in the way he thinks.

Osric's been on her ass from the moment she came aboard, letting loose his bile. It was mild, at first. A comment here, a snide remark there. But now, after everything came out about her, he's worse and worse the closer they get to the end of the mission, like some sick and twisted time bomb, revving up to explode the moment they reach port.

A part of her wonders if he isn't dreading the return home, but that sure as hell isn't her problem. She only wishes he wasn't so bent on making her suffer.

It was easy to brush it off at first, but now…?

Halfway up the access ladder, which leads to mid-deck, her eyes catch on the overhead alert light, still flashing yellow.

And still no intercom from the captain?

Odd.

She climbs.

She hops off the metal ladder onto mid-deck and climbs the next one, up to upper deck.

With every step farther away from Osric, she feels her blood pressure lessening. There's no point in losing her cool over him. She knows this. She just has to buckle down, keep her trap shut, and it'll soon be over.

Down upper deck hallway, she eyes the grated ceiling, checking the long metallic tubes for the electrical circuits, plumbing pipes, and communication wires. She takes a mental inventory. Each one gets visually inspected as she moves down the hall.

It all looks fine. A little dusty, dented, rusty in spots and dated, but functional. Still, it's abnormally warm on upper deck. The ventilation grates along the ceiling might not be blowing enough air. She reaches up and tries to feel the cool breeze. There isn't one. She'll have to check that later.

When she reaches the spacewalk preparation chamber, she opens the thick sliding doors and locks them in place. Then she activates the pressurization gauge from the work console and heads back across the hallway to the airlock.

Ensign Tamsin arrives, smiling widely. "We really must stop meeting like this," she jokes.

Raina grins in return but isn't up for their usual playful banter. Something about Osric's rant today got under her skin.

Maybe it's just the heat.

Raina's thankful when Tamsin gets busy and doesn't push her. Tam sits at a console and starts the process of downloading the camera feeds and sensory readings from the space suit's computers, but Raina catches her watching out of the corner of her eye.

"What? No Osric today?" Tamsin asks.

"Nope, just me."

Tamsin winks, then sets back to typing. "Well, isn't that refreshing? Let's handle this without the usual drama. Shall we?"

"Amen to that," she agrees and watches Tamsin work.

Tam's usual beaming smile mutes behind a thin mouth as she concentrates. She's wearing her altered uniform, the one with the sparkly belt and a multitude of glittery bead necklaces around her neck. Tam has her long stick-straight blond hair knotted on the top of her head, held up with an alligator clip.

Raina resists the urge to reach over and mess her hair. She's a good kid, although she seems too much of a free spirit for the Space Corps. But maybe that's just her age. At eighteen she's the youngest of the ensigns, compared to the others, who are all in their early twenties. All except Raina, that is, who's the old lady at twenty-seven.

Still, for someone so young, Tamsin's wicked smart. She's got a photographic memory, is a freakishly quick study, got accepted to the Academy two years early and graduated after only two cycles, which is more than Raina can say. It took her seven.

With a click of a button, Tamsin activates the airlock. "Ta-da!"

Raina smirks and makes her way to the doors, feeling a rush of adrenaline. This is always interesting. There hasn't been a single walk that hasn't resulted in a mechanics malfunction of some kind.

The first happened only three months into the mission. On descent, the freighter pod got stuck to the airlock with the walkers inside, and Osric and Raina had to suit up and manually release it from the ship's exterior. It'd been Raina's first spacewalk. Osric managed to blame her in the official report, claiming she hadn't properly inspected the freight pod before departure, which was an all-out lie. Osric had done the inspection himself and missed a bent docking clamp.

But she knows the crew is well aware she was the one that fixed it. In fact, a few weeks after that, when the pod door got jammed re-attaching to the airlock, the crew didn't even bother calling Osric. They sent for her.

It amazes her how Osric has advanced as far as he has within the Corps, being as useless and abrasive as he is. But if the last two years are any indication, she's sure he's done it on the backs of his ensigns.

Lazy, sexist jackass.

She'd love to tell him just what she thinks of him, but it'll end her career faster than a shorted circuit breaker box. She'd considered going up the chain of command about him, but after everything else, she gave up the idea. Maybe on her last day she'll tell Osric what a dim-witted dumbass he is. He certainly has it coming. The thought makes her smile.

She shakes her head and listens as the airlock rises up the chamber. It churns along at a snail's pace. So far, so good.

Tamsin hums to herself and types away at her console, then hits the release with a click.

The airlock gears labor and crank to a stop. It's loud and grinding but operating as it should. Raina steps forward and uses the control panel on the wall and starts depressurization. It takes a full sixty seconds.

Tamsin sighs. "I miss cheese."

Raina turns from the airlock doors. "What?"

Tam twists her head to one side. "I think the thing I miss most about Earth is the cheese. When I get home, I'm eating the largest block of Gouda I can get. What about you? What do you miss most about home?"

She thinks a moment, her eyes going back to the airlock controls. "My family, I suppose. I have nine brothers and sisters, so I guess I miss them."

"You guess?" Tamsin giggles. "You never told me you had nine siblings."

"I have over twenty cousins, too."

"Sheesh." Tamsin gapes. "Sounds crowded. I think if I were you, I'd run away to a desert island."

"Why do you think I joined the Space Corps?" Raina smirks.

Tamsin purses her lips and nods. "Point taken."

The depressurization is complete. Raina hits the control panel again and the two sliding doors slowly hiss, then crank open. They get stuck once, but Raina kicks them, and they keep going.

Inside, she can make out the three walkers in their tan-colored suits. Each wears a head-to-toe encasement, complete with an oxygen tank, gravity-assist boots, and a large round helmet. Raina smiles at them and is about to welcome them back when she notices Sergeant Pollux's face. Inside her helmet, her eyes roll back. She's not smiling. She looks like she's about to pass out.

The second the door is completely open, Pollux pitches forward.

Raina catches her, but crumples under the weight. They both crash to the hallway floor.

Still inside the airlock, Corporal Gayla and Ensign Avram shout over the top of each other.

"Help her!" Gayla bellows, her light eyes wide. "Get her open!"

"Get her open!" yells Avram. "Now!"

"What happened?" Tamsin hollers, then uses the intercom to call a medical officer.

Raina slides out from under Pollux's suit and rolls her over. One check of the suit's controls at Pollux's hip and she can spot the issue.

"She jumped off a boulder and ever since then she's been complaining about the heat and passing out," Gayla shouts. She tries to step out of the airlock, but Raina has Pollux on the floor just outside the doors, and there's no room to get around.

Raina whips out her screwdriver and pops off a control casing, loosens the screw holding the power wire, rips a new copper lead from her tool belt, and switches them out. She then reroutes the power from the planetary gravity-assist controls to the temperature gauge.

Raina straddles Pollux's body to gain a better view of her face as she waits for the body temperature gauge to reboot.

"Hey," she says, tapping on the helmet. "Can you hear me?"

Inside the suit, Pollux sweats profusely, fogging the helmet's glass. She's breathing heavily and whispers something about itching and backwash. Raina can barely hear what she says.

"Medical officer to the space prep room – stat!" Tamsin shouts over the intercom again.

Heavy boots pound down the hallway from behind Raina. She looks over her shoulder and sees Airman First Class Valda approaching.

"Más vale que sea bueno. Report, Ensign," he says to Raina.

"She's overheating, sir," she says. "Just give the suit a minute, the temp gauge has to recalibrate."

"What are her vitals?" he demands, standing over them. "Crack her open."

"She hasn't been switched to proper oxygenation," Raina says.

"Then do it fast!" he orders, muttering something to himself in Spanish. "Where the hell is Osric?"

"I'm sure he's hiding under a bridge and scaring small children for sport," Avram quips from inside the airlock, but everyone ignores him. "Wow. Tough crowd."

Raina grabs Valda's hands and shoves them down onto Pollux's shoulders. "Here, watch her. I'll get the oxygen."

"Watch her? ¿Qué demonios?" He bends over Pollux.

She scrambles to her feet, skirts around Pollux and Valda, lightly shoves Tamsin out of the way, and snatches a pair of oxygen tanks from the locker. She drags them back and flicks the valve open.

With the oxygen on, Raina rolls the dial on the tank to the proper levels and attaches it to the coupling on Pollux's suit. Moving on, she hooks Gayla to the other tank.

Avram throws up his hands. "Hey! What am I, chopped liver?"

"She's coming around," Valda says. "Pollux, can you hear me?" He taps on the glass of her helmet and she slowly nods. "Ensign," he says to Raina. "Now?"

Raina checks Pollux's temperature gauge and the oxygenation levels – back to normal. "Crack it."

Valda grips either side of her helmet. With a sharp twist he snaps it loose and pulls it away. Pollux gasps for air.

Once the helmet is off, Raina approaches Pollux, rips out the temporary wire in the temp gauge, and runs it back to the planetary gravity-assist controls.

As Valda shines a light in Pollux's eyes and asks her to recite the alphabet for him, Pollux's suit powers down.

Without pausing, Raina turns to Gayla, checks her oxygenation levels, then clears her for helmet removal as well. Gayla pops off her helmet and shakes her bobbed hair loose, just as Raina starts the process of removing the oxygen tank from Gayla and attaching it to Avram.

"Last but not least," he muses.

"What a disaster, eh?" Gayla says, peeling off the space suit a bit at a time. She drops a glove to the airlock floor.

Avram twists off his helmet and blows out a lungful of recycled air. "This is what you get for showing off, Pollux. Wouldn't you say?"

Pollux moans something from the floor and then lifts the middle finger of her gloved hand in Avram's direction.

He smiles brightly then drops his helmet. He bites the fingertips of his gloves and yanks them off next. "Well, that was fun. For your next trick let's go into oxygen shock."

Gayla giggles, fussing with her hair again. "No kidding, eh?"

"I'm taking Pollux to the sleep chamber for examination," Valda says, removing Pollux's spacesuit a piece at a time so all that's left are her boots and sweaty uniform. "Despasito."

Pollux manages to get to her feet, and she and Valda amble down the hallway together.

In a matter of moments, Gayla and Avram are gone too, slapping each other on the back and laughing about close calls. All that's left is Raina and Tamsin standing over a dozen pieces of spacewalk suits, cluttering the floor like garbage at a landfill. Tamsin bends over, picks up an empty oxygen tank, and eyes Raina.

"Lucky you were here," she says. "I don't think Osric would have thought to reroute the planetary gravity-assist controls."

Raina purses her lips. "You noticed that? Just wait. He'll report me for unregulated repairs again."

"Let him," Tamsin scoffs. "She was going to roast in that suit."

Raina lugs two helmets back into the space prep chamber, stacks them in an open containment locker, and locks them down.

Tamsin's right, but Raina knows it doesn't matter. Osric will spin it, just like he always does. With all the complaints he's made against her, she'll be lucky if she isn't demoted. It's possible she'll have to repeat her exit exams at the Academy again and they'll make her train under Osric for another two years.

She stifles a growl.

"I suppose I'll have to cover for Valda at the data processing controls if he's taking Pollux to the sleep chamber," Tamsin notes, checking the clock on the wall. "You mind if I take off?"

Raina waves her off. "Yeah, go ahead, I got this."

"Thanks." Tamsin steps over the pile of equipment and skips down the hall toward the access shaft.

Raina watches her go, grinning to herself. *That girl is far too chipper for her own good.* Raina sets about cleaning up and is nearly halfway done when she smells something putrid.

"What the hell happened here?" Osric eyes the suits on the floor. He's purple with fury all the way to the tips of his fleshy ears.

"There was a suit malfunction," Raina says, then hastily adds, "sir."

"Do you know how much each one of these suits costs?"

Of course she knows. Raina sets down Gayla's suit pants into the appropriate compartment, locks it, and turns around to face him.

He keeps opening and closing his mouth like he's gearing up for an oration. The whites of his eyes are huge and pulsing.

Raina puts her hands on her hips, presses her lips together and sighs.

Here we go. Let's count how many fucks I give…. One…. Two….

"You can't just leave these suits on the floor in the middle of the hallway," he keeps on. "What the fuck have you been doing up here?"

"*Your* job," Raina says quickly, then regrets it.

His face contorts with disbelief and wrath like she's never seen before. The dome of his head slicks with sweat and grease. "You can't speak to your superior officer like that. What the hell is the matter with you?"

Words play on the tip of her tongue, but she bites them back. "What's the matter with me?" she asks finally. The sentence echoes off her mind with thunderous reverberation.

What's the matter with me?

With me?

Despite the voice inside her head shouting: *Calm down, take it easy, don't forget to breathe, give him a second before speaking* – images of another two years with Osric, of having to return to the Academy as a failed ensign, of every foul, sexist, and cruel comment he's ever made while she was on board – they flash through Raina's mind like lightning, burning the back of her eyes with searing heat.

If he demotes her, which she's pretty sure he's about to do, and she fails her exams again, she'll have to retake all the mechanics courses. She'll be almost thirty by the time she's done. Again.

A thirty-year-old ensign?

Good god.

Her career will never amount to anything at that rate. She'll be lucky to crack corporal by the time she's forty, doing grunt repairs and shit assignments until she's old and bent.

In an instant, Raina's face flushes with mountains of unspoken words – pent up like magma under the Earth's crust they push out her mouth with steam and lava. "What's the matter with…*me?*"

Osric's eyes shoot wide as her volume builds. He opens his mouth to speak again but she beats him to it.

Mount Raina erupts.

"You know what?" she says, kicking a glove into the air. It hits the wall beside Osric. "Fuck it. I'm done. Done. Yes – I know how much these fucking suits cost. And yes – I know they can't be left in the middle of the fucking hallway. What the hell do you think I've been doing? Does it look like I'm just standing here, picking my fucking nose? There are three suits to put away and sterilize, and the team *just* left! So, I apologize for the mess, you fucking *dumbass*. But I was too busy saving Pollux's ass from boiling to death in her suit after her temp gauge was damaged. But of course, you wouldn't know that – since you weren't even fucking here!"

Osric blinks but recovers quickly. "What did you call me?"

"I called you a fucking dumbass," she repeats gladly. She slows the next part down like she's addressing a dim child. "That's D-U-M-B-A-S-S. Don't forget the B."

Osric's face deforms. Anger slides down his face like melted wax. "You can't speak to me like that," he says, visibly shaking in his boots. "You're just an ensign – a fucking, stupid cunt ensign. And I'm your superior officer!"

"What're you going to do?" Raina asks, not thinking and waving her arms. "You going to write me up? Again? You're going to do that no matter what I do anyway! You know what? I really don't see the point of even talking to you." She turns her back to him and raises a palm in his direction. "You're useless. You seriously don't know shit. Just leave me alone and let me finish this in peace. It's the least you can do given that I've been doing your fucking job for the past two years." She hears the rage in his voice but doesn't bother to turn around.

"When I'm through with you," he says, "you'll be lucky to get stationed as a chef's assistant. You want to spend your life peeling potatoes? You got it! It's all you're good for anyway."

"So you keep saying!" Raina shouts back, finally turning around to face him. She takes a grim satisfaction in seeing sweat beading on his scalp. He's gone beyond purple with his anger and is now pale. "You want to know what you're good for, Osric? Nothing. Abso-fucking-lutely nothing. You're a worthless, lazy, stupid-as-fuck dumbass. You're the worst trainer in all of the charted *and* uncharted universes. I haven't learned a damned thing since you've been my commanding officer. And, you know what else? You fucking smell like a rotting corpse." Leaving the suits scattered, she stalks down the hall toward the access shaft. "Fuck it. Do this yourself. I'm done. I'm done. I'm done!"

Fuck it. Fuck it. Just fuck it.

"Get back here!" Osric yells after her. "You can't walk away from me!"

"Just did!" she says down the hall over her shoulder. "I'm off to the galley to start my career as a chef's assistant and peel some fucking potatoes."

"You're finished in the Space Corps!" Osric shouts as Raina climbs the ladder to upper deck. "Finished!"

"You bet your dumb ass I am!"

Climbing up the ladder, Raina's hands shake. She hasn't the slightest idea how that just happened. Her momentary rush from telling off Osric recedes with each step toward upper deck. Her head spins. What did she just do?

She's finished. Her career is over. She's proven everything Osric ever said about her correct.

I am *a fucking moron.*

CHAPTER FOUR

Demeter
30.8.2231 AD
1000 hours

There is nothing Pollux Tate hates more than being treated like a woman. As if they are somehow weaker and less durable than a man. What little men know. To her, that extra bit of compassion a woman receives from a man when she's injured is the worst thing in all of the cosmos – just above black holes, flying through a nebula, and when a star burns out.

Yet, that's exactly what Valda is doing, and it's driving her insane.

"Watch your step," he says, then whispers something in Spanish. "How are you feeling, okay?"

"Fine," she grunts, although she feels far from it. She's not sure how hot she got while Raina was messing with her suit, but she feels as dry as a shriveled prune. Her head is a mile wide and weighs twice as much as it normally does and her arms itch something fierce. She's so drenched in sweat she can feel it pooling in her boots.

She's not about to tell Valda any of this, however, or he'll order her to rest for the next twelve hours, and she's pretty sure the boredom will kill her faster than anything else.

"Lightheaded?" Valda presses.

"No." A lie.

"Oh dios mio, esta mujer. Do you feel weak? Would you like me to help you walk?"

"No."

"Here, let me get the door for you."

"Jesus Christ, Valda, lay off."

"Hey – I know you outrank me, but I am still the chief medical officer on this pile of caca. So, calmate, vieja loca."

"I don't know what the hell you're saying."

Valda taps the controls to the sleep chamber and points inside. "Just get in there and let me scan you."

"Whatever you say, boss."

Inside the sleep chamber, each bunk is encased in a small, closet-sized compartment, complete with a small sink, a footlocker, and a cot flatter than a strip of plywood. Pollux hates every square inch of this chamber but has never been so glad to see it in her life. She ambles through the central room, reaches her compartment, then stumbles through the open door.

She hates that she's limping. She collapses onto her bunk a little harder than she means and groans as she hits the mattress, regretting that as well. But damn, it feels good to lie down.

"All right, hold still," Valda orders her, and takes his scanner from his utility belt. He gives her the once-over. "You're dehydrated, but otherwise fine. No organ damage. At least, none that this scanner picks up."

"Dandy. Now leave me alone."

"I should set you up with an IV."

"Do what you gotta do, then get out," Pollux mumbles as Valda exits to retrieve the IV. She unlatches the buckles on her boots and grabs hold of the safety belts on her bunk. She straps herself in and groans again.

"Quit that," she gripes.

"I didn't say anything," Valda insists, returning to the sleep chamber with a small bag of saline and a tube.

"Wasn't talking to you."

Valda smirks and rolls up Pollux's right sleeve. "¿Qué diablos es eso?"

She's too exhausted to tell him to shut up.

"What is this?" he asks again.

She peels her eyes open to see what he's babbling about and sighs as she inspects her arms. The rash has gotten worse. It's spread down both her arms and even covers her fingernails. "I don't know. It's been there a while. Just some rash." Why doesn't he leave?

Damn, it's hot.

"Let me take a skin sample and run it through the lab," he says.

"Will you stop acting like a mother hen and *go away*?"

He sighs, then runs the line into the soft part of the inside of her elbow. Attaching the bag to a rusted latch beside the cot, he mutters, "I'll get you some hydrocortisone when you wake up. Try and relax."

Lost somewhere between sleep and consciousness, Pollux calculates just how long she'll allow herself to rest before her next shift. She's due in the greenhouse in an hour. She's supposed to analyze the algae Giggling Gayla collected. But as plans come into her mind, they slip back out like a cloud, and she's unable to grasp them.

"Now, if you're okay," Valda says, standing in the doorway, "I've got to make sure Ensign Tamsin has covered data processing."

"Yeah, yeah," Pollux mumbles, fighting the blackness that grows behind her eyelids. "I'm fine. Get the hell out of here. Go."

She doesn't notice when he leaves.

★   ★   ★

Raina slouches at one of the tables in the galley and sucks down the slop inside the plastic meal bag. It's chipped beef on toast; if you call flourless bark 'toast' and canned meat substitute 'beef'. But she's too pissed to taste how awful it is.

I've really done it this time.

All that training at the Academy, wasted.

Seven years of flunked tests, repeated classes, late-night cram sessions, and enough money spent to buy a moon colony – gone. Almost two years of wordlessly putting up with Osric's abuse, and everything else, down the wormhole in a flash of word-vomit.

Raina, two weeks shy from obtaining her first commission as an actual mechanic, and her career is shot. And she's the one that blew it up.

Typical.

What will her family say? She hates to even imagine. They'll be so disappointed. But, sadly, probably not surprised.

Hadn't her father told her joining the Space Corps was a mistake?

Hadn't he insisted she was being reckless? But no, she had to prove him wrong. She had to show him that she was just as brave and smart as her brother – him, with all his awards and medals and fatherly approval.

But she was just stupid. *So* stupid.

She should have kept her fucking trap shut. She should have gone into the private electrical trade like one of her uncles had suggested. She should have done a great many things differently. But no. Self-sabotaging Raina strikes again.

Unable to think about it any further without choking, she sucks another mouthful of mush onto her tongue, hardly chewing.

To her left, she eyes the cook, a paunchy, gray-haired sergeant named Niall. He's messing with the heat console on the range, keeping the packets warm, but he looks more interested in watching the yellow alert light flash above the door. He casts a worried look at Payload Specialist Sorrel, who burps as he tosses his discarded packets into the waste container.

"Weren't you supposed to go to the flight deck a half hour ago?" Niall asks him.

Sorrel shrugs. "I was hungry. Probably just another asteroid." He chucks his carton into the other basin, splattering the air with particles of white gravy.

Niall grimaces.

Poor guy, Raina thinks. *These space jocks are slobs.*

She takes another swallow from her packet but gags. Needs more salt.

"I've got to drop a log, then I'll head up," Sorrel mumbles, and wipes his mouth on a napkin. "Who put you in charge anyway?"

Niall doesn't look amused.

"Now, now, Sorrel," Avram jokes, his mouth full of food. "Play nice. You must admit yellow alert is a bit suspect." He sits at one of the three tables in the galley, and slurps mush from his packet without hesitation. His dark skin and floppy hair still glisten with sweat from the spacewalk. Given the way he's eating, Raina doesn't think he's too affected at having almost watched his superior officer roast like a Christmas turkey. That's something she and he agree upon, even if he doesn't know it. He coughs once and wipes his nose on his sleeve.

"You don't seem worried about the yellow alert," Raina says to Sorrel.

He's already halfway out the door and shoots his words over his shoulder. "They've got it covered, I'm sure. You know the captain." And then he's gone, taking his gravy-stained pants with him.

Niall stops messing with the heating unit long enough to wring his hands. "That's the problem."

Raina nods. Sorrel's last words don't sit well with her either. She'd like to believe yellow alert is no cause for alarm, but she knows the captain has never gone to yellow alert before. Never. It's always red, or nothing. She asked him about it once. He said, "Why bother with yellow, an 'almost' catastrophe?"

The captain is cold or hot. All or nothing.

Raina watches Niall reluctantly go back to work. She guesses he's thinking the same thing.

The galley door slides open and Osric stalks inside. He looks as mad as a hornet. His bug eyes search the room and lurch to a stop when they find her.

Raina's stomach gurgles in protest.

"There you are," he growls.

"I told you I was going to the galley. It wasn't a grand mystery."

His face flushes.

She shuts her mouth. There's no sense in digging a deeper grave. Besides, it's one thing when he belittles her and it's just the two of them. It's doubly horrifying when there's an audience. She eyes Avram. He's doing a terrible job of pretending he's deaf, examining the ceiling like it's the Sistine Chapel.

"Don't get comfortable," Osric snarls at her. "You still have work to do before you start your new position, *Ensign*." He gets packets of slop from Niall, then plops down at a table across the aisle from her. He glowers and jams his napkin into the collar of his uniform. It looks like a deranged ascot.

Avram's dark eyes widen. "Did you get your commission, Raina?"

She shakes her head. "Not even close."

Osric snickers maniacally. "No. I've dismissed her from the mechanics department and placed her as a chef's assistant." He takes a swig of food and dribbles down his chin.

Avram scoffs. "You're kidding, right?" Raina shakes her head at him, but he doesn't get the hint. "This bucket of bolts wouldn't be flying if it weren't for her. Remember when the ventilation system shut down on HD 85512b? We'd all have suffocated if it weren't for her creating that makeshift atmospheric filter."

Osric spits gravy as he speaks. "You mean that convoluted pile of shit that was completely unsafe and against every safety code in Space Corps history and short-circuited the lighting on mid-deck?"

"It worked, didn't it?" Raina says.

Avram puts up his palms as if signaling defeat. "Easy there, Toro. I'm just saying, I'd rather be alive and bypass a few safety protocols and fumble around in the dark, than suffocate while following repair guidelines. You know what I mean?" He looks to Niall, but he's too busy staring down the yellow alert light.

Avram turns to Raina instead and winks. "Come on. Am I right?"

Raina presses her lips together and shakes her head again. He'll get no help from her. She's had enough bickering with Osric. There's no sense in it. It's like repeatedly sticking your head inside a booster exhaust and wondering why you keep getting burned.

Avram goes back to his mush. "Jesus. Never mind."

With a gush of kinetic energy, Tamsin arrives in the galley and heads straight for the food, her ponytail swinging like a pendulum. "Do we know why we're on yellow alert yet?" she asks without bothering to say hello. "I mean, why yellow?" she adds, looking to Raina.

All Raina has to do is cast her gaze to Osric and Tamsin nods.

"Oh, right," Tamsin grumbles with disgust.

"The yellow alert means we're supposed to start wearing our fall colors," Avram says. When no one laughs, he shakes his head, then stands to get more food. He wipes his nose on his sleeve. His nose is reddened and his dark eyes almost look glassy, they're so watery.

He sniffs loudly and coughs – right on the packets at the serving station. Raina wonders if he's picked up a virus from the spacewalk. Great. They'll all be sick within the week. "I still say we should intercom the captain about the alert," she says, getting back on topic.

"You mean no one has?" Tamsin asks.

"Man alive, girl." Osric gives Tamsin the same look he gives Raina whenever he's about to call her a moron. "Don't you ever shut up?"

Tamsin blinks at him, seemingly unaffected. "Don't you ever shower?"

Avram bursts out laughing, wordlessly raises his palm, and Tamsin slaps it.

"Point for the ensigns!" she cheers.

Osric curses at them both but Avram only laughs as Tamsin shrugs it off and grins devilishly at Raina, who hides her smile behind a carton of recycled water.

These two.

When these last few weeks are over, and the crew scatters across the Space Corps fleet in their new assignments and promotions, and as Raina will probably be spending her days opening cans of meat substitute and recycling urine into drinking water, she's going to miss these two, and pretty much only these two.

Sunshine Tamsin and Smart-Alec Avram. Always rays of color on a gray ship.

You'd never guess Avram is good at what he does, given his constant sarcasm, and beanpole-esque physique. He towers over Raina and most of the crew and he's not much to look at. But he's a good tech. Raina's seen him in action. It's why he's the only ensign allowed on the planet surface with the rest of the botany team. He's also always on time, always there with a quick joke and helping hand. Unlike so many others on board.

"You should have heard Valda talking about your heroics earlier, Raina," Tamsin says, sitting down with her food on the other side of Raina, and flipping her bead necklaces back. "I spoke to him in the hall afterward. He was so impressed he's thinking of recommending you for a commendation."

Osric scoffs. "Let me guess. It was completely against code."

"No, really," Tamsin pipes up, despite the warning glare she gets from Raina. "Pollux would have died if she hadn't been there."

"I'm sure there was nothing heroic in what she did," Osric says. "More like she didn't do a proper systems check before departure."

"The damage happened on the planet's surface," Tamsin argues, playing with the tip of her ponytail, "when Pollux tried to jump a ravine. It had nothing to do with the departure inspection."

Osric grumbles with a mouth full of mush. "Yeah? Well, I don't recall it being any of your damned business."

"It is if you're blaming Raina for something that's not her fault," Tamsin says.

Osric scoffs again. "Ha. According to Raina, *nothing* is ever her fault."

"How do you even know? You weren't there," Tamsin says.

"Well, neither were you."

"I was in the hall when they got back. What's your beef with her anyway?"

He rolls his eyes. "You need to back down, kid. This isn't your fight."

"Who you calling a kid?" Tamsin says, her voice rising an octave.

"You see what's she's doing?" Osric points at Raina. "She's just sitting there, letting you fight her battles. Now, sit down and eat your packets and quit getting played."

Tamsin sets her jaw and twists her beads in her fingers. "You really don't get it. She saved Pollux's life. I mean, how hard is that to understand? Are you stupid or something?"

"Hey!" he shouts. "You better watch yourself. I'll write you up."

"Oh, give it a rest," Tamsin says. "You've written so many people up nobody even cares anymore."

"I'm serious," he says.

"Go right ahead. I'll outrank you in a year."

"Hey," someone says. "Leave any of that slop for me?"

The last of the ensigns, Morven, enters the galley. He saunters his tall and muscular frame through the door as if there hadn't been a shouting match not two seconds before.

Osric scowls, as does Tamsin.

"Slop?" Niall says. "What are you calling slop?"

Raina watches Morven as he glides across the galley toward the food.

His eyes find hers and she suppresses a frown. She really isn't in the mood to deal with the likes of him. But it's unlikely Morven will cut her any slack, not that he ever did before.

"Oh, come on, old man," Morven says. "I didn't mean anything by it. Lay it on me." He snatches twice the ration of packets.

"Cripes, Osric," Avram says, then moves aside so Morven can get by. "You going through 'the change' or something? Simmer down."

Meanwhile, Osric curses at Tamsin under his breath. She just smirks, but Raina keeps her attention elsewhere.

She watches Morven. His hair is a mess, and his lips look chapped. He must have had a rough night.

Good.

Niall hands Morven a carton of water and the ensign grimaces. Even though it's been processed and sterilized, everybody knows where it comes from.

Raina tries not to think about it.

Avram grins maniacally and raises his carton as if to clink glasses. "Bon appetit!"

"So, now that the inventory is complete," Morven says to him, talking loudly enough so that the entire room has no choice but to listen, "how long will it take you and Pollux to finish the analysis?"

Avram plops back down at the table with his fresh packets of food. "In case you hadn't heard, Pollux is taking the next shift off." He wipes his nose on the napkin then tucks it in his lap. "You know, because of that whole near-death experience a half hour ago."

Morven doesn't look impressed. "How long will it take for the algae analysis to be finished? Two days? Three?"

Avram sniffs. "I dunno. Three or four, maybe. What's the rush? We've got time before we port."

"Why will it take so long?" Morven asks.

Avram raises his unibrow at him. "Hey. It's done when it's done. If you have a problem with my performance speed, here's my official 'I don't give a fuck what you think' and take it up with Pollux."

Raina smirks.

Pollux won't take kindly to having one of her ensigns question her productivity, least of all Morven, and everyone knows it. Avram has basically told Morven to take a hike. It's yet another reason why Raina likes him. He doesn't put up with Morven's bravado.

Morven spots Raina's expression and frowns, then slaps his packets of food onto the table and slides his bulk into the chair next to Avram. Morven's twice the size of anyone aboard, and his shoulders are so wide, Avram has to scoot over.

"I'll be sure to mention it to Pollux when she gets up from her afternoon nap," Morven says with clenched teeth.

Raina's face flushes. The man never lets up. Ever. Especially now. She takes a swig of water and looks the other way. Her eyes catch Tamsin, who crosses her eyes and sticks out her tongue in response. Raina chokes on a laugh and thoughtlessly sucks down another mouthful of food. She sputters at the taste.

"Do you suppose the United Space Corps science headquarters will take special interest in our report once you get off your ass and finish it?" Morven asks. His packets sit untouched, getting cold.

"Tell you what," Avram says, his almost empty pack an inch from his mouth. "You let me eat my meal in peace and I'll be sure to make a special notation in the footnotes about how your inventory list of the collected alien plant species was so instrumental to the completion of this mission, that we all vow to give you our firstborn. How's that? That work for you? And who knows? Maybe they'll give you a medal for listing the plants in alphabetical order."

"Thank you," Morven says. "I appreciate that."

Avram scoffs.

Tamsin looks up from her food and eyes the door. "Has anyone seen Kris?"

"She's on deck, I think," Raina says.

Osric slams his water down on the table. "Will you stop yammering and get your ass down to the airlock and clean up that mess?"

"What mess?" Tamsin chirps. "Do you want my help, Raina?"

Raina stands and drops her trash into the appropriate bin. "Don't worry about it, Tam. I'm done eating anyway. The stench ruined my appetite."

The cook raises an eyebrow, but Raina waves it away as she exits. "Not the food, Niall. The stench of dumbass."

She just hears Osric's words, "What did she say?" then the galley door closes behind her.

On her way to the airlock, she can't help grinning. Yes, her career is shot, but at least she'll end it in a blaze of glory.

She doesn't take five steps before she hears the ship's intercom buzz alive.

Good. Maybe the captain is finally going to explain this yellow alert business.

"Ensign Raina to data processing," Corporal Gayla says over the speakers.

Raina turns on her heel and heads the other direction. So much for dramatic exits.

CHAPTER FIVE

One Month Ago….

"Hello."

Raina freezes in position at her workbench. It's in the corner of the mechanics workstation, an out-of-the-way bar-height table Osric begrudgingly allows her to use. It's the collecting ground for her special pile of tidbits. Old parts, pieces of broken equipment, bits and pieces of a little of this and little of that, old tools she's manipulated into newer, custom-built ones, and odd space junk.

Morven's in the door. He looks small, which is difficult for a man of his size to accomplish. His shoulders slump, and his face hangs low. He stands with his weight all on one leg.

She wonders if he's here to make trouble, but given his expression she doubts it. A part of her knew this was coming. Honestly, it's a surprise it's taken him this long to get around to it. It's too bad she still doesn't feel prepared for what's coming next.

"I miss you," he says.

There it is.

She doesn't answer. What can she say? She misses him too. Well, at least parts of him. She misses the softness, his teasing manner. She misses the way he used to look at her, like in the beginning, when she was his salvation.

Now, she's his curse.

He smiles meekly, which melts her heart slightly. She quickly puts a front up, trying to look like he doesn't have any effect on her. She's a horrible liar, this she knows, but she has to try.

"How are you?" he asks.

She swallows, not leaving her position at the workbench, not moving. Hardly breathing. "Fine."

"What have you been doing with yourself? I don't see you around."

"The captain said I should keep my distance, so I am."

"I don't want you to keep your distance," he says, stepping forward. He's practically beside her now and her muscles tense.

She feels a dull ache in her ribs and without thinking puts a hand on them.

He notices. Of course he notices. He's always been good at seeing everything she does. It used to be very sweet, how he was so in tuned in to her every mood and word, until it wasn't.

"You shouldn't be here," she manages to say.

He steps closer again. She sees tears in his eyes and fights to stand her ground. She has to stop herself from reaching out and stroking his cheek.

This isn't him, she reminds herself. This isn't *all* of him, at any rate. You can't have only half of the equation.

"But I miss you," he whispers, pleading with his wet eyes.

"Morven…."

"People fight all the time," he says. "That's normal. Arguments happen, people move on. Can't we just move on? I can't sleep. I…."

Her face goes hot. "If that's your normal, then I'm going to pass."

"No, that's not what I'm saying at all," he says, stepping forward again until he's right beside her. They're practically touching and her heart races.

Is it fear? Or is it something else? She can hardly tell the difference anymore.

"I'm just saying I think we can get past it, that's all. I know we can," he says. "If you let us."

"I can't," she says, as firmly as she can muster. She takes her hand off her ribs and rests it on the soldering iron that smolders on her workbench. It's comforting to hold it in her hands, familiar and powerful.

He notices and steps back. As his face hardens and his mouth contorts, he says, "That's how you're going to play this?"

"You should leave."

In an instant he's fuming. His hands clench. "Fine. But whatever's coming, it's all on you."

"What's that supposed to mean?"

He backs out the door, slamming his hand against the control panel on his way. The door hisses closed when he's gone.

Raina lets her breath out slowly and swallows the growing lump in her throat, then releases the soldering iron in her fist.

This is so far out of control, it's not even funny. She only wishes she'd stopped it before it ever started, but it's too late to go backward now.

★   ★   ★

Demeter
30.8.2231
1030 hours

No matter how many times Pollux falls asleep on her bunk, she always tries to roll over onto her stomach. It's the only way she can truly get a solid sleep. But every time the safety restraints yank her awake, she remembers where she is.

It's a rude awakening.

Somewhere in sleep her subconscious traveled back home. She'd been cataloging specimens from the Planetary Conservatory back on base, a task she hasn't been assigned since her days as a junior science tech at the beginning of her career. She hasn't the foggiest idea why she's thought of that now. It feels a lifetime ago, back when she was young, spry, and full of world-conquering ambition. Before she took the assignment to collect alien plant life and left the comfort of terra firma and got fucking old.

She runs her hands through her cropped hair, rips the IV from her arm and studies the rash. It'd started on her palms a few weeks ago but now it's all the way up her arm, past her elbow and creeping up and around her neck.

Nasty fucking itch.

The raised white bumps must be an allergic reaction of some kind.

With all the plant specimens in the greenhouse there's no wonder she's covered in welts. This one's a whopper, though. The hydrocortisone she snagged from the med kit a few days ago hardly touched it. It's probably time to have Valda take a skin sample like he requested.

After unlatching her restraints, she sits up. Her head hurts and her red and splotchy skin is covered in sweat that makes every pore sting, and no wonder. The sleep compartment feels as hot as the greenhouse.

That good-for-nothing piece of shit Osric. He couldn't fix squat to save his life.

She tosses her legs over the side, then squeezes into her damp boots. She reaches above toward the vent in the ceiling. Nothing comes out. Not even hot air.

Goddamned worthless asshole.

She wishes she could toss him out the airlock.

Add the vent system to the long, long list of neglected repairs. If Osric had any brains in him he'd have fixed it before it was even an issue. But the asshole won't lift a finger without a fucking work order, and who's got time to babysit that mole? Certainly not she.

Pollux snatches her towel from the clasp by her sink and hits the control panel on the wall to open her door. Her heart's pumping light and fast and she'd love to punch something – anything to release some of this pent-up frustration.

God, she's pissed. That nasty itch is driving her batty. A cold shower might calm her down, although the way she's feeling, it doesn't seem like she'll ever feel right again. It's got to be a hundred and ten degrees, minimum.

Fuck, her head hurts – it pulses with every heartbeat and every inch of her skin feels like she's rolled in steel wool. She's half tempted to track down Valda and ask for a cortisone shot and migraine med right here and now, but he'd only insist she rest afterward and it's not worth it.

She can practically hear her mother in her head saying, "Weakness is for girls."

She checks over her shoulder as she leaves.

The yellow alert lights flash.

What the hell?

Why yellow? That doesn't make sense at all. Is that because of her? Did her little episode at the airlock raise the alarm?

She's surrounded by idiots. There have been malfunctions after walks before, and the alert level hasn't budged. Why'd they do it this time?

Come to think of it, they probably didn't. It's got to be some asteroid that got too close for comfort. It's the only logical explanation, not that anything on this fucking ship is ever logical.

Was there an impact? Did she miss something while she was passed out?

Leave it to the captain to fuck it up. He's so desperate to end this boring trip he's hardly aware he's still aboard the ship.

She shakes her head and regrets it when it throbs. She'll check on him later. If she approaches the flight deck like this, he'll probably give her orders, and right now, she doesn't want anything to come between her and a cold shower.

Stumbling through the door, she feels an odd sensation, like she's being watched. She glances over her shoulder again, but there's nothing in there but that stupid broken air vent and a sweat-drenched bunk.

★　　★　　★

Raina enters the workstation just down the hall from the galley and spots Corporal Gayla tapping her fingers on the keyboard at the first console. Her fingers are flying, her bobbed hair swinging with the rhythmic motion. Given the grin on her face, Raina can tell she's loving it, which is an odd thing to consider. How can data processing be so much fun?

"You called for maintenance?" Raina asks.

Gayla points to a workstation in the corner, her eyes not leaving her monitor. "The data port is busted. Have a look, eh?"

"Sure thing, Corporal."

Raina ambles over and inspects it. It appears someone's jammed the wrong-sized data chip into the port and now the prongs are bent. She takes out her screwdriver and a spare port from her utility belt.

Valda enters, looking a little disheveled. "¿Qué paso ahora?"

"Nada," Gayla answers, still tapping away at her keyboard. "The data port in two is busted, that's all."

"Oh. I thought maybe there was something wrong with the data from the walk."

"Nope. So far, so good," Gayla says, giving a little giggle. "Although Pollux's data is a bit jumbled, it's translatable. How is she?"

"She'll live. I think her pride is wounded most of all."

"Poor girl," Gayla sighs.

"Don't let her hear you say that."

Raina finishes up swapping out the bent port, then turns to the others. "Is there anything else while I'm here?"

"Damn, eres rápido."

"Excuse me, sir?"

Gayla giggles. "He says you're fast."

Raina raises an eyebrow and stares back at the workstation. It was a simple repair. "No big deal, ma'am."

"Ha! If Osric were here he'd still be figuring out which end of the screwdriver to use." Gayla continues to type at lightning speed.

Valda plops down at the second workstation and boots it. "Yeah, thanks. Good work today. And don't worry about Osric. When we get back to Earth, I'll be sure to set the record straight about how things really go around here."

Raina feels a lump in her throat but swallows it down. "I'd appreciate that, sir." It's a little too late for that considering she's already quit. But it's still nice of him to offer.

Gayla stops typing and rotates in her chair to face her. "Don't worry about it for a moment, eh? You've got my report and Tech Sergeant Pollux's report on the incident too. We've got you covered."

Raina nods, afraid of what she might say if she speaks aloud. It's sweet of them to say this but she also knows Osric's report will hold more weight with the Space Corps Commissions Committee than theirs, given he's her direct superior.

Fuck. If only she'd kept her mouth shut this whole thing could have blown over.

She wordlessly exits the workstation and crosses the hall, down to the space preparatory chamber and the airlock. Raina gathers up the last of the remnants of the uniforms from the hall floor, locks the compartments closed, then activates the sterilizations. It's meant to remove any toxins the team may have picked up from the planet's surface but is more of a precautionary measure.

She waits, watching the valves dance as the computer isolates and neutralizes a specific isotope. She leans against the wall.

She's going to miss this, funnily enough. Aside from Osric, and putting up with Morven, she actually likes working for the Corps. There's a certain satisfaction in keeping this piece of space junk floating.

The helmets finish their sterilization, so Raina activates the suit compartment. The entire process only takes a few moments, but she closes her eyes, listening to the computer do its job. The ship's engines throb at a low idle and she can feel the slight vibration from the stationary boosters through the soles of her boots.

Why haven't we left orbit yet?

That must have something to do with the yellow alert level, but she hasn't a clue what it's about. She's surprised the flight deck hasn't at least contacted Osric to let him know if there's a malfunction aboard. She debates activating a work console and checking for a communiqué when she hears someone approaching. She turns and looks, and has to stop herself from groaning.

The other asshole.

Great.

Morven's got a smug look on his face. No doubt he's come to pour salt on her wounds and remind her of her many failures: him being one of them.

"Look," she says, hoping to chop Morven's insults off at the knees, "if you've come to cause trouble you can just bugger off."

"I heard what happened," he says, looking smug and hot at the same time. It's not fair at all. "Osric said a mouthful after you left the galley. Why the hell are you cleaning up if you've basically quit?"

She rolls her eyes at him, not answering.

He smirks back like a superior shit.

She knows he has a point, but it's not everybody else's fault that Osric popped her like a pimple, and she'll be damned if she'll make anybody else clean up her mess. It's a cinch Osric won't do it. "Just getting it out of everybody's way."

"You're pathetic."

"Being considerate isn't being pathetic," she says. "Of course, you wouldn't know that, seeing as how you've never done anything nice for anyone." It's meant to wound him but he only laughs. She begins the sterilization on the glove compartment.

"You didn't used to think that," he says, smirking. "In fact, if I remember right, you used to love me. A lot. And often. Although, not very well."

Raina doesn't dignify that comment with a response. She taps the gauge on the glove sterilization to loosen the needle.

"Besides, this isn't being considerate," he insists, not letting it go. "This is letting Osric win."

"He's already won. He's my superior officer."

"Not anymore he's not."

"He is while I'm aboard this ship. He can do whatever he wants to me, and I have no recourse. You get it? None. The only thing I can do is get my job done, just the way he wants me to, even if it's the stupidest job ever, because that's my duty. My job isn't to think, to tell him how to do things, to show him anything new – his job is to boss me around. So, that's what he's doing. And by shutting up and doing whatever he says, I'm doing my job. So don't stand there and tell me I'm pathetic. I'm an ensign. Ensigns are pathetic by design. And this includes you, *Ensign* Morven."

This doesn't sit well with him. He crosses his arms across his massive chest and shifts his weight. He doesn't like to admit he's got no real power, and Raina knows this. Sure, he puts up a brave front and pretends he's above the rest of the trainees, but in truth, he's fresh out of the Academy just like the others, and if Pollux told him to clean out the toilet with his toothbrush, he'd have to do it.

If he came to rub salt in her wounds, Raina can do the same right back. She really isn't in the mood. "Why are you even here? What do you want?"

He shrugs. "Nothing from you," he says. "Not anymore." And then he ambles down the hall, back toward the access shaft. "Just offering up some friendly advice."

Raina stares after him.

Asshole.

★   ★   ★

Sorrel climbs up the access shaft ladder toward the flight deck, his lunch rolling around in his belly like a caged animal. Even after his extended trip to the bathroom, his stomach is still upset. Maybe he should have skipped that third ration. The four cartons of recycled water aren't helping either. Every time he considers the source his gut turns over.

Just as he's lamenting that the airlock doesn't go all the way up to the flight deck, he notices a gravy stain on his pants. His last unstained uniform. Well, not anymore. At least it's near the end of the tour. He can stock up on new ones when they reach port. He might get the next size up. The clasps on his shirt are so tight it's almost painful.

He climbs up the ladder, lost in thoughts of tight uniforms and neglected exercise regimens, when his left hand touches something sticky on the ladder rung. He stops, pulling his hand away, slightly horrified.

Upon further inspection, he's even more repulsed.

Is that *blood*?

Not wishing to wipe the blood onto his flight suit, or grasp the ladder with the soiled hand and risk spreading the blood around, he holds the hand aloft, and uses the other and his legs to ascend the ladder. He focuses on the wall so as not to lose his balance.

"Hey up there!" he calls. "Did you cut yourself shaving off that ridiculous mustache, Captain?" He chuckles to himself, proud of his little jibe. When no response comes, he feels a touch of panic and climbs faster. "Cap?"

A sour sweat soaks Sorrel's neck as he climbs faster still, huffing and puffing like an old-fashioned steam train.

He ascends, keeping his eyes on the growing number of blood droplets on the access shaft wall.

Oh god.

"Cap?"

Then, from above, he feels the unmistakable sensation of fingers touching his hair. Lurching to one side, he looks up.

He notices the hand first, then the arm. But it's not an arm attached to a body; it's just an arm, sliced as if by a butcher's blade right at the shoulder.

"Oh god," he pants. "Captain?"

He stumbles up the ladder but stops a second to inspect the severed arm. What disturbs him the most is that it wears the sleeve of a flight suit and has the pilot's patch where the shoulder should be.

He calls the pilot's name, because surely, that can't be her arm. That would be ridiculous. They have to be messing with him. "Davenport? Report, please!"

He slips on more blood splatter. His eyes focus again on the access shaft walls. It's everywhere. Speckled like splattered paint. His heart quickens so fast his left arm has begun to ache and he's feeling lightheaded. He slows his climbing to a snail's pace and, forgetting the blood on his hand, grips the ladder tightly with both palms to keep from fainting.

One more look at the pilot's severed arm as it dangles over the edge of the access shaft and Sorrel's lunch makes a hasty escape from his stomach.

Vomit splashes across the access shaft walls, splattering Sorrel's uniform, and cascades down the ladder in a wretched wave. Sorrel grips tightly and holds on as he heaves. When his stomach is empty, he wipes his mouth on his shoulder, panting.

"Captain! Report! Captain!"

He labors up the ladder. Almost there. As he climbs, he strains his ears.

There's nothing. No moaning. No breathing.

In a mad rush of courage, Sorrel climbs the last few feet of the access shaft ladder and emerges onto the flight deck a blood-covered, vomitous mess.

The scene stops him dead in his tracks.

What is left of the pilot lies crumpled in a pile of flesh and bone to the side of the shaft, on his right. Her insides appear to be missing, and all that remains are her limbs, the shell of her torso, and her limp head. Her empty eye sockets stare at him blankly.

"Oh god. Oh god. Oh god." Sorrel whispers it again and again. He climbs inside the deck. He steps to the left toward the captain's chair, where his hollow corpse lies flayed wide open just under the observation window.

Sorrel reaches across the captain's body and checks to make sure the autopilot is deactivated. It is.

What should I do? Where are we again? How far is the nearest station?

The nav computer.

Sorrel teeters on his feet, corrects his balance, and then turns to face the navigation console. There, Kris's headless corpse slumps against the backside of her chair, the inside of her torso as clean as a carved pumpkin. He can't see where her head has gone, but he recognizes her just the same. She had a nice rack.

Sorrel steps over her legs and flips the switch, triggering red alert. He feels another surge of bile in his gut and leans forward to press his finger to the intercom, but the button sticks, and as he opens his mouth to speak, he sees a portion of the captain's chair move.

It looks to be some sort of fluffy blue pillow, the exact same shade as the upholstery on the command chairs. Then the pillow moves again. The fur adjusts to its surroundings, first looking like a pillow from the chair, then a part of the captain's console, and then an extension of Kris's bloody empty body.

He stares at it. Dumbfounded.

"Oh god. Oh god."

Then he sees the eyes.

He opens his mouth to scream.

His finger jams down on the stuck intercom button.

CHAPTER SIX

Raina taps the last of the sanitation commands and leans against the wall. She watches Morven as he saunters away, down the hall toward the access shaft. She's trying not to notice the contours of his muscular backside as he disappears from view.

Such a waste.

He looks back and winks at her like he knows she's watching.

She glowers at him.

From farther down the hall, Pollux ambles toward them, a towel in her hand. The space prep room also doubles as the ship's bathroom, so Raina guesses she's on her way to take a shower. She looks haggard. A good rinse might do her good.

"Sarge," Morven says to her as Pollux limps by.

"Ensign," she responds, and continues past him, barely lifting her eyes to meet his.

Morven shoots Raina a satisfied smirk. She can almost hear his sarcastic jab at Pollux in her head. She forces her eyes away, shifting them to the yellow flashing lights. Suddenly, the hue fluctuates, changing to red. Rays of crimson bleed across the wall with ominous strokes.

The speakers overhead crackle to life. "Red alert!" a man's voice shouts. "Oh god! Red alert! Foreign biological! I repeat, foreign biological aboard—!"

The intercom crackles and stops.

From down the hall, Morven stands, frozen. "What the fuck?"

"Was that Sorrel?" Raina asks.

Pollux has stopped in the middle of the hall, her towel dropped to the floor. "Come on!"

Without thinking, Raina leaves the space preparatory chamber and jogs down the hallway toward them. Her boots pound the metallic floor with every step. "What do we do? Should we go up to the flight deck and check it out?"

Pollux shakes her head and then grunts. "Negative." She makes for the ladder. "We get to the armory. Now. That's procedure."

Raina can't help but feel at odds with the look of excitement on Morven's wide face. "Yeah," he says, looking almost childlike. "Get the lead out."

Pollux is already halfway down the access shaft to mid-deck, but she stops after a few steps to scratch her arm.

Morven cuts in front of Raina and goes next.

There's a sick feeling swelling in her gut. But without hesitation, she follows.

★ ★ ★

With almost the entire crew gathering in the armory, it's cramped tight. Standing shoulder-to-shoulder, Raina notices the rest of the crew's expressions are grim, as well she supposes they should be. Foreign biologicals are cause for alarm. This could get very bad, very fast.

Raina watches as Pollux takes a laser rifle from one of the armory lockers. She's all business as she yanks a rifle from the wall and inspects it, but Raina can't help but feel sorry for her. She looks like hell and her face gleams with sweat, not to mention the bumps on her hand that look like a bad case of hives.

Still, Pollux checks the power cell on the rifle, then snaps the cell back into place and hands the weapon to the nearest person. It's Tamsin, who twists her beads in her fingers and acts as if she's just been handed an atom grenade.

"What's this for?" she asks.

Osric jeers at her. "What the fuck do you think it's for?" No one dares mention he still has his dinner napkin tucked into the collar of his uniform.

Raina watches as Pollux pulls another rifle off the wall and checks its cell.

"Any idea what we're dealing with?" Niall asks the rest. His droopy eyes dart to the door and back again with shards of panic.

"Foreign biological, just what Sorrel said," Pollux says, handing him a laser rifle. She turns to the wall to snag another rifle, inspects it, then hands it to Gayla, who stands beside Raina. "That's what I heard. That's what the consoles read too."

"We haven't left orbit, eh?" Gayla says, slipping the strap of her rifle over her shoulder.

"What does that mean?" asks Tamsin.

"It means," Pollux responds, an edge to her voice, "that we're floating in circles, burning fuel."

"Why would the captain do that?" Raina asks.

"Buena pregunta," mutters Valda.

"It's procedure," Avram says. "When faced with an unknown biological it's standard operating procedure to hold position until the biological can be contained."

"The yellow alert?" Tamsin asks.

No one answers.

Raina bites the inside of her cheek. Goddamnit, she *knew* something was wrong.

"We hold until it's contained. They don't want us bringing it back to port," Pollux adds tersely, handing Morven a rifle. He takes it quickly.

Raina tucks a wayward strand of hair behind her ear and notices her fingers shake.

"Bring what back to port?" Tamsin asks, and recoils when Osric groans.

"The foreign biological, you idiot," he says.

Tamsin sticks her tongue out at him, and he glowers back at her.

"Here's what we do," Pollux says, and no one questions her, since she's the highest-ranking officer in the room. "The officers and I will head up to the flight deck and figure out what's happened. Meanwhile, Niall, take the ensigns to the galley, and barricade yourselves in until we get the biological contained."

"That's it?" Morven looks unimpressed. "That's your big plan? You hunt it down while we hide like children?"

Pollux's humorless expression speaks volumes. She digs at her shoulder like she's about to peel off her skin. "How much combat experience do you have, Ensign?"

He doesn't answer.

"That's what I thought. Now shut the fuck up."

Raina watches Morven's face. She can tell his cooperation takes a vast amount of control on his part. He's gripping his rifle with white knuckles.

"Are we clear?" Pollux emphasizes.

Morven nods stiffly. "Yes, ma'am."

"Good boy. Now let's go," Pollux orders.

"Good luck!" Tamsin waves cheerfully as Pollux, Gayla, Osric, and Valda exit the armory.

Once they're gone, Niall wipes his palms on his apron, and glances over the remaining people. He sighs. Raina doesn't blame him for looking dejected. All that's left is a flunky mechanic, a space-case, a skinny geek, and a hothead.

Niall snatches a second rifle from the wall. "Just my luck. Come on."

Tamsin follows, cradling her rifle.

Avram sneezes and trails behind her. "Do you suppose a foreign biological growls with an accent?"

Before Raina can continue the line of people, Morven reaches out and wraps his fingers around her arm with his large hand. "Wait a second."

On instinct, she yanks her arm away. The look of intensity on his face is far too familiar. "Don't."

Morven's expression immediately hardens and the blood vessel on his temple surges. "I was just trying to—"

Raina takes a step back. "Don't start, okay? Just don't. Not now."

"I wasn't—! Don't be such a bitch." His face flushes red.

Memories of their breakup flash across Raina's mind and she flinches. It's been weeks but it still feels raw. "I don't like this any more than you do," she says. She doesn't like having him so close. Alone. At least at the airlock he was mocking her – that she can handle. But when he's gazing at her like this, with those eyes full of emotion, it feels…dangerous.

"You don't like what?" he asks.

"I don't like the idea of being locked in a room with you," she tells him, and feels a tug of guilt for having said it. It's harsh, but true. She takes another step toward the door, but he blocks her.

"Raina—" Morven blurts again, but she cuts him off.

"Just don't, okay? I don't know what you're doing, but just don't."

"I'm not doing *anything*," he says, like he's addressing a rebellious child.

Raina's temper rises. How does he do that? How does he make her feel like such an idiot? "Can we just *go*? We're falling behind."

Morven's face is as still as stone. "All right. Fine. Only you forgot one thing."

"And what's that?" she asks sharply, regretting her loss of control when his face reddens again.

He squints at her. Then, spinning on his heel, he exits the door, leaving her alone in the armory. "You forgot your rifle," he says, touching the console and closing the door in her face.

Raina jolts backward.

Son of a—

She checks her shoulder.

Christ.

Pollux never handed her a rifle. Raina snatches a pair from a locker and slings the straps over her shoulder. She steps forward to exit but hesitates.

What did she see in him again? Ugh.

Raina glances around the armory. Standing alone in the middle of the chamber, she's suddenly aware of the silence. It's eerily soothing. No Osric. No crew. None of them arguing over recent political decisions coming down from the United Space Commission, or the evils of cloning and planetary colonization.

It's completely quiet. She feels her heart rate instantly relax. It could almost be peaceful, if it weren't for the foreign biological hidden someplace aboard the ship.

She reaches out and opens the armory door. Once she has checked to make sure the hallway is clear, she heads for the access shaft.

Her only hope of avoiding another scene with Morven is if the officers can contain the biological quickly and cleanly. Based on her and Morven's state of mind, she doesn't think being locked with him is going to end well.

Nothing with them ever does.

★   ★   ★

Technical Sergeant Pollux is no soldier, and she knows this. She's a botanist, a scientist, the first in her class at the Academy, in fact.

She's the middle of three siblings. The only girl sandwiched between two rough-and-tumble boys, she had a mother who was meaner than a drill sergeant. Pollux has earned the Scientific Achievement Honor, twice, for her work collecting alien plant life from the planets listed as potentially habitable by the United Space Corps Planetary Habitations Committee. She's met the Brigadier General. She's shaken hands with the United Space Corps Admiral. All this before she was forty years old.

But nothing could prepare her for what she's about to see on the flight deck of the *Demeter*.

Nothing.

There isn't a class that covers how to deal with a massacre.

Climbing hand over hand up the access shaft ladder, Pollux takes notice of every droplet of blood on the wall, every chunk of vomit on the rungs. With each step her heart pounds faster, and her skin crawls anew. If only her head would stop pulsing maybe she could think straight, figure out what to do. But the smell is horrendous, and Osric climbs so close behind her he might as well crawl up her ass. She has to force herself not to kick him in the face.

She knows one thing for sure: whatever happened on the flight deck, it's going to be bad. It doesn't take a rocket scientist to figure this out.

If the captain is dead, then she's in command – and she knows it's going to take all her guts and brains to pull the rest of the crew through. She's not afraid of responsibility, just of fucking up. She's only a scientist, damnit.

And hell, if her head and that stupid-ass rash aren't driving her mad.

When Pollux breaches the top of the shaft and enters the flight deck, her worst fears are realized. She sees them all, in horrifying detail. Not just the captain, but four corpses.

The captain. The pilot. Ensign Kris. Specialist Sorrel.

Their bodies lie slumped against consoles, splayed across chairs, and cover the floor like broken limbs off a dilapidated tree. Their abdomens are sliced open and eaten clean out – empty hollow logs.

Pollux swallows vomit down the back of her throat. She steps up and off the ladder, and then over a severed arm. She makes room for the others, who climb up behind her.

It smells like death.

"Jesus H. Mother of Christ, what the fuck happened in here?" Osric asks, gaping, as he exits the shaft. "What is that smell?"

It's ironic, coming from him, but Pollux doesn't comment. His eyes have gone wide and his pallor shifts to an even sicklier hue. If Pollux didn't know any better, she'd think Osric was feeling actual emotions.

"What the hell kind of biological is this?" he asks.

She doesn't have an answer. Truth is, she's afraid to speak. There's a pulsing rage pumping through her that's getting harder to control. It's got to be the stress of the situation causing it, but she can't lose her shit – she's in command.

It's like she can hear her mother's voice in her head.

Pull it together, Polly.

The other officers enter behind Osric. When Valda's head pops up from the shaft, his face turns green. Pollux points to the navigations console. "Find out where we are," she says to him.

Valda only nods, although she hears him pray in Spanish. She also notices he's brushed up against the shaft walls on his way up, and that he has blood and vomit on his uniform, but she keeps that to herself.

"Osric, do something with these bodies. We're out of room," Pollux says.

The mechanic sputters, "I'm not touching them. What if the biological's saliva is poisonous, or radioactive?"

"Then put on your gloves." She pulls the captain's body away from the command chair so she can check the interior monitors. "Gayla," she calls.

"Get up here and make sure we're out of the asteroid field."

"We're out by two klicks," Valda says, reading the nav computer over Kris's headless remains.

"Thank god for small favors," she lets slip out.

Nobody comments. Seems they agree.

The last of the officers arrives. Gayla stumbles onto the flight deck and chokes on a sob. No one mutters a word against her. They're all feeling it. She crawls over chunks of body and slides a fire extinguisher to the floor. Flopping into the pilot's chair, which is covered in foam, she reaches up to attach her safety restraints.

"Don't," Pollux says, and reads the command controls. "We're not staying."

Gayla nods. "Want me to re-enable the autopilot, eh?"

Pollux sees Gayla's face streaked with tears and resists the urge to groan.

Yes. There's a bright idea. Take us to the most populated area you can think of.

Honestly, a part of her wishes they could do that. But it isn't right. No matter how much she hates to admit she wants it. As much as the thought of keeping the ship stationary pisses Pollux off, she knows she can't bring the biological back to Earth. They have to follow procedure and remain immobile until the thing is contained, even if it means the death of them all and trapping the biological within the ship. The United Space Corps has seen it before and has learned this the hard way.

Pollux doesn't want to be another space commander blamed for a station bloodbath. That won't be her legacy. "No," she says, and no one but Osric makes a sound.

"Fat son of a bitch," he curses, tossing Sorrel's body to the side like a sack of potatoes.

"Muestra un poco de respeto!" Valda barks at him.

"Fuck you," Osric snaps back.

Pollux bites back her reply and tastes blood. She tries to formulate plans, but it's hard to think surrounded by so much death and with her head pounding like a fucking jackhammer. On top of that, the temperature has to have gone up again. She's sweating so much it drips from her nose.

She checks the controls. It's a hundred and five degrees. When this is all over, she's handing Osric's ass to command for allowing the air system to fail so horrendously, and at such a critical time too. Truthfully, someone should have done that ages ago. "Valda," she finally calls, scratching her shoulder. "Sync that portable unit on your left to the interior sensors so we can take it with us and track the biological from anywhere in the ship."

"Yes, ma'am." Valda goes to work.

Gayla wipes the tears from her freckled face. "Where is it now?"

Pollux checks one last time on the command controls and faces the others to inform them, but her thoughts cloud with a single phrase.

Four dead.

Three of them officers.

There are only four officers left, not counting Niall, who is with the ensigns, none of whom have seen a speck of real combat.

Four dead. *Four officers left.*

Even after they kill the biological and re-engage the autopilot, how are they going to dock without a pilot? The captain also knew how to port, but he's gone too.

Plus, the quarantine and decontamination process....

They're so royally fucked.

Pollux shakes her throbbing skull. The situation is as bad as it gets, and if any of these idiots are sharp enough, they know it too. Given their reactions, she guesses they've figured it out.

These aren't good odds.

Plus, if the foreign biological has killed the first four this easily, how are they going to do any better? She absently touches the rifle at her hip. At least they're armed.

"Where is it now?" Gayla asks again.

All eyes turn to Pollux and she fights to control her breathing. She concentrates on the living faces looking toward her and tries not to see the blank stares of her former shipmates that gaze at nothing.

Four dead.

No pilot.

Fucking bad odds.

CHAPTER SEVEN

Three Months Ago....

The greenhouse alert wakes Pollux at three o'clock in the morning, and she slaps it silent. Without much thought, she quickly pulls on her uniform, squeezes into her boots, and makes her way down the access shaft.

It's probably one of the sensors come loose again, but she has to check, even at this hour. Too bad the alert can't go to either Morven or Avram, but truthfully she doesn't trust them as far as she can throw them, so she doesn't mind being the one never getting a full night's rest. She's not a deep sleeper anyway – she never is while she's on a mission, and besides, she's not about to trust those two monkeys with anything this important.

Heaven forbid something crucial should happen with a specimen and she isn't there to take proper records. The whole point of this mission is to try and find viable specimens that can be duplicated back at Earth and on the colonies, and if the ensigns muck up anything, even the slightest detail, the whole mission could get scrapped. She'll not have that on her military record. It's practically flawless.

Pollux hops off the last ladder and runs a hand through her hair, pulling it away from her face. Maybe that blue vine that's grown up the enclosure, the one they picked up on Gliese 667Cc, has finally bloomed?

There are motion sensors throughout the greenhouse floor. It's possible the movement of the flower petals opening set it off. Either that or the humidifier coupling sprung a leak again, or some sprinklers banged against each other when they turned on. That's happened before too. The possibilities of the alert being nothing of consequence are pretty high, but still, Pollux thinks it's better to check herself than have something blundered. And the way Avram and Morven bicker like little children, she wouldn't trust them to handle it right if her life depended on it – even the replacement of a loose sprinkler head.

She taps the control panel and enters the greenhouse. The air feels dry. Is the humidifier broken again? She'll have to ask Ensign Raina if there isn't a way to pump it up. Even though the setting is all the way up, the air still doesn't feel damp enough.

Suppose some static sparked and set off the motion sensors? On this turd of a vessel she wouldn't doubt it could be something as stupid as that.

Deeper inside the greenhouse, Pollux pulls her tablet out of her pocket and checks the monitor. There's an alert coming from the corner, over by the glass enclosure, just as she figured. Those damned blue vines.

Weaving through the aisles, she resets the alarm on a five-minute delay, then keys the code into the enclosure keypad. The doors hiss open, and her eyes search the blue vine overhead.

Hmm. No blooms.

She checks the sensor readings again, and sure enough, the alert came from the enclosure. It's not until her eyes rest on two spherical seed spores that her eyes widen with shock.

One of them has opened. At a meter wide and another meter tall, it resembles a spherical cushion, peeled open from the inside. One pod lies on its side, a gaping hole right in the center.

She steps forward and gingerly peels back the shredded fibrous coat to peer inside, but forgets about the clear odorless slime that covers each of the pods, sticking to her fingers like tacky paste. She rubs her fingers together to try and loosen it, but it only hardens.

Cold and rubbery, the slime doesn't bother her at first, but within seconds she feels the tips of her fingers prickle. She flicks the slime free, wipes the remnants on her sleeve, and peers inside the spore.

"Shit."

Leaving the pod where it lies, Pollux dashes through the greenhouse to the control panel back at the door. "Captain, protocol 23292 is in play. We have a contamination in the greenhouse."

There's a delay as she waits by the panel. A few moments later the speaker crackles to life and the captain's voice booms against the walls.

"All right," he mumbles. He sounds like he might still be asleep. "Where in the greenhouse?"

"The enclosure," she answers, pressing the com button to speak, then letting go.

"Well, that's fortunate. Seal the enclosure, turn on the circulatory system, and shut the vent. Were you exposed?"

She taps the com with quick irritation. "I'm in the greenhouse, what do you think?"

"Oh, right. Take a sterilization wash and decontaminate your uniform, just to be safe."

She shakes her head but doesn't argue with him. Honestly, he's acting like she's a fresh recruit straight from the Academy. She knows all this. She's the one who wrote the contamination protocols, for fuck's sake. "Yes, sir."

"I want a full report in the morning. 'Night." The com spits static into the air then falls quiet.

Pollux frowns and scratches her palm. Sure, don't send any help – leave her to deal with it all by herself. She's not just been exposed to an unknown alien contaminant.

"Prick."

She turns on her heel and heads back to the enclosure, shaking her head with a slow-building rage.

Honestly, if you want something done right….

*   *   *

Demeter
30.8.2231 AD
1100 hours

Raina adjusts the laser rifles on her shoulder and climbs the access ladder as quickly as her bulky boots allow. The galley is on upper deck, between the flight deck one floor up, and the armory, one floor down. The shiny silver metal of the access ladder is cold in her hands, and she rushes, feeling exposed.

When she reaches upper deck, she checks over her shoulder, toward the shaft that leads up to the flight deck. She can't help but wonder how the officers are doing, and if they've already engaged with the foreign biological. Even though the ship is relatively small by comparison to other cargo ships in the Corps fleet, sound doesn't travel from one level to the next aboard the *Demeter* due to the heavily reinforced walls.

It doesn't sit well that the others are so close, and she has no idea if they are in the middle of a heated battle. She pushes the thoughts from her head. She has her own battle to contend with.

Checking over her shoulder again, she pulls out one of the rifles, just in case, and flicks on the power cell. There's an electrical squeal as it powers up and heats in her hands.

Poking her head around the corner, she checks to make sure the area is clear. When she's confident in the silence, she dashes across the open space between the ladder and the airlock, and then quietly makes her way down the hall, past the workstation full of computer consoles, and then to the galley.

The ship feels eerily quiet.

When she rounds the bend she spots Morven. He stands inside the galley door, watching her approach.

She lowers her rifle to her side.

"You made it," he says.

She could swear he sounds disappointed. She opens her mouth to reply but stops when his eyes narrow and the galley doors slide closed, not a foot from her approaching nose.

What the…?

When the lock clicks, her hands clench onto her rifle so hard she feels as if she could crush it.

"Damn it, Morven."

Lifting the rifle strap back onto her shoulder, she pounds on the galley door with her free hand.

"Hey, let me in!" She presses the controls on the wall beside the door, but since it's locked from the inside this accomplishes nothing.

He wouldn't dare.

Feelings of panic settle inside her gut. She's suddenly aware of how much noise she's making. If the foreign biological is nearby, she surely is calling attention to herself with this racket.

She's alone. She's locked out. She's toast.

Maybe that's what he wants.

No. He wouldn't.

No matter how bad the end had been, and it had been pretty bad, he surely doesn't want her dead. Morven's a shitty boyfriend, but he isn't completely heartless.

She considers her next move. Reaching into her tool belt for her screwdriver, she hears a hiss. The galley door slides open.

Tamsin stands just on the inside beside the interior controls, twisting her beads in her fingers. "See?" she says, shooting her words over her shoulder, into the galley. "I told you it was Raina. Foreign biologicals don't knock."

Morven stands by the sink beside Niall, who's twisting a dishrag in his palms. "It's a good thing for you, Tamsin," Morven says. "Otherwise you could have killed us all by opening that door."

Raina's face flushes with heat. "You looked right at me as you closed the door."

He shrugs like he's made an honest mistake. "Must have just missed you. Sorry."

She hates how those words hurt. She should be past the point where he can hurt her. But the way he's leaning against the counter with that smug smirk on his face – it makes her blood boil.

He was hoping she'd get attacked.

That sick son of a bitch!

Losing all control for the second time in one day, Mount Raina erupts anew. In a flash, she's across the galley and slaps Morven's cheek so hard the air vibrates.

Tamsin gasps.

Avram shouts like he's at a sporting event, "Ooohhh! Good shot."

This only amplifies Morven's rage.

In his humiliation, his fist pulls back. Niall grabs hold of Morven's elbow, but despite his best effort, the old man isn't strong enough to hold it back. Morven's fist swipes in her direction.

She dodges. He misses by millimeters. She feels the air breeze on her face just as an arm – someone else's arm – pulls her back and away. It's Avram.

"Whoa!" he shouts. "What the hell, Morven?"

Raina's back is against Avram's chest; his arm remains protectively around her waist. She pulls away, but he holds tight. Her eyes find Morven's, and a dread so dark and foreboding makes her shove Avram away with both hands.

"Get back!" she bellows.

Morven's face flushes crimson. Like a wrecking ball he plows straight at her, tossing chairs out of his way, knocking Tamsin aside with a shriek.

Recollections of Morven's temper send Raina into a defensive stance. Her anger morphs into fear. She twists to escape toward the galley door. But Avram is behind her, and in her haste she knocks them both over.

Tangled in each other, Avram and Raina struggle to stand, but Morven reaches them first. Using his meaty arms, he wrenches them to their feet with a single hand.

"No! Don't hurt him," Raina yelps.

"Enough!" shouts Niall.

"Don't you touch her!" Morven bellows at Avram, and then he shoves him so hard he hits the floor and slides backward, slamming into a table.

Tamsin bursts into tears. "Stop it!" she squeals like a child watching her parents argue. "Stop it!"

Raina still has one arm locked in Morven's grasp. He's staring at her, panting like a wild animal, and hurt like a wounded one. She yanks her arm but can't break it free. For a moment, she stands there, heaving and confused. Just a minute ago he tried to deck her, and now he's mad some other guy has touched her?

She comes to her senses enough to say, "Leave Avram alone." Angry tears threaten her burning eyes. "He was only—"

Morven's hurt twists on his face, and he wrenches her arm like a demon. Her words stick in her throat. "Are you fucking *him* now? Is that it?" He's panting so hard he spits in her face.

Raina's dumbstruck. Her arm is screaming for release, but all she can see is the torment in his eyes. For a moment, she's at a loss – unable to make sense of all her feelings as her heart whirs in her ear like a turbine.

She feels sorry for him. Her arm throbs with pain. She's afraid of him. She hates him. She wants to kiss him until his lips bleed.

He still loves me.

"What's your malfunction, Morven?" Avram asks, back upright. He's rubbing his head where it knocked into the table. "Let her go."

With his other hand Morven points at Avram and shoots him a look of death. "Mind your own damn business."

Raina takes the opportunity and yanks her arm free. She walks backward toward Niall, rubbing the bruise that's forming on her bicep.

Niall has one of his rifles powered and aims at Morven's head.

"No, I'm not *fucking* Avram," Raina says. "Not that it's any of your business."

"Ensign Morven, stand down!" Niall shouts, and for once he listens. Morven stands in the middle of the galley, a ring of destruction around him.

Avram inches toward him but Niall points the rifle at him instead and he freezes.

"Stand down. All of you!" Niall shouts again, his arms shaking as they grip the rifle to his shoulder. "That's an order."

Nobody moves.

"Now, I don't know what this is about and I don't care," Niall says through clenched teeth.

"Morven locked the door in my face," Raina says, and Morven glowers at her like she's betrayed him.

"She slapped me," he says.

"You could have killed me."

"He tried to punch her in the face," Avram protests.

"It doesn't matter!" Niall says, and although Raina strongly disagrees, she speaks no more.

"It was an honest mistake, shutting the door just then. Right, Morven?" Niall leads.

Morven reluctantly nods.

Raina opens her mouth but stops when Niall raises a shaking palm in her direction.

"Then Raina went hormonal and Avram was just trying to calm her down, right Avram?" Niall asks, although Raina knows it isn't really a question.

"Fine," says Avram, his expression saying otherwise. "But this is bullshit. He should be written up."

"I'm not *hormonal*," Raina objects.

"Enough!" Niall shouts. "Just drop it. All of you. We've got bigger problems than this, and we're going to be in here for a while. So everybody needs to calm down. Is that understood? Do you all hear me?"

Raina understands completely. As always, nothing will change. The officers will smooth things over as if nothing is wrong. They'll placate Raina and take no action against Morven, just like before.

She absently rubs her ribs.

It's a pattern that will never go in her favor. It never has.

Since no one answers Niall, he shouts again, his voice vibrating with every jagged breath. "Is that *understood*?"

One at a time the others answer, "Yes, sir."

Although the words taste bitter, Raina says it as well.

"All right then," Niall continues, shouldering his laser rifle and stomping to the cooling unit as if nothing has happened at all. He whips open the door and bends over as he rummages around the containers. "Who wants pie?"

★　　★　　★

Demeter
30.8.2331 AD
1130 hours

The sensor readings take Pollux and the others down two access shafts to mid-deck. After circling the level twice, they're still unable to locate the foreign biological.

This makes no sense to Pollux at all. There has to be something wrong with the portable unit, she reasons, because even though it reads the beast is right in front of them, there's obviously nothing there.

That happens twice, once in the mechanics station and again at the armory. Both times they stand there staring, squinting – at a blank wall. Each time, it brings her patience closer to the edge, and damned if her head won't stop pounding.

She knows it's not going to be easy to contain the foreign biological, but it never occurred to her that it would be just as difficult to find the fucking thing. Given what it did on the flight deck it's not exactly docile. Eventually, the creature will get hungry again and go back on the hunt. But still, that doesn't explain why it's hiding now.

Maybe it's full?

The thought makes her shudder.

"What the fuck," Osric groans. "This is annoying."

"Duh." Turning the bend in the hall again, away from the access shaft, she's back around for a third time. It's not that she's in a hurry to engage with the creature, but it sure as hell beats walking in circles for an hour, looking for something that is apparently too quick to be seen.

She passes the planetary lab with Gayla and Valda at her heels. Osric is in the back of the group, which is for the best. He stinks to holy hell and having him too close makes her so furious her nose runs.

Out of the corner of her eye something moves. She twists around, scanning the wall. For a second she's unable to register what she's looking at. It almost appears as if the wall has swollen and grown hair.

In a flash she spots four beady yellow eyes glaring back at her. With a growl, the creature bares its teeth.

"What the fuck is that?" Osric shrieks.

Gayla is the closest to it. She raises her rifle to fire. She snaps the trigger repeatedly, but nothing happens. "Crap!"

"Get behind me, get behind me!" Pollux shouts so loudly she can feel her words echo off the base of her skull.

Gayla skirts behind her, flicking switches on her rifle.

Pollux raises her own weapon, squeezing off two shots. Valda, beside her, gets off two shots as well.

Lasers pierce the hallway and penetrate the wall, leaving charred circles around the creature. But the biological swivels on its legs and dodges each shot, bending its torso as if it were made of rubber. Then it moves up the wall, slaps the cover off the air vent, and disappears inside.

"What the hell was that?" Osric squeals again. His rifle aims at the wall in front of them, but Pollux can tell his weapon hasn't been fired. "Did we get it?"

"We?" Her rifle feels hot in her hands.

"No sé," Valda says. "I don't think so."

Pollux glares at the wall where the creature sat and swallows. It was right there. If it hadn't moved its eyes, she never would have even seen it. No wonder they missed it twice. How could they have been so stupid? The fucking thing is camouflaged.

"Should we go after it?" Osric asks.

"And go where, eh?" Gayla asks. "Through the air vent?"

"Let's wait a sec," Pollux says, checking her rifle's power cell. "Give Gayla a chance to power up."

Gayla looks sheepish as she powers her laser rifle.

Valda frowns at her. "How could you not have your rifle powered, señora loca?"

"I'm sorry," Gayla says, and she holds up the butt of her weapon to show Valda that it is fully powered. "I meant to do it on the flight deck, but I just, the bodies...."

Valda persists. "You had a clear shot! ¿Qué es lo que te pasa?"

"*You* had a clear shot and you *missed*!" Gayla shouts, and the rest of the group shush her.

"All of you shut the fuck up!" Pollux hisses. "Is everybody okay?" She counts. Still four.

"Yeah, we're fucking swell," Osric says. "Any idea what that was?"

She shakes her head. "No idea. I don't recognize it from any of the research on the planets we cultivated. Did the mobile unit find any record of it?"

Valda checks the portable unit on his hip. "Nada. It just reads, 'unknown'."

"It looks like a cat, if you ask me," Gayla says, her hair swaying as she speaks.

Pollux nods. "Moves like one too."

Osric snarls, "Is that why you hesitated, Corporal? Because it's fluffy?"

"No!" Gayla sounds more like a child than an officer. "My rifle wasn't powered."

"Jesucristo salvanos," mutters Valda.

"Did you see the mouth on that thing?" Osric asks. "It has teeth like a shark, in rows."

"I'm more concerned with the fact that we didn't see it until it moved," Pollux notes. "Where is it now?"

Valda checks the portable unit. "I think it went back up."

"You *think* it went up?" Gayla breathes.

Pollux sighs.

"It's got to be moving via the air vents and shafts," Valda explains. "Or it's crawling through the electrical conduits in the wall. It's going to be tricky to track it. This unit doesn't recognize life signs quick enough."

"If it's moving through the electrical conduits," Osric says, "the ship could be in worse shape than it looks. Who knows what that *thing* is ripping apart in the interior of the control panels and consoles while it moves around inside the walls?"

"Use that portable's infrared," Pollux says to Valda. "Track its heat signature. It'll give us a better idea of where it's been and where it's going."

"Hecho." Valda cracks a few switches on the unit and watches the monitor. "That's better. It went through that vent, up that wall, and is now back on upper deck. Should we notify Niall?"

"No, come on," Pollux says, jogging down the hall toward the access shaft, feeling her head pulse with every stomp of her boot. "If we can get there first, we can end this."

CHAPTER EIGHT

Raina glances across the glossy galley table. "Pass the salt."

Morven shifts in his seat and his utility belt clanks against the chair. "What kind of freak puts salt on pie?"

When he doesn't move, Tamsin reaches across him and hands the salt carton to Raina.

Given his expression, Raina thinks she's lucky he didn't flatten her arm with his fist.

Niall plunks another pie packet into the middle of the table and sits down with a grunt. Where he's found the pies, Raina doesn't know. She's afraid to ask. Two years in space and Niall hasn't served pie once. Not once. Maybe it's his private stash, or maybe he was saving them for their last meal of the mission. Either way, she's halfway through a Dutch apple packet that's soothing her nerves well enough.

She looks around at the others. They're all sucking down packets like there's no tomorrow. Depending on how things go with the foreign biological, there might not be. The others seem oblivious to this fact.

"I never fully appreciated you and Morven until I got ringside seats. You're a barrel of laughs," Avram says, his mouth full of coconut cream. "Other than shouting at each other and smacking each other around, do you do party tricks too? How about Who's on First?"

"You should probably shut up now." Raina sprays more salt into her pie packet.

Tamsin blinks. "Who's on first?"

Avram sneezes and wipes his nose on the cloth napkin in his lap. He snorts. "And What's on Second." Tam looks at him like she doesn't know what he's talking about, so he just shakes his head.

Niall chews, saying nothing. He runs his fingers over his wrinkled face and grimaces. If Raina didn't know any better, she'd think the bags under his eyes have doubled in size since they arrived in the galley.

She frowns, and her eyes find Morven's hands from across the table. One holds his packet like he's dumping a shovel into his mouth, the other rests softly on the slick top. He taps the table with the long strong fingers on his free hand and she forces herself to look away. It's too easy to remember his hands, his touch. When he was nice about it.

Raina takes a swig of recycled water and swallows loudly. She looks up and sees him watching her, as if he's sensing her thoughts of him.

He smirks. His pearly smile glistens with pie.

A while back that sexy grin would have sent her into the cosmos with lust, but now it makes her head throb. She stands up, taking her empty packet with her, then shoves it into the waste bin. There are still gravy stains on the side from this morning's breakfast.

"You're on cleanup duty," Niall says to her, and Raina's frown deepens.

She unbuttons the sleeves on her uniform to roll them up. It reminds her of all the times she'd been relegated to kitchen duty while she was still living at home, which became more and more often as her younger siblings grew up and moved out, leaving her there, wondering what to do with her life, buried in the bulk of the chores. Now Raina is out in the universe, traveling amongst the stars just like her brother the golden boy, and she's still stuck doing the dishes. How's that for irony?

"Avram, are you sick?" Tamsin asks, and all eyes go to him.

He sniffs loudly. "No. Just allergies."

Raina hopes the conversation will end at that. Chatting among this crowd could lead to another incident. But this is Tamsin, and she doesn't leave much unsaid. That's a bonus as far as Raina is concerned, usually.

"What are you allergic to?" Tamsin continues.

"What does it matter?" Morven asks.

She shoots him a look. "I'm just making conversation."

Morven grumbles and squeezes more pie into his mouth.

"I'm allergic to bullies and buzz haircuts," Avram says, and Niall snickers.

"You're a scientist, how could you *not* know what you're allergic to?" Tamsin asks, flipping her ponytail in the air and chewing on her beads.

He shrugs, wiping his nose again, this time on his hand.

"Disgusting." Morven grimaces, and tosses him the napkin from his own lap.

"Thanks," Avram says, snatching the napkin in midair and blowing his nose into it. "I'm not sure what happened. It's gotten so much worse lately."

"Why don't you run a panel and find out what's causing it?" Tam suggests. "Or take an antihistamine?"

He shrugs again. "Well, I've been busy. In case you haven't noticed, we've got over fifteen hundred specimens in the greenhouse. They don't take care of themselves, you know. It's a lot of work pulling alien weeds. Which, funnily enough, is *not* what I thought I would be doing when I joined the science program at the Space Corps. I had visions of exotic planets and scantily clad green women who had not yet heard the term 'geek'."

"You're a disgrace," Morven grumbles.

"Meh," he says, "can't blame a guy for trying. And it's a hell of a lot better than cataloging and measuring how tall alien plants grow. Wouldn't you say, Morven?" He raises his unibrow at him. "Tell me, is that why you joined? To pull weeds and measure plants?"

"Of course not. Don't be an imbecile," Morven says.

"Can't do that," he answers. "That's your department."

"Now, now," Tamsin says. "Don't start that up again."

"He joined for the honor," Raina says, and suddenly all eyes are on her. She realizes she's breaking a confidence that she and Morven once shared by volunteering this information, but that's over now, and she suddenly has the urge to knock him down a few pegs. "He joined because he wants to be a hero."

"I do not," he says, turning red. "You don't know what the fuck you're talking about."

"Don't I?"

No one contradicts her, not even Morven. He turns back to his pie and chews so hard Raina can hear his teeth hitting against each other. Her disgusted reaction is a far cry from how she used to feel.

She can still picture him in bed with her, late that one night after a particularly bumpy and aggressive asteroid field had banged up the ship and put them all on edge. Raina had spent the better part of a twenty-four-hour shift listening to Osric blame her for every crack and break aboard, and after a hot and heavy evening with Morven, she spent a good ten minutes feeling sorry for herself. That was, until Morven had given her a speech about the honor of joining the United Space Corps, and that she was doing a service to the whole universe, and she needed to pull herself together, for the sake of the mission.

"Stop your damned whining," he added, with just a hint of sadness.

Raina ran her hand up his arm and stroked his face. He was probably thinking of his father.

Morven traced the curve of her breast with his fingertip so gently it made her quiver. "Who knows what cures and discoveries lie inside those alien plant specimens," he said. He ran his palm down the contours of her hip. "*We* are a part of that," he whispered in her ear.

Arching her back, she dug her fingernails into his shoulders.

"We're making a difference," he said. "*We're* making history. Don't let that fuckhead Osric ruin it for you."

Raina let out her breath, almost forgetting what they were talking about.

"You mean *he's* making history."

Morven frowned.

"Don't forget," she explained, stroking his ear. "Ensigns won't show up in the official reports. Osric and all the officers will get the honor."

He took her hand away.

Thinking him not in the mood, she rolled onto her back and continued, "Meanwhile, I'll get demoted and sent to fix flickering light fixtures in bathroom stalls for the rest of my tour, and you'll get a medal for being the best lay in the cosmos."

He'd gotten furious with her then, shoving her out of bed and tossing her clothes in her face. She didn't understand why, at the time. She chalked it up to his fiery temper and having his feelings hurt because she'd called him a good lay. She'd slunk silently back into her own sleep chamber and forgot all about it.

It wasn't until just then, sitting in the galley with the others, and listening to him call Avram an imbecile, that she understood why he'd gotten so angry with her back then.

Yes, his feelings had been hurt, but it wasn't why she had thought.

His ego had been bruised.

Above all else, she sees now, Morven wants *credit*. He wants his part in their mission to be *known*. He didn't join the Space Corps to be treated like a second-class citizen. He craves recognition. He wants to rewrite his family's history, wants to be thought of as a hero.

"Better to join for honor than to run away from home," Morven digs back at her.

Raina shrugs, unaffected by the truth. "At least I got what I wanted."

His face flushes.

Before Morven can reply, Tamsin interrupts. "Avram, back to your allergies. How long does it take to run a blood panel? I mean, really?"

Raina nods. It's an innocent enough question to which they all know the answer. It takes no time at all. Not with their scientific capabilities aboard.

"We could run one now," Tamsin suggests. "Then we could figure out how best to treat it."

"Can't do much from here," Avram notes and he's right. There aren't any consoles or workstations inside the galley – just the kitchenette, the cold storage unit, and a few tables with chairs. "Besides, we can't do anything now, we've been benched."

"Did you have allergies back home?" Tamsin asks.

"Christ, can't we talk about something else?" Morven waves his hand holding the pie packet. "I'm eating!"

"Animal dander," Avram says, ignoring him.

Raina stops scrubbing gravy stains off the waste container and twists around. "Wait. What?"

"Avram!" Morven shouts and they all stare at him as he sniffs.

"What?"

Morven gets to his feet. "Why didn't you mention this before?"

"Mention my allergies?" He looks confused.

Raina dries her soapy hands on a dishrag. She's surprised to see Niall continue to slurp his slice of rhubarb pie as if nothing is wrong. Doesn't he understand? From the look on Morven's face, Raina knows he's had the same thought she's had, which is disturbing to her on a whole other level.

"How long have your allergies been this bad?" Morven asks. His eyes squint at Avram's confused face.

He shrugs. "I don't know, a few weeks maybe."

"A few weeks!" Raina exclaims.

"What? I don't get it! What's the big deal?" Avram asks.

"You're allergic to animal dander and there's a foreign biological loose on board, you dipshit," Morven says.

"So?" he says, and Raina inches toward him, in case Morven loses his temper and gets physical again.

"So," Morven seethes. "You didn't think to mention this to the captain when it started?"

Avram scratches his watery eyes. "I figured one of the specimens had set me off. I still don't get what the big deal is."

"But you're not allergic to plants," Tamsin says.

"Not usually. But they're *alien* plant specimens. We're still analyzing what kind of pollen they release. There could be any number of things floating through this shitty ventilation system, setting me off. Honestly, I'm surprised we're not all sick with something. In fact, come to think of it, we had a spore split open, and we had to quarantine it for a week just to make sure it didn't emit any toxic fumes. It was probably that."

Morven's face goes ashen. "The open seed spore."

Avram nods. "See? Morven gets it."

"But it's not just anything setting you off," Raina says, taking another step closer to the table. Her eyes meet Morven's. "It's animal dander."

"It's not a seed spore at all," he breathes. "It hatched from there."

Tamsin looks confused. "Hold on. What hatched?"

"The foreign biological," Raina says.

"Now, just wait a minute." Niall holds up his hands like he's stopping traffic. He'd been so quiet, Raina had almost forgotten he was there. "You're getting ahead of yourselves. None of this could mean anything."

"Or everything," Morven says, and Raina nods in agreement. "We need to get to the greenhouse and check out that spore. Avram, did you finish the analysis after the quarantine was lifted?"

He shakes his head, suddenly realizing the seriousness of the situation. "Pollux was supposed to do it."

"And did she?"

"I don't know. She's my superior. I can't exactly *ask*."

"Did you see any report?" Morven turns to Tamsin. She has her moments, but the entire crew is well aware of her photographic memory. The report would have crossed her desk and as a top-notch Data Processing Ensign, Tamsin never forgets one iota of information she's heard or read. It's one of her strengths, and weaknesses.

"Nope," she says, "never saw it. Valda must have processed it."

"We need to get to the greenhouse," Morven says again, and he makes a move toward his laser rifle, which is slung over the back of his chair. "We have to know if that's where the foreign biological came from. If we know where it came from, we'll know better how to kill it."

Niall labors to stand, grunting with the effort. "Now, hold on. Nobody is going anywhere."

Avram snatches up his rifle. "Weren't there two spores?"

"Yes," Morven says, powering up his weapon. "But the other one didn't open."

"If it does, that means there could be two foreign biologicals aboard," Avram says.

Raina moves to retrieve her rifles.

"Hold on!" Niall shouts. "Just wait – damn it. Attention!"

The room snaps still as everybody in the room stands stiff as a board.

"We are under orders to stay in this room until we hear otherwise," Niall reminds them. "We'll only get in the way. We can't go gallivanting off like a bunch of cowboys. Nobody is going anywhere. Am I making myself clear?"

There's a smattering of 'yes, sirs'.

"Very good," Niall says, and he gives the 'at ease' order, relaxing the others.

"But, sir—" Morven starts.

"I said that's enough," Niall insists, and he sprays half the table with pie as he speaks. "If it'll make you feel better, I'll send a communiqué to Pollux letting her know about these spores. Let the *officers* take care of this. It's their job! They know what they're doing."

Raina's eyes flick toward Morven and she can tell from his expression that he's thinking the same thing she is.

Let's hope so.

CHAPTER NINE

Five Months Ago....

"Were you, or were you not responsible for the injuries to Ensign Raina?" the captain asks again.

Raina sits at her designated table in the galley, jiggling her legs underneath. There's only the three of them there, and she wishes Pollux was with her. At least for moral support, if nothing else. But the captain had ordered the hearings closed, which meant it was her word against his, and she didn't like the captain's tone at all.

Morven stares straight ahead like the captain hasn't just asked the same question twice. "That depends on your point of view."

"Don't get smart with me," he says. "This medical report was quite damning. She claims, and the ship's cameras confirm, these injuries were sustained at your hand. You were the only one in and out of her sleep chamber during this time frame. I fail to see how this could be anything but your fault."

"Captain, if I may, I was provoked."

"Provoked!" Raina shouts. She gets to her feet so quickly her chair falls back. "How can you stand there and—"

"Ensign Raina!" the captain says. "Sit down."

"But you heard what Sergeant Pollux said, Captain," she persists. "You can see the medical report. No matter what I supposedly did to provoke him, surely that doesn't justify what he did."

"Nothing can justify violence against another crew member, that's a given—" the captain starts.

"I lay on that floor for an hour before Tamsin found me, Captain. I was unconscious for an *hour*."

"I am well aware of your condition, Ensign," the captain says. "Now, sit down."

Raina reaches behind, picks up her chair and flops into her seat. This is the biggest load of shit she's ever witnessed in her life.

Never mind having to deal with Osric for the past year and a half, this takes the cake. Why Morven wasn't immediately jettisoned from the ship the moment the security cameras were reviewed is beyond her comprehension. It's not as if she did it to herself.

"Your injuries were egregious," the captain continues, "but if Ensign Morven was provoked...."

"She struck me first, sir," Morven says.

"You lying sack of shit. He had me by the arm!"

The captain raises his hand, stopping her cold. "I am not interested in participating in a 'he said, she said'. This unfortunate event is nothing more than the fruits of your own misjudgment, the both of you. Fraternization aboard this ship is strictly forbidden, and I have no tolerance for those who break the rules and then complain when they must suffer the consequences."

She can barely believe her ears. "But Captain!"

"I have heard all I want to hear on this matter. As per protocol when a complaint of this nature is brought forth, the two of you will not be alone together, or communicate with one another for the remainder of this voyage – except for on official business – and both of you will have disciplinary marks on your record due to this incident. Dismissed."

"But Captain!"

"Ensign Raina," he says, standing from his chair and leaning against the table with his palms. "I don't want to hear another word about this from either of you for the remainder of this mission. Understood?"

Morven nods stiffly. "Yes, sir."

The captain, apparently satisfied, stalks across the galley and exits – leaving Raina alone with Morven. Two seconds after the hearing and they're already in violation of the captain's orders.

Raina's tongue is so dry it sticks to the roof of her mouth.

What the fuck was that?

Morven beats her unconscious and *she* gets disciplined? She's just barely back on duty from sick leave and she feels like he's beaten her all over again. Every bone in her body aches.

"Can you believe that shit?" Morven laughs.

She turns her head so slowly, it's as if the moment lasts minutes.

He's laughing.

He's fucking *laughing*!

Thinking quickly, she spins on her heels, ducking out the galley door so fast she almost smacks her face on the door as it hisses open.

The sound of Morven's laughter follows her down the hall.

★   ★   ★

Demeter
30.8.2331 AD
1200 hours

Morven moans and slams his fist against the galley table so hard it makes everybody jump. "What the hell is taking them so long?"

No one dares to answer him, except Niall. He turns from the sink and eyes Morven with a steady gaze. "It's a big ship," he says evenly, his arms covered in soap bubbles up to his elbows. He'd gotten so frustrated watching Raina do a horrible job washing the water cartons he's taken over. She doesn't mind.

She sits on the other side of the room with her legs propped up on a chair and watches.

Morven looks about ready to burst wide open with nervous energy. "It's not that big!" he protests, and he turns on his heel and paces in the other direction.

"Big enough," says Avram. "Sit down and meditate, or something. There's nothing we can do."

"That's the problem," Morven says. "There *is* something we can do, but *he* won't let us." He nods toward Niall at the sink. "Did Pollux respond to your communiqué?"

Niall grunts in response. "Not yet."

"It's no wonder she hasn't responded. I doubt she's checking her messages right now. It was a stupid idea," Morven says.

"Our orders were to wait," Raina reminds him, and Morven's fiery eyes briefly flash at her before they return to boring holes into Niall's back. She looks away. Sometimes the way he gazes at her still wrings her heart like a wet towel.

"If we coordinate with the officers, we can trap the foreign biological between us. This whole ordeal could have been over by now if we'd gone out together," Morven says.

"You surprise me." Raina chooses her words with care. "You're usually such a stickler for rules and regulations."

"Yeah, well," he flounders, looking uncomfortable at the personal comment. "Only when the orders make sense."

"Pollux is just following command regulations," Avram says. "Any of you have combat experience?" When no one answers his question, he continues, wiping his runny nose on the napkin in his hand. "When faced with an unknown life-form, the subject is to be engaged by combat-experienced personnel only. Am I right, Tamsin?"

"You're right. Section 1.186.9 of the *United Space Corps Rules of Engagement*," she confirms. "Page five hundred and fifty-four, paragraph six."

"See," Avram says, and he raises his unibrow at her. "I'm always right."

A tiny grin etches across Tamsin's small face as she sits at one of the tables, and she looks so young and scared just then, Raina's heart lurches. She's just a kid, really.

Still, even with the other ensigns being a few years older than Tam, none of them have any battle training either. There was basic assembly and fire of a laser rifle instruction at the Academy, but Raina knows that won't be enough to track and contain a foreign biological of unknown origin. They'd only get in the way or get killed.

Although, part of her hates to admit she agrees with Morven. If they were out with the officers they might be able to help in some respect, versus just waiting in the galley like fish in a barrel.

Raina shifts in her seat. She watches Niall scrub the same container for the second time and knows he's stress cleaning. It's just as well. At least he has something to do to keep busy.

She runs her hands across the back of her neck as a chill prickles her skin. Instinctively, she turns around, expecting to see someone behind her. No one is there.

She turns back around to face the others, but when she has the sensation again, she drops her feet to the floor and rotates in her chair, facing the wall behind her.

Avram sneezes loudly, causing them all to jump.

"Gesundheit," Tamsin says.

He sniffs. "Danke."

Raina can't help it. She stares at the wall behind her. Something isn't right, but she can't place it.

"What's wrong with you?" Morven asks.

"Nothing," she answers, and forces herself to turn back around. "Just a chill."

Morven shakes his head in annoyance. "Leave it to you to get a chill when it's a hundred degrees in here."

She rolls her eyes at him. There isn't much she can do that doesn't annoy him.

Avram sneezes again, this time harder. The force of that sneeze doubles him over in his chair. When he sits back up, he wheezes with a sudden intake of breath that stops in his throat. "I…can't…breathe…."

Morven sighs. "That's not funny."

Avram chokes once, and coughs. His face goes scarlet.

"I don't think he's joking," Raina says.

"He's not." Tamsin's on her feet the quickest, but she doesn't go to Avram. Instead, she heads straight for the sink and moves Niall out of the way so she can rummage in the cupboard underneath.

Avram's wheezes worsen and he grips his throat.

"What's happening?" Raina cries. Avram's lips turn blue. "Avram, what's wrong?"

Avram chokes in response and falls from his chair, hitting the floor.

Tamsin comes up from the kitchen cupboard with an injector and without hesitation, crosses the room and puts it to Avram's neck. She presses the release button with her thumb and it hisses like a snake.

Immediately, he gasps for air and the wheezing softens. His lips turn a healthy shade of pink. Tamsin helps him sit up, although he still looks woozy.

"What was that?" Niall asks, shaking bubbles from his thick arms.

Avram jiggles his head, unable to talk.

Tamsin loads the injector with another vial. "Anaphylactic shock."

"An allergic reaction?" Another chill breezes Raina's neck. "To what?" She turns around slowly this time, sensing a presence behind her. This time she sees it.

A creature with fur the exact color of the wall crouches just inside the tiny air grate at the ceiling – watching her with all four of its yellow beady eyes.

She lurches with a shriek and falls to the floor, then crawls backward on all fours, skittering away. "The air vent!"

Morven doesn't hesitate. He has his rifle ready and shots ring out. He misses. The wall sizzles where the laser strikes around the vent grate.

The creature pops its head and shoulders out the vent and growls, sending the grate clattering to the floor. The beast retreats, easily dodging two more shots from Morven's laser.

In a flash of fur and teeth, it slithers backward into the shaft, practically flattened all the way down.

Morven gets off one more shot, as does Niall – both of them miss. The beast is too fast and dodges each one. The wall smolders with laser welts.

"Damn it all!" Niall curses. He lowers his rifle, makes his way across the room to the door console, and presses the ship's intercom button. "Foreign biological is in the air vent system, upper deck. It's headed away from the galley toward the access shafts and sleep chamber. Sergeant Pollux, do you copy?"

"Did you see how long it was?" Tamsin whispers, terror in her eyes.

Raina gets to her feet and holds the table to steady herself. She feels the unmistakable sensation of fear as her eyes dart back to the exposed air vent. It had been right behind her. Right there. She'd felt its breath on the back of her neck.

She feels so naked.

Avram wheezes beside Tamsin and she hits him again with the injector.

"Sergeant Pollux, do you copy?" Niall says into the intercom.

"What if they're already dead?" Morven asks.

★　　★　　★

Pollux is the first off the ladder and onto upper deck. Valda, Gayla, and Osric follow closely behind. They stand just off the access ladder, and twist their bodies around, rifles at the ready, searching for what is almost invisible.

Pollux's head pounds like a piston as her heart rate increases. It's even hotter up here. She resists the urge to let go of her rifle and massage her pulsing temples.

Pain is for sissies.

A trickle of sweat drips down her bangs and stings her eyes. Pollux uses her arm to brush it away and fights to keep her vision sharp. The ship still feels over a hundred degrees and there so much sweat pooling in her boots her feet squeak with each step. The skin on both arms and her chest burns with a fierce itch. She's not sure how much longer she can go on like this. It's nearly unbearable.

Passing the sleep chamber on her left, she pops the door open and circles inside, then back out. Seems clear. Before she closes the door, Pollux checks it again, trying to catch sight of the yellow eyes.

Nothing.

She turns around and faces the hallway. The others stand by the access shaft, whispering to one another. When they catch sight of her watching, Gayla steps away from the men and looks at the floor.

"You got something to say?" Pollux challenges them. "Say it."

The wall moves over her shoulder. She twists and spots it. The foreign biological has crawled out of the air vent leading off the galley and hangs there, peering at her.

The ship's intercom crackles to life. Niall's strained voice announces, "Foreign biological is in the air vent system, upper deck. It's headed away from the galley toward the access shafts and sleep chamber. Sergeant Pollux, do you copy?"

"Wait – that would make it...." Osric says.

"Right here," Pollux finishes, and moves exceptionally slowly and carefully toward the beast.

The creature's fur matches the wall and transforms with each of its steps. It glides on six legs like a pocket of air with the agility of a sidewinder snake in the sand. It has no tail, just a round end and a slender, tubular torso. The rib cage juts from side to side as it silently pads aslant across the wall.

The three of them had been standing right across from it and had been too busy gossiping about her to see it.

Pollux swallows the bile in the back of her throat. "Two o'clock," she whispers, and she raises her rifle to her shoulder.

"Where?" Gayla whispers back.

"I don't see a damned thing," Osric grumbles.

"Yo lo veo," Valda says.

"Fire!" Pollux gives the order and opens fire.

She and Valda each get off two shots, three of them hitting the wall beside the animal and burning a hole. The other shot strikes the biological with a black sizzle between the eyes. A faint scorch mark appears on the beast's head where the laser hit, but the creature shakes its head as if to get rid of an annoying insect, then slithers back up the wall toward the ceiling, bending and slinking at a casual pace. It disappears again into the air vent headfirst.

"You got it!" Gayla cheers.

"Madre de Dios."

"It barely flinched," Pollux says. "We need a higher wattage." She fumbles with the controls of her rifle.

"Copy that," Valda says, doing the same.

"To maximum," Pollux adds.

"The rifles will burn out too fast at that wattage," Osric says, squinting at the wall where the biological had hung. "Where do you think it's going?"

With a burst, the creature ruptures from the vent again, landing sidelong on the wall like a spider.

"Motherfucker!" bellows Osric.

With its teeth bared, the beast growls from the depths of its throat. A tiny dribble of clear sticky slime drips off its lower lip.

All hell breaks loose.

Laser rifle fire erupts again, ripping through the air like ribbons of flame. Valda prays in Spanish as he shoots. Osric curses. Gayla screams and backs up, firing from the top of the access shaft.

Pollux's rifle burns out with a hiss and she steps behind Osric, frantically attempting to remove one of the extra rifles from his shoulder. But he's too busy using both his arms, firing at the biological, and won't stop long enough to allow the strap off his shoulder.

Pollux struggles with the strap clasp but keeps her eyes on the creature across the hall.

The wall behind it sizzles with laser holes and the beast itself is hit many times. It barely moves each time it is struck. Several shots hit the same spot on its back, leaving a small open wound. Even then, the animal appears unaffected. The wound, surrounded by singed fur, reveals purplish muscle mass underneath. Yet, it hardly winces.

Pollux presses her thumb against the rifle strap release and yanks the strap from Osric's arm, but still her eyes watch the creature.

Valda hits it between the eyes again. To Pollux, it seems to only aggravate the thing more. As far as she can tell, even using maximum laser wattage hasn't made a difference. They'll never wound it mortally if they continue like this. The thing is too still, even in the barrage of laser fire. It does not appear to be feeling any pain.

Pollux blinks back sweat and watches as it inches forward across the wall, slowly stalking toward Gayla.

If she doesn't think of something fast things are going to get ugly.

Come on! It's just a stupid cat! Think!

With a heave from its back legs, the biological lands on the floor about a foot from the access shaft, with its back to Pollux and the others. The creature's head faces Gayla.

"Oh Jesus," Pollux whispers, finally powering up the extra rifle and tossing the strap over her head. Down the hall, the animal has separated the corporal from the rest of the group. "Gayla! Get around it!"

Valda and Osric fire their weapons repeatedly, striking the foreign biological and the floor of the hallway. Crossing leg over leg, they shift their position in an attempt to fire upon the beast from multiple sides. But the animal is still unmoved by the laser wounds. The only evidence it feels anything at all is the occasional shift of fur as it ripples across the animal's body, adjusting and readjusting the camouflage to its surroundings.

Gayla backs up all the way to the top of the access shaft ladders, but has nowhere left to go.

Pollux can only watch as the realization crosses Gayla's face. She's trapped. "Wait!" Gayla shouts, panic rising. "Wait!"

With a snarl, it pounces onto Gayla's chest.

Thick and metallic-looking claws launch from the animal's paws and swat Gayla across the shoulder, knocking her rifle clear across her body and into the wall, and slicing her flesh with the precision of a blade. She shrieks in agony.

Her tendons severed, her arms slacken and she loses her grip, collapsing under the weight of her own body. Gayla falls backward down the access ladder and disappears from sight. The beast jumps down after her.

"Gayla!" Valda cries.

"Go, go, go!" shouts Pollux. Osric and Valda get to the ladder and slide down the sides of it like a pole.

Arriving last to the ladder, Pollux snatches Gayla's discarded rifle from the floor and slides down after the others. Landing on her feet, she reaches mid-deck with a thud. Behind her are the sounds of rifle fire.

"Aim at the fucking eyes!" shouts Osric.

When she turns to face the action, Pollux gasps.

Gayla's body dangles from the foreign biological's jaws, which are clamped around her crushed skull. Chunks of brain matter and Gayla's stark red blood plops everywhere the animal crawls, dripping a trail of horror on the floor in goopy lumps.

Pollux drops to one knee and concentrates her fire on the beast's yellow eyes, but she misses. It moves with lightning speed, slinking up the wall with ease, and dragging Gayla's body from the head. The creature knocks off the vent grate with a swipe and squeezes back end first into the vent.

Gayla's head, still clamped in its jaws, collapses enough to fit inside, but her body protrudes from the vent at the shoulders like a limp doll.

"Jesus," Osric and Valda both say.

The rifle fire stops once the beast disappears into the vent.

Gayla's body shakes and jolts as the beast pulls and tugs, but no amount of yanking will make Gayla's body fit inside the air vent.

"Oh god," Pollux says, too repulsed to move. She desperately wants to free Gayla's body but she's rooted to the floor in terror.

With a final tug, Gayla's head snaps off and the rest of her body hits the floor with a splat.

Coming from just inside the vent echoes the sound of the beast's teeth scraping across the corporal's skull.

CHAPTER TEN

Demeter
30.8.2231 AD
1220 hours

Inside the galley, Morven tilts his head to one side. "Did you hear laser fire?"

"Yeah," Raina confirms. "They're on our floor. That's the only way we'd be able to hear them."

"What did you hear?" Tamsin asks. She sits beside Avram, twisting her beads in one hand and monitoring his vital signs with the other. Although Avram can breathe and his color is improving, he is still sniffing like a madman. Tamsin hands him a fresh napkin, which he takes willingly. A pile of spent, snotty cloths is heaped on the table in front of him. He spots Raina watching and gives her a thumbs-up.

"I think it was rifle fire," Raina says, sensing Morven is too annoyed with her question to say it again.

Morven stands at the far corner of the room, his rifle at the ready as he stares at the air vent.

"They're just outside," Niall says. He noisily sips a carton of coffee and grunts as he shifts his weight in a chair by the door. "It'll all be over soon."

"I hope they got it. I don't think my respiratory system could take another pummeling like that," Avram says.

"Only one way to find out," Morven says, and he moves across the room toward the door control panel.

"No," Niall insists, and he sounds stern enough to mean it.

Morven stops midway. "What if they need backup?"

"They'd ask for it."

"Not if they're too busy dying," Morven says. His hands go straight for the control panel.

Niall is on his feet and snatches his hand. He moves awfully fast for an old codger. "We're under orders, Ensign Morven."

"In time of battle," Morven quotes, "members of the United Space Corps are given leeway to disobey direct orders. Particularly when the chain of command is disrupted. Isn't that right, Tamsin?"

"3.876.5 of the *United Space Corps Rules of Engagement*, paragraph—"

"Shut up, Tamsin," barks Niall, and the harshness of his tone stills the room. "Nobody leaves."

Morven pulls his arm out of Niall's hand. "They're just outside."

"You don't know that."

"You just said it yourself!"

"They could have moved on." He turns to the others. "I'm sure they've got it covered. Nobody. Goes. Anywhere."

"We're not safe in here," Morven says. "That thing can move through the air vents. We're sitting ducks!"

Hesitation flits across Niall's face. He looks to Raina as if she'll agree with him. She doesn't. She finds herself in the uncomfortable position of siding with Morven. They're no safer in the galley than they are in the rest of the ship. If they truly follow the United Space Corps terms of engagement, they should be altering their orders to fit the situation.

All eyes are on Niall. As senior officer, it's his call. Their lives are in the hands of the ship's chef, and he looks too petrified to move.

★　　★　　★

"Where's it going?" Pollux shouts. She stares at the air vent where the creature has disappeared. "Damnit!"

"There it is!" Valda says, pointing to the next air vent farther down the hall. "It's heading toward the lab. Prisa, vamos a seguir!"

"Fuck it!" Osric labors down the corridor.

"Wait up," Pollux says. The last thing she needs is for the slowest member of their diminishing troop to take point.

She casts one last glace at Gayla's headless corpse slumped against the wall, then jogs after the biological, passing Valda and Osric on the way.

Three left.

Bad odds. Bad fucking odds!

She reaches the entrance to the planetary lab, and without waiting for the others to catch up, taps the door control panel with an open palm.

The doors slide open to reveal the beast, standing on the floor just on the inside. Pollux catches a quick glance of the bent vent grate lying on the floor beside the creature, and several pieces of lab debris shattered at its feet, probably from when the animal crawled down the wall. Gayla's crushed head sits beside it. She's missing both eyes.

The beast turns and looks at Pollux. Its fur ripples and changes color again. All she can see is its eyes.

Instead of firing, she dives for the controls. Her palm slaps the panel and the door starts to close. But the beast leans back on its haunches and leaps off the floor with a whisper, crashing into the sliding metal, and slicing through it as if it were made of paper. Pollux scrambles backward, pushing her body against the wall of the hallway.

The animal lands on the ground at Pollux's feet, sniffs the air and then turns away. It focuses on Valda and Osric, who run toward them both.

"Holy shit!" Osric skids to a halt.

Valda slams into Osric's back and they both careen forward.

Pollux readies her rifle and shoots at the beast twice. She hits it once on the back, once on the shoulder. But the animal ignores the rifle fire and stalks past her toward Valda and Osric. Both are on their knees, firing. Even getting pelted from both sides, the creature doesn't stop. They might as well be throwing water balloons.

There has to be some way to stop this thing!

Pollux turns on her heel. Behind her is the planetary lab. She pries the sliced doors open and shimmies through. There's got to be something inside she can use. There has to!

The lab is normally used to prepare the botany team for specimen gathering. Calculations, research, and past exploration records of the alien planets are analyzed and scrutinized before the botanists suit up and spacewalk down to the planet to collect new plant life.

Pollux scans the room. There isn't much besides work consoles, chairs, database storage units, and atmospheric experimentation equipment. The only moveable items are the chairs.

She hears a shriek from the hallway and snatches one. It's made of metal, and is heavy and large. Shouldering her way back out the broken door, she drags the chair behind. She arrives back in the hallway just in time to see the beast bury its face into the soft cushion of Valda's abdomen.

"No!" she cries.

Valda bellows in agony. The creature presses him up against the wall and chews its way through his gut. Valda's arms flail and his legs lift off the ground an inch.

"Jesús salvsame!"

Blood and flesh splatter him, Osric, and every inch of the hallway like a sprinkler.

Osric has given up firing his rifle and uses it as a club, beating the biological in the head repeatedly, cursing with every swing.

Pollux drags the chair down the hall, and with a great heave, lifts it as high as she can. Using every ounce of her strength, she crashes the chair down onto the back of the animal.

The chair crushes the creature flat, popping its head out of Valda's bloody torso like a cork. Valda's feet hit the ground but are unable to hold his weight. He pitches forward, face-first onto the metal-grated floor.

Just to the side of Valda, Pollux gapes at the beast's flattened tubular body.

"Yes!" Osric cheers.

The biological writhes on the floor, snapping and popping loudly. It jerks from side to side, wriggling like a lizard that lost its tail.

"Die, you motherfucker!" Osric jeers. He stands on the other side of Valda, still holding his rifle like a bat.

Neither one of them can move to help Valda, who lies on the floor in a pool of his own entrails, gasping for air with shallow, gurgling breaths. The beast is in their way and still flops all over. They can only stand frozen in their awe and terror, inches from him, waiting for the creature to die.

It snaps its jaws, biting nothing but hot air, growling.

"Is it dying?" Pollux asks aloud, to no one in particular.

"Come on, die!" Osric taunts it.

Suddenly, there's a crack.

The biological's shoulder bone slides up from under its skin and pops back into place just below the neck. Then follows the spine. In a wave of dominoes, the vertebrae rotate and reassemble back into position – like some sick and twisted antique clock rewinding itself. Last come the hip sockets. They snap back in place with the sound of splitting sticks.

"No!" Pollux cries.

Having re-expanded its flattened body into a tubular shape, the beast twitches its head to one side with a pop, as if realigning its neck.

Pollux watches, transfixed, stunned. Her mouth gapes open. Tears flood her eyes.

This can't be!

When finished, the creature shakes like a wet dog, re-camouflages its fur, then scuttles its feet on the floor, spinning around.

Pollux drops the chair from her numbed fingers.

There's no killing it.

We're dead. We're all dead.

The beast faces her, then turns toward Osric, who also gapes in utter disbelief. Coming to his senses, he swishes his rifle through the air, aiming at the biological's head again.

"Son of a bitch!" he bellows.

With a direct hit to the animal's skull, the rifle breaks into pieces. The creature barely flinches and pauses its approach for only a sliver of a moment. A desperate-looking Osric smacks the beast repeatedly with the rifle shards.

Pollux quickly bends down, grips the chair again, hoping to toss it over Valda and back onto the biological. But she only gets it off the ground an inch or two when the alien pounces onto Osric's shoulders. It slides its claws down his body like nails on a chalkboard, slicing him to meaty chunks.

"Motherfu—!" is Osric's last gurgle before Pollux watches the light escape his eyes and his body pieces cascade to the floor.

The chair slips from Pollux's fingers.

There is nothing left to do but die.

She hears shrieking and realizes it's coming from her. She turns her watering eyes to Valda, who gasps slowly, so very slowly, looking white and ghostly. His lips move in a pool of his own blood. He whispers to her, "Corre, chica. Run."

★   ★   ★

Six Months Ago....

Pollux snaps gloves over her hands and laces her fingers together to fit them snugly. With a trained eye she studies the most recent specimen. It's odd really, for a seed spore.

She and Gayla found a batch of them in a crater on Kepler 22b. It's spherical, quite large, shaped almost like an egg, but hard like a seedpod and devoid of life signs. She wanted to take the lot of them, but the captain insisted on only gathering two. All her preliminary theories about the spores, from their colorful exterior to their location beside a large batch of red treelike saplings on the planet's surface, leads her to believe they're seeds for the tree species.

What a feather in her cap this would be, bringing home the seeds of a previously failed species. The last expedition had only brought back a few saplings, but those had died in transit. But if she's able to preserve the seed spores and bring them back to Earth, maybe the Space Corps Scientific Division at headquarters will be able to grow viable samples.

She takes a swab from the tray beside her in the enclosure and dabs it into the clear gel-like substance that coats the exterior of the pod. It's rather gooey, to tell the truth. Like sticky saliva or something you'd style your hair with. She's never seen a seed spore with a coating before, but then again, it *is* of alien origin. One has to keep an open mind.

She seals the gel sample into a test tube, pulls off her gloves, and exits the enclosure, securing the door behind her and making her way to the lab.

After tasking Morven and Avram to set up the sample for a full breakdown in the processor, she heads up to the data station. As she expects, Valda and Gayla sit at their work consoles. Gayla grins like an idiot and types so fast Pollux has to wonder if she's making a million mistakes and doesn't even notice.

"Hey guys," she says.

Valda looks up but Gayla keeps typing.

"Hola chica. Que pasa?"

"He wants to know what's up," Gayla translates.

"That one I know." Pollux puts a hand on her hip. "Got a new one for you."

Gayla's fingers stop moving. "Have you run it, eh?"

"The coating is running now, but I still have the full spectrum scan to do. Should have the preliminaries in a few hours. It's probably those red trees we saw on Kepler 22b, Gay, but if they're not, I was just curious how you want me to input them into the inventory."

She's got both their attentions now.

"Well, I guess we'll know where to list it once you get the genus specified," Valda says. "In the meantime, list it in the addendum and I'll recategorize it later."

"What if there isn't a category for it yet?"

Gayla's eyes widen. "You mean it could be *brand* new?"

Pollux grins. What a bunch of nerds they are, getting excited about a tree. "Could be."

"Oh, how cool is that?" Gayla squeals. She turns back to her typing, a wide smile on her face. Her bobbed hair dances as she nods. "Don't forget, I'm the one who saw them first."

"Excelente!" Valda says, looking back at his monitor. "We'll make the Universal Feed with a find like that."

Pollux chuckles. She seriously doubts that anyone beyond the science division will care, but it's cute of them to pretend on her behalf. "Here's hoping."

Valda gets back to work. "Let me know what the com says."

"Will do." She heads back to the lab, a slight spring in her step.

Truth be told, she'd been doubtful about coming on another mission with Captain Cabano. The last mission they took was a total bust. But this time she could actually make a difference. If this tree bears edible fruit, she could even alter the future of planet colonies for centuries to come.

On her way down the access shaft back to the greenhouse, a laugh escapes her lips.

She could make history. Maybe they'll name the tree after her.

So, coming on this mission?

Best. Decision. Ever.

*   *   *

Demeter
30.8.2231 AD
1250 hours

Raina taps the control panel with her palm and opens the galley door.

"This is such a bad idea," Niall says, and she's worried he's right.

Immediately out in the hall, evidence of a gun battle peppers the walls and floor. A burned-out rifle is strewn on the ground, and laser holes dot every square inch of the area.

It doesn't look good.

Raina had hoped to find the officers cleaning up the area and laughing about the trouble they had containing the foreign biological, but another part of her knows that would be too much to hope for. Nothing is that easy.

She levels her weapon to her shoulder and inches her way into the hall. Morven does the same just behind her, as does Niall. Tamsin, who has the medic kit slung over her shoulder, helps Avram in the rear.

They fan out once they exit the false safety of the galley, and trickle down the hallway toward the workstation on upper deck, which is as far as Niall has authorized any of them to go.

Insisting that they are to research the origin of the suspect seed spore, and no more, Niall finally caved to Morven and Raina's pressure. They cannot sit idly by, he eventually agreed, especially if they can be of some help to Tech Sergeant Pollux and the others.

After skimming down the hall without incident, Morven touches the control panel for the workstation and enters first. He circles around the room, searching under and above the consoles, and flashing a light into the air vent. "Clear," he says.

Tamsin twists her beads and assists Avram as he plops into a station chair. "Easy as pie."

Niall raises a heavy eyebrow at her.

Raina stations herself at the door and keeps her eyes peeled. She knows this is just the beginning.

At the work consoles, Morven and Avram power up the units and immediately set to work pulling up the greenhouse inventory. The flashing lights from the red alert weave scarlet rays across the monitors and set Raina on edge. They somehow look more ominous out in the open than in the galley.

"How long ago did it hitch a ride?" Avram sniffs. He sounds awful. He's breathing through his mouth and is as pale as a sheet. She wonders how many hits of the epi-injector Tamsin has given him.

"Quarantine on the spores was lifted a few weeks ago, so it has to be over a month. Maybe more," Morven says, his fingers attacking the keyboard like it's to blame for their predicament.

Avram reads the planets aloud one at a time and Morven grunts in reply as he rejects each.

"Hurry up," Niall says, and Raina notices he's almost as pale as Avram.

"We're going as fast as we can," he says.

Morven's large hands pound the keyboard in frustration, causing them all to jump. "Damnit, the search engine in this workstation is as slow as zero gravity."

"I got it!" Avram coughs, and Tamsin reads the information over his sagging shoulders.

"Kepler 22b," Tamsin reads aloud. "Pollux made the report. Two seed spores with multicolored exterior: green, brown and red – picked up six months ago."

"Who cares about the color?" Morven says.

Tamsin glowers at him. "I'm just reading what it says."

"What else does the report say about it, Tam?" Raina asks, and shoots Morven a silent glare, shutting him up.

"It's about a meter high, and a meter wide," she reads.

"What else?" Niall asks.

"The spores were found in a crater. One opened after three months. It was hollow on the inside. No seeds or organisms were found. And as they said, quarantine was lifted last month."

"That should have been reported to the captain," Raina says.

"It was noted in the weekly report," Tamsin reads over Avram's shoulder. "So he knew."

"What else?" Morven asks.

"No toxic fumes, no poisonous extracts from the interior, although an analysis of the exterior gel was inconclusive. The spore was classified a dud, and results from the remaining labs all came back relatively normal. The report does specify that the ecosystem on Kepler 22b is mostly rock, and there's little to no humidity in the air, but I'm not sure that's relevant."

"Well, this was a wasted trip," Niall moans. "I'm so glad we risked our lives to find out absolutely nothing."

"There is one thing," Tamsin says. "After quarantine was lifted, Pollux made a note in the addendum about striations on the interior of the spore."

"Striations?" Raina asks.

"Four parallel striations at varying depths and intervals on the inside of the pod," Tamsin reads.

"What does that mean?" Niall asks.

"Lines, four parallel lines. Like grooves," she explains.

Morven's face falls and Raina feels a momentary wish to reassure him. The urge ends abruptly as his next words come off his thick lips. "Stupid bitch."

"Excuse me?" Tamsin gasps.

"Look, it's not her fault...."Avram says.

"Not you," Morven says. He stands from his chair and kicks it over. It clatters to the floor.

"Quiet!" says Niall, but Morven isn't listening.

"That stupid bitch, Pollux!" he seethes.

"Keep it down!" Niall says.

"Why is Pollux stupid?" Raina asks, and takes a step away from him, out of habit.

"Don't you get it? Four parallel striations!" He stalks around the workstation like an ape.

"Shhh!" Niall waves his hands in the air.

"Why is he flipping out?" Tamsin cries.

Avram shrugs and spins his finger around his ear.

"Morven," Raina says, her voice slipping easily into that soothing tone she's taken on so many times before. She hears herself use it, and hates it as memories of bedside conversations and intimate heated moments crowd her head. How many times has she calmed him down from a tirade? How many times has he kicked a chair, or punched a wall when something doesn't go his way? How many times has she used creative techniques to divert his attention?

She recalls one time specifically, way back when they'd first gotten together. While he was yelling and ranting about not being able to go on planetary expeditions like Avram, she stripped down naked and he fucked his frustration out on her so hard she was sore for days.

Raina shakes the images away. "Morven!"

He snaps his face to hers, and for a brief second, she sees the fear and vulnerability in his eyes. That same look he's always gotten when he's scared and hurt. It's the Morven she loves. Loved. There he is. He's the one who used to nuzzle her neck and hang on her every word, as if she were the most interesting person alive.

Raina's breath catches in her chest with a jab. She can see the old him now, in his hazel eyes, as they gaze at her. She used to call that Morven 'Moe'. She thought he had gone.

"Stupid, fucking Pollux!" Morven yells again, and Raina's mind instantly clears.

"Enough! You're not making any sense," she shouts back at him, and his eyes harden like stone.

"Four parallel striations," he says, and he holds up his hand into the air and swipes it down like a claw in front of her face.

"Oh fuck," Niall says.

Morven gives them all a hard stare, and kicks his chair again for good measure. "It's a talon mark. The damned thing clawed its way out of the pod. It's been here all along, and we never even knew it."

For a moment the room is silent as they digest this realization.

Raina can understand his anger; she's heading in that direction herself. Here they are, nothing but ensigns and a cook, and they've already figured out where the foreign biological has come from, and how long it's been onboard. Yet the officers had all this information before, and never thought it cause for concern. Or, if they had, they didn't bother to share it with the rest of the crew.

"What do we do?" she asks, although she suspects that no one has the slightest idea.

All eyes go to the senior officer, Niall. He stands by the door panel, looking pale and doughy. From the look on his face, she knows he's at a loss.

"It's been inside the ship for months?" Niall asks, confirming Raina's worry. He's obviously having a hard time grasping the concept.

Morven is ruthless and snaps his fingers in front of the old man's beleaguered face. "Catch up, Grandpa!"

"And if we don't hurry," Avram says with a sniffle, "there could be another one."

Raina and the others watch as Niall struggles with his panic. He casts a longing look out the door and she wonders if he's missing his kitchen and the comfort of his pie packets.

"We have to go to the greenhouse, don't we?" Niall asks, and Morven scoffs.

"Of course we do."

"We could put the other spore in the airlock, then move it up and out the top bay doors," Raina says.

"Why don't we shove it out in the freighter pod?" Niall suggests.

"That's operated from the inside," Morven points out.

"It's gotta be the airlock. I don't see we have a choice," Avram agrees, and he sneezes into the soggy napkin in his hands.

"What if we send it out in the escape pod? That has external controls,"

Tamsin says, stroking her ponytail like it's a baby blanket. "Or, better yet, we all climb aboard the escape pod and let the biological have the ship."

"What about the other officers?" Raina reminds her.

"We're not running away," Morven says.

"And what about the plants?" Avram wheezes as he takes a breath. "Are we just going to bail on two years' worth of research?"

Morven's eyes meet Raina's. He's looking for her to back him up. It worked before, when they had to convince Niall to leave the galley and head to the workstation. But this unspoken alignment between her and Morven isn't a source of comfort. She looks away from his piercing eyes. It's too familiar.

Risky.

"It means climbing down two decks," Niall says, looking terrified. "That thing could be anywhere."

"But if we don't go, there'll be two *things*," Morven says, and he gazes at her again with that look.

She can almost hear him thinking. *Come on, Rain. Back me up, Rain.*

"Morven's right, Niall," she says, the words tasting bitter. "It's the right thing to do."

"We're all willing to do it, right guys?" Morven turns to Avram and Tamsin.

"I'm in," Avram says, and coughs once. "But I want it on record I'm not happy about it."

Tamsin's eyes are wide and scared, but she nods. She twists the beads around her neck nervously. "Yeah. Okay."

Niall leans against the wall and eyes the floor. "The right thing to do would have been to retire two years ago like I was supposed to."

With a wry grin, Morven reaches out and slaps him on the shoulder. "Think of it this way, old man. After this is over, you can retire with honors."

Niall looks grave.

Raina has a feeling he knows better than to hope for that.

CHAPTER ELEVEN

Down the hall to the access shaft, any confidence Raina may have felt about their plan evaporates. There's evidence of a fight around every corner, and Raina's worst fears are realized when they reach mid-deck.

Brain matter and chunky blobs of blood carpet the walls and floor. A headless corpse slumps against the wall just below a mangled air vent. The head is nowhere in sight.

Tamsin bursts into sobs and Niall bends over, losing his pie. A puddle of vomit pools at his feet and mixes with the blood on the floor, creating a smelly, sticky goo.

Avram leans against the wall, but manages to stay upright, just barely. "Gayla," he says softly.

Raina looks away from the body and fights to stop her own tears from coming. She's overcome with revulsion and fear. Every fiber of her being wants to run in the other direction and never stop. She forces herself to look back.

The mangled bones of the body's spine poke out like a white saber from the top of the corpse. She can't even imagine the shock and pain the officer must have felt at the last. "How can you tell it's Gayla?"

"By her rank," Morven says, and she looks again. The body has a corporal's insignia on its shoulder. Gayla is the only corporal aboard. Or, was.

She looks away again. Her eyes focus on the red alert light flashing on the ceiling.

"What do we do?" Tamsin cries. "We can't just leave her here." She steps away from Niall and through the others, bending at the knees. She takes Gayla's bloodied and limp hand into her own and pats it gently, stroking it with her fingers. She chokes on a sob. "Poor Gayla."

"We're not looking to contain the foreign biological anymore," Morven says. "The mission has changed. Now, we kill it. Right, Niall?"

The man just nods. He heaves once and retches again at his feet.

"Come on," Morven says, and he gestures away from the body.

Tamsin's face flushes. "But what about Gayla?"

"We'll have time for burials after the biological is killed," Avram says gently, and he steps toward her in an effort to collect her. Something on the body catches his attention. "Wow. I've never seen anything like it."

"Avram, none of us have," Raina says. "Let's get out of here."

"No, wait," he insists, and he bends over, inspecting the corpse. "Look at the cuts across her chest. The biological sliced the tendons on her arms so she couldn't hold her rifle. It's a smart sucker, whatever it is."

"You don't know that, you're just talking out your ass," Morven says. "It got in a lucky blow. That's all. Let's go."

"Just hold on a second," Avram says with a sniff, pointing at the slash marks. "Look for yourself. It's a perfect swipe straight across and it takes out both her arms."

Tamsin buries her face into Gayla's hand, shaking with sobs. Niall grumbles something that Raina can't hear, then steps forward and takes Tamsin by the shoulders. He guides her back to her feet and away from the body. Raina isn't sure who is comforting whom.

"I'm just saying," Avram's nasally voice continues.

"Let's hold off studying the corpses and make sure we don't get eaten first," Raina says. The edge in her voice catches Morven's attention and they look at each other again.

His eyes are wet. She stops herself from patting him on the shoulder and instead steps away, down the hall.

"Look," Avram says, getting to his feet, "if we want to make it through this, we need to study what we're up against – I was just making an observation. The biological is intelligent, it might not be so easy to kill."

"Obviously," Niall mumbles.

"Just, quit hovering over her!" Morven says to Avram. "Show a little respect."

His eyes shoot wide. "That's rich coming from you."

"Can we debate this later?" Niall whispers harshly, patting Tamsin as she sobs on his soggy shoulder. "The thing killed Gayla, and probably more. Haven't you noticed how the captain, or Sorrel, or even the pilot haven't come across the intercom? We need to move. Now."

"Kris is up there too," Tamsin cries. Tears trickle down her nose. "She's going riding with me when we get back to Earth."

"Don't think that's gonna happen," Morven grumbles and Tamsin bursts into full-fledged gasping sobs again.

"Morven!" Raina chastises him, but he only shrugs.

"Come on," he says. "Let's get moving."

"So where's Pollux, Osric, and Valda?" Avram asks.

"Probably down one more level, in the greenhouse," Morven guesses. "This is good, we'll meet up with them and come at the biological as a full unit. Better chances of survival."

"Can we go then?" Niall asks.

Raina eyeballs each of the group, then back to Gayla's body. Concern washes over her. She can't shake the feeling that they don't have a chance. How can they? Just look what it's done!

We should run.

They should use the escape pod while they still can, let the officers handle containment. They should get out while the getting is good. What chance do they have against a creature that can do *that* to a human body?

She looks back over at the others in her group. It's not comforting. Niall is old, Tamsin's a mess, Avram can hardly breathe, and Morven is, well, Morven.

The only way she sees they're going to live through this if they stay aboard is to find a way to outsmart the foreign biological. Maybe Avram is right. Maybe they should study the body more, even though the idea makes her sick. A different idea comes to mind instead.

"Maybe we could trap it," she says, but Morven ignores her and Avram steps by and crosses himself.

"Didn't know you were religious," Morven says and turns back in the direction of the access ladder.

Avram sneezes once and sniffs loudly. "Couldn't hurt."

Raina stands in the back of the group and sighs. It reminds her, ever so briefly, of the many times she stood among her enormous family and tried to say something, only to have her words fall on uninterested ears. "I said, I think we should trap it." But the group still moves away, as if they don't hear her.

"We can't leave Gayla!" Tamsin cries anew.

Niall tries to pull her along, but she yanks out of his grasp. She steps by them all, and over to Gayla's body, where she reaches over her head and pulls a strand of colored beads from the collection around her neck. She places a single strand in Gayla's cold, dead hands.

"Yeah. That'll help," scoffs Morven.

"These were my favorite." Tamsin sniffs, and she stands, staring at the body. "Gayla once told me she liked them."

"Can we go now?" Morven asks.

Raina steps forward and takes Tamsin's hand in hers.

Niall walks off in the other direction, abandoning his puddle of vomit.

Raina tugs Tamsin along.

On the bottom deck of the ship, the greenhouse is murky, and the humidity level feels low to Raina as they enter, but it's still hot as hell.

Morven wants to patrol the aisles inside, just in case the foreign biological is close, or the senior officers, but Niall shoots him down.

"That could take hours. Focus on the task at hand," he says. "We'll know soon enough if they're here, or if the foreign biological finds us." Niall steps past them, leading down the aisle, and farther into the thick air of the greenhouse.

Sprinklers snake across the ceiling like tentacles, and Raina immediately starts to sweat. Greenery covers every shelf space available, and the group of them crowd around the door, gaping at the enormity of the place. It takes up the entire level, complete with a glass enclosure and its own lab, with a workstation, and storage area.

"I'm guessing Pollux and the others are someplace else," she says, imagining a pile of more corpses farther into mid-deck, or back up on upper deck.

"Hmm," Niall grumbles and no one else dares to comment. "Where are the spores, Avram?"

"This way." They follow him single file to the left, bending around crowded corners and taking several sharp turns.

The greenhouse is a like a hedge maze, with nothing but shelves stacked atop shelves, all of them full of the odd colors and shapes of alien plant life, stuck into hydroponic pools or soil pots. It's hard for Raina to keep track of where they are, and where they're going. It all looks the same to her.

Avram stops short of a glass enclosure that seems to come out of nowhere and taps a code into the keypad beside the handle. When it beeps, he slides the door and leaves it open. Inside the enclosure, vines and flowery webs have grown all the way up to the glass ceiling.

Despite Tamsin's crying she still manages to say, "Pretty." She reaches out and touches the petal of a flower on some blue alien vine.

Avram stops at a sack-like orb. Splotches of color cover the pod's exterior, as if it's been rolled in paint. If Raina didn't know any better, she'd call it beautiful. It appears thick as rock but collapses like an alligator egg when Avram touches it. When he rolls it over on its side, they can see it's split wide open and hollow. "Bingo."

The inside looks deep and ominous.

"Nice," Morven groans. "Right under our noses."

Avram peers inside the pod and frowns. "See?" He points inside. "Four striations."

"Damnit," Morven swears.

"It's smaller than I thought it'd be," Niall says.

Morven squints at him. "The biological has grown since it hatched."

Raina nods, recalling the long tubular body of the beast they saw in the galley. Given the state of Gayla's corpse, they'd be smart not to underestimate it.

"Here's the other one," Avram says, and he nods toward an identical orb beside the split one.

Thankfully, it's fully intact. It shines under the fluorescent lights of the greenhouse and gleams with an exterior layer of glossy odorless slime.

"Lovely," Raina scoffs.

"Come on." Morven brushes past her and comes up alongside Avram. "If I remember, this thing was slippery when we brought it in, and we were in our spacesuits, which has grippers in the gloves. This is going to be tricky without that. Help me lift it."

The both of them struggle to pick up the pod. Due to the layer of slime, it slides from their fingers and they nearly drop it. It takes two tries, but they finally get a good enough grip, and the two of them muscle it out of the enclosure and labor slowly toward the airlock doors on the other side of the greenhouse, which sits beside another lab.

It takes Morven and Avram a few good minutes, as they weave around the aisles of plants. They lose their grip three times. Each time it's a struggle to get it back up and moving. When they're on the go, the spore leans against both their arms and chests. At one point Morven collapses to his knees and allows the slipping sphere to land on his thighs to prevent it from hitting the ground. There's a good amount of swearing involved.

When they near the end of their slow journey, Tamsin runs ahead and activates the controls on the airlock. They wait as the airlock descends from the space prep room on mid-deck, then the alert rings. Tamsin hits the controls again and the doors slowly labor open and hiss to a stop.

Coming up from behind, Avram and Morven, now thoroughly covered in slime, struggle by her and bend at the knees to gently place the pod on the airlock floor.

Satisfied, they amble out and Tamsin taps the controls again.

All five of them stand and watch as the doors slowly slide closed.

When the airlock doors seal with a hiss and a pop, the group visibly relaxes.

"Good job, guys," Tamsin says with a small smile.

Morven wipes his slimy hands on the pants of his uniform and grunts. "Yeah. You were a big help."

"Now what?" Niall asks, and Raina immediately realizes the problem with their plan.

"We can send the airlock up to the top bay doors but can't open them from here. To release the spore into space, we have to get back to the flight deck. The bay door controls are there," she says.

"Ah, hell," Niall whispers. The terror creeps back onto his face.

"We can't leave the spore in there," she says. "What if it hatches? You saw what the biological did to Gayla. It could be strong enough to break through the doors, or breach the hull, and then we'd all be screwed."

"Can you hack an override from the lab workstation?" Morven suggests, and Raina does her best to hide her surprise. By-the-books Morven wants to hack the ship's computer system?

As if hearing her thoughts, he explains, "Desperate times call for desperate measures. Can you do it, Tamsin?"

Tam sniffs a few times and thinks. Raina's relieved to see she's gotten a handle on her emotions, for now. "Not sure. But I can try."

Avram reaches out and taps the controls on the door panel beside the airlock, sending it upward. "Well, points for getting this far."

Morven leads the way back through the labyrinthine aisles of the greenhouse to the laboratory, which is sealed inside a steel room, so as not to corrupt the computer system with the greenhouse humidity. To enter the lab, they pile into a middle compartment first, which seals them in and dehumidifies the air. Then, and only after the process is complete, the lab doors can open.

Once inside, Tamsin seats herself at a workstation, powers the unit, and types feverishly.

The rest have no choice but to sit and wait.

★ ★ ★

After an hour in the greenhouse laboratory, Tamsin makes an announcement. "You know what?"

"Are you finished yet?" Niall asks.

She twists in her chair and smiles at him. "No. But I have an idea."

The others stare at her. When no one asks what it is, she frowns and continues. "I think we should stay here until help from the United Space Corps comes. It's cozy in here. Safe."

Avram turns his head to one side, contemplating. "We don't know if the Corps is coming. What if the officers never sent out a distress signal?"

Niall shifts around in his position on the floor by the door. "They wouldn't have. Procedure states to send a distress signal only after the beast is contained. And we're not authorized to do so without approval from the captain or the pilot."

"But what if they're both dead?" Morven asks. "That makes no sense."

Tamsin flinches.

"Surely they sent one out already," Avram says with a sniff. "They had to have notified command of our situation."

Raina shrugs. "I doubt it happened. We went straight to the armory after red alert sounded. I don't think they had the chance."

"Well, I don't believe we're not allowed to contact command ourselves. I've never read that rule," Tamsin says obstinately, turning back around in her rotating chair and focusing again on the screen before her. "And I remember everything."

"Just focus on getting that bay door open," Niall says.

"Yeah, yeah, yeah," she says. "I'm on it."

Raina relaxes back into her chair. She can't help but wonder about the ship's intercom, which has been ominously quiet. Too quiet. It's a bad sign.

If the officers aren't responding to Niall's communiqué, she doubts they've sent a distress signal, which can only mean the biological still isn't contained.

Maybe Tamsin is right. It wouldn't surprise Raina if Niall is making that up to keep them from breaking ranks. But if he's so determined to stick to the rules, none of them have the authority to question him. He is the most experienced one among them. Surely, he knows best. Right? Honestly, she's not sure. And as time passes, and Tamsin types, the more Raina thinks about it. The more she thinks, the deeper her resentment festers.

Niall should let them send a distress signal anyway. Why is he so worried about breaking procedure? If it's even true. If it saves their lives – what does it matter? Besides, they're attempting to hack their own computer system right now. Why is he so bent on following that protocol, but not this one?

If he were any other officer, this whole ordeal might have gone differently. But he's all they've got, and for better or worse, they're relatively unscathed compared to the others. So, she supposes Niall has that in his favor.

Still, she can't shake the feeling that their time will come if they don't change their tactics soon.

She knows hiding in the greenhouse lab isn't a long-term solution.

All it's doing is wasting time.

★   ★   ★

Tamsin works at the console steadily for a while longer, typing, tapping her feet on the floor, and occasionally humming to herself. Every now and then, when someone opens their mouth to speak, she shushes them and the room goes quiet again.

A few times Raina catches Morven staring at her. She pretends not to notice.

When finally Morven can't seem to wait any longer, he snatches his rifle from its resting place against the laboratory wall, and signals for Raina to follow him.

"I need to talk to you," he whispers, and Tamsin shushes him loudly.

"I don't think that's a good idea," Raina says.

"It's not about that," he says, and his expression confirms it.

"You're not helping!" Tamsin sings from her chair at the console.

"We won't go far, just the dehumidifying chamber," Morven offers.

Niall, who slumps in the corner of the lab, looks defeated. He waves them off. "Make it fast. I'm not sure how much longer I can take this."

Raina eyes Avram palely sniffling at the other console chair and then reluctantly follows Morven into the chamber.

He waits for the doors to seal shut before he speaks. "I don't think she can crack it."

"Maybe if we give her more time?"

He shakes his head. "She would have done it by now. I've been watching over her shoulder. The safety protocols are stopping her at every turn. Right now, she's trying to override one at a time. But no matter how good she is, that creature is loose on the ship and god knows what it's doing while we sit here. What if we have no ship left by the time she's done? What if it breaches the hull? We have to act now."

Raina sighs and crosses her arms, settling deep into thought. He's right. She hates that. What makes it worse is that he's just repeated almost every thought in her head from the past hour. "What are you thinking we should do?"

"Don't you think it's odd we haven't heard from the officers yet?" He casts a look out the other window and into the greenhouse. The sprinklers have turned on and the window is so fogged they can't see a thing on the other side. Just gray air. "Something has gone wrong."

"I think so too."

He sets his jaw. "I think they're all dead."

She swallows the saliva collecting in her mouth with a thick gulp and nods. "That means Niall is in charge of the ship."

"Exactly. Now, I don't know about you, but I'd rather not count on the old man to get us out of this. He's too afraid."

Not wanting to admit that's exactly what she's been thinking, she says, "What do you propose?"

"Technically, since I'm first ensign under Pollux, I'm senior officer under Niall," he says. "I should assume command." He sets his jaw, and now she sees where he's going with this.

"You want command?" she repeats, because she's unsure how else to respond.

"Someone needs to take charge, and it can't be Avram – he's about to croak any minute, and Tamsin is a ditz. No offense, but you're only a mechanic."

She smiles to herself. She's almost glad for the insult. It's a reminder of just who he really is. "That leaves you."

"Exactly," he says again.

It could be only her imagination, but she swears he puffs out his chest like a deranged superhero. She wishes she could have a moment alone so she can think this through – without his meaty fists and intense eyes drilling holes into her psyche. Her intuition tells her that him in command would be a terrible mistake, but she also has to factor in that she has personal feelings mixed with the equation, and it's blinding her from a clear view, much like the fog on the outside of the greenhouse window.

He is the highest-ranking ensign, she reasons. He's also tougher than any of them, and not afraid to make hard choices. But choices that serve whom? That remains to be seen. She knows him well enough to understand that he *wants* command of the ship, and this doesn't sit well with her.

"What about Niall? Think he'll go along with it?" she finally manages to say.

"I doubt it. Which is why I need your support."

"You're talking about mutiny."

This hits him harder than she meant. His face flushes and he takes a step back. His hands have reddened, looking splotchy, and clench into fists. Her eyes immediately find the nearest exit.

"It's not a mutiny," he spits, and she can tell she's hit a nerve. "I'm trying to save our lives!"

"Okay, okay."

"Don't do that, don't placate me," he says. He paces back and forth in the small room, scratching his palms.

She shakes her head in frustration. "Well, what else would you have me do? You're about ready to punch the damn wall again."

This stops him. He looks down at his hands and consciously unclenches them. "I am not."

She can't help but scoff. "Could have fooled me."

"Damnit, Raina – what else can we do?"

"I don't know," she says, and her apparent agreement stops his pacing in an instant.

"Then you agree I should take command?"

"I don't disagree."

"Then you'll back me?"

His eagerness bothers her. It's almost as if he's enjoying this. "Hold on. Say Niall gives you command. What's your plan?"

He seems dumbfounded, like the answer is obvious. "Kill the thing, of course."

"Yeah, well, that's all well and good, but isn't that what got the other officers killed? Assuming they're dead, which I don't think is an unfair assumption. We have to be smarter than them. Niall's right about one thing: gallivanting off like a posse of cowboys is like lambs to the slaughter. Look what the foreign biological did to Gayla. And she fought in the Colonization Wars. She's a veteran. With experience! I don't think Tamsin has shot a rifle in her life, Avram can barely breathe, and Niall is about to have a heart attack. You and I can't kill it alone, Moe."

The rest of her words catch in her throat. She hadn't meant to call him that. She can tell from his expression it's hit him like a meteor shower.

He's giving her that look. That wounded vulnerable one that cuts straight through to her heart. "Sorry," she says. "I didn't mean...."

"It's fine," he says, and the stone slowly returns to his face, but not completely.

She's half afraid this will open a dialogue they've been avoiding these last few weeks, but he mercifully returns to the original topic.

"So, you won't back me?" he asks.

Raina purses her lips. "I'll back you if you come up with a plan. Something other than shoot, shoot, bang, bang. And Niall has to agree to it."

"Okay," he says, and he makes for the door leading back into the laboratory. "We have a deal."

CHAPTER TWELVE

Back inside the laboratory, Morven clears his throat and addresses the group. "Hey, listen up."

"I just need a few more minutes," Tamsin says, not taking her eyes off the monitor.

"Tamsin," Raina says gently, and Tamsin turns to look at her. "This isn't working."

"It's taking too long," Morven says. "We need a Plan B."

Niall sighs and labors to his feet. "Yeah? And what's that?"

"I think it's fair to say the other officers are dead," Morven blurts, and Tamsin gasps. "We're all that's left, and we need to find a way out of this mess."

"You don't know that," Niall says.

"There's the escape pod," Avram volunteers, rubbing his palms on the legs of his uniform.

"Not an option," Morven says. "We're not going to abandon two years' worth of hard work and labor, everything the officers worked for, because of one foreign biological. Maybe two now, because we've just wasted hours trying to open the bay doors, when we should have just gone to flight deck and done it manually."

"I agree," Niall says. "But we don't know that the other officers are dead. We only found Gayla. In fact, this whole ordeal could be over with, and we wouldn't know because we've been in here, hiding."

"Wake up and smell the pie, Niall." Morven glares at him. "The other officers are dead. *That's* why we haven't heard from them. They would have used the intercom to issue an all clear, and they haven't. It's been too long. We're on our own."

The logic of Morven's argument doesn't sit well with Niall. He looks doubly pale. Raina half expects him to faint.

"What do we do?" Tamsin asks, fresh fear trickling down her face in the form of tears.

"Well, first thing we do is establish a new chain of command," Morven says, and the room becomes so quiet the only sound heard is Avram's wheezing.

"Is that right?" Niall puts his hands on his hips. "You think a deadly foreign biological has slaughtered your bosses and mentors, real people that I've served with for almost ten years, and you want to have a meeting to create a command flowchart?"

"I don't think you can do it," Morven says, and Niall is visibly shaken. "Excuse me?"

"No offense, but when's the last time you shot a rifle?"

"A few hours ago in the galley, genius," Niall says.

"No, I mean...." Morven looks to Raina for help, but she's at a loss as to how to handle this. This isn't the way she would have done it. She thought Morven would take Niall aside in the dehumidifying chamber and have a private talk, but to stage a mutiny in front of the others is a critical error on Morven's part. This isn't what she agreed to at all.

"You want to be captain?" Avram asks with a sniff.

"Just temporarily," he says. "I'm the highest-ranking ensign, technically."

"You little prick," Niall says, and Morven's face pales. "You want a promotion? You're actually asking for a promotion in the middle of all this? The senior officers' bodies aren't even cold, and you have the gall to ask for command? Are you out of your fucking mind?"

"No, sir," Morven says, squaring his shoulders. "I just want to live. And I don't think you're up to the task."

"Is that right?"

"Yes, sir. How old are you? Late sixties? Ever been on the field during battle? When's the last time you went to the range to practice your marksmanship? When's the last time you took a class on battle strategy? Thirty? Forty years ago?"

"Two years ago before we departed on this mission, you self-important egotistical jackass," Niall says. "The same time you did. Marksmanship and battle strategy courses are required for every member on board before each mission. And since I've been a Space Corps cook for forty years, that means I've taken those classes over twenty times. How many times did you take them, Ensign? Once?"

Morven's jaw clenches and his eyes look to Raina.

She can almost hear him. *Come on, Rain. Back me up, Rain.*

But a louder voice inside her head answers him back. *Not like this.*

"Is that what you two were talking about in there?" Niall asks. "Were you two conspiring to further your careers?"

"It's not like that," Raina says, and the disappointed look Niall gives her makes her cringe. "We, we need a plan. A way to trap the…the Kepler."

"The what now?" Avram asks.

"It's from Kepler 22b," Tamsin says at almost a whisper.

"Whatever you call it," Morven says, gaining back confidence in his voice. "I don't think hiding in here, or barricading ourselves in the galley to eat pie, will end well. We need to think bigger. We need to think smarter." He casts a look at Raina as if she's a traitor.

She turns away. So much for working together. That didn't take long to fall apart.

"And Niall," Morven says, "you may be the oldest and most experienced officer here, but—"

"I'm the *only* officer here!" he corrects him.

"But you're not the fastest, and you have no engineering or scientific training. You're a cook. If we needed someone to bake a cake, we'd put you in command – but we need someone who has the knowledge of this ship and the ability to physically see it through. That's not you." He finishes and waits for the others to respond.

"Unbelievable," Niall mutters. "Do you all feel this way?"

Avram is the first to respond. "What's your plan, el Capitán?" he asks Morven.

"Na-uh. No way," Niall interrupts. "You can't decide this. This is not a vote."

"Sorry, Niall," Tamsin says. "I vote Morven."

"I just said this is *not* a vote!"

Morven nods to Raina. "And you?"

"As long as you're smart about it," she says. "Sorry, Niall."

"Son of a bitch," Niall says, and he punches the air with a right hook.

Avram sneezes. "I trust you, dude, even if you are an ass. What's the plan?"

"Are you kidding me?" Niall fumes. "Are you guys fucking kidding me?"

"First we get those bay doors open from the flight deck," Morven says.

"And then?" asks Tamsin. Raina can tell the answer terrifies her.

"We see how many of us are left to try and trap the...Kepler."

Tamsin moans.

"Where?" Niall asks. "Trap it where? Have you thought of that? Have any of you thought of that?"

Morven adjusts the rifle on his shoulder and breezes by Niall toward the exit. "I'm still working that part out."

★   ★   ★

Back in the greenhouse, Morven leads the others through the maze of plants and greenery. The mood is palpable.

Niall grumbles to himself like an old lady. Avram wheezes, and Tamsin sucks back her tears so loudly the repetitive sniffing is starting to get on Raina's nerves.

Meanwhile, seemingly oblivious, Morven marches – a man on a mission. His eyes face forward and his jaw is set. Raina can't help but notice there's the slightest grin playing on the corner of his lips.

He almost looks happy. And why shouldn't he be? He's in command, just like he's always dreamed about. She knows it's all he's ever wanted. She just wishes he didn't have to look so smug about it.

When they reach the greenhouse door leading to the access shaft, he stops short. "Hear that?"

Everybody stills to strain his or her ears.

"Sounds like...."

"Crying," Tamsin says, finishing Raina's sentence.

Morven snatches his rifle off his shoulder and aims at the door. He fans his other hand out, indicating for the group to seek cover.

Raina takes position, crouching beside the door control panel. Tamsin, Niall, and Avram scatter behind her, disappearing into the shrubbery.

Morven inches forward and peers through the small glass window on the greenhouse door, but the glass is badly fogged and he shakes his head, signifying that he can't see the source of the sound. He motions to Raina and she taps the controls, then aims her rifle at the opening.

The door slides open with a hiss.

There's an audible gulp, and the crying stops.

Morven signals wordlessly for Raina to follow him. Quickly, he leads her out into the hallway where the body of a woman lies slumped against the wall. Her flushed face is streaked with blood and tears.

"Oh my god. It's Pollux," Raina says.

"Sergeant?" Morven calls.

Raina lowers her rifle and goes to her, kneeling beside the woman. Her breathing is steady, and her eyes are open – but her expression is vacant. "Pollux, can you hear me?"

"Is she wounded?" Morven asks. He scans the access shaft with his readied rifle.

Apparently satisfied that the area is clear, he steps back in through the greenhouse door, leaving Raina alone with Pollux in the hall.

Raina stifles her irritation. It's not like she could use the cover. "Pollux? Can you move? It's not safe here."

The sergeant's eyes look glazed, but from what Raina can see, she has no visible wounds, although her uniform is splattered with blood and chunky globs of guts and gore, and her hands still have that rash. Pollux's rifle lies beside her, powered down, and she makes no move to stop her when Raina picks it up and slings the strap over her own shoulder.

"Ensign Raina?" Pollux whispers, her eyes slowly coming to life. "What are you doing here?"

Raina wraps Pollux's arm over her shoulder to help her to stand. Morven makes no move to assist, and stands just inside the greenhouse, watching them struggle.

As the two women hobble toward the door, a motion catches Raina's eyes. Morven's pink hand slowly moves toward the controls on the inside of the greenhouse. It floats above the door panel ominously. His fingers twitch.

She stops and a chill travels up the length of her spine.

He wouldn't dare shut the door on me again.

She can tell he's thinking about it. His eyes look to the control panel and linger on his hand, hovering just above the controls. He blinks three times in rapid succession.

All it would take is one slight motion and Raina and Pollux would be locked outside. If he leaves them exposed and alone, not only would Morven guarantee he would retain his newly found command over the ship, he'd also rid himself of the two people he hates most in one swift move – his boss and his ex-lover. Gone. Just like that.

They wouldn't stand a chance.

Raina clears her throat and Morven's eyes snap to meet hers. His hand drops to his side, and he impatiently waves them in, as if he hadn't just considered murdering them both.

Raina narrows her eyes at him as they both stumble inside the door. "I saw that."

He feigns confusion. "Saw what? You were taking forever."

Tamsin, who cries fresh tears at the sight of Pollux, reaches across him and taps the control panel, closing the door behind them.

Pollux collapses and hits the greenhouse floor, taking Raina to her knees.

Niall surges forward but stops short of touching Pollux. Avram reaches above and pulls vapor tubing from the snakelike tendrils on the ceiling used for the sprinkler system. He brings it down to her level. Ignoring the water that pours out from above into a specimen bed, he hands the other end of the dripping tube to Raina, and nods toward Pollux. "Water," he says.

Raina grasps the tube and holds it to Pollux's lips. She swallows roughly, water dribbling down her shaking chin. Then she cups some in her spotted palms and washes her face.

Raina turns away from her and eyes Morven with distaste. He's looking at the floor, unable to meet her eyes again.

Good.

She hopes he feels a mass of guilt. What she'd really like to do is deck him, but she has other, more pressing, matters to consider. Pollux, for one.

Tamsin claws her way through the others and wraps her arms around Pollux, encircling her in a constricting embrace. "I'm so glad you're okay."

Pollux grunts.

"Easy now," Raina says, and she pries the girl's arms off the sergeant.

"We were so worried!" Tamsin cries at Pollux. "I'm so happy to see you."

"Are you hurt?" Niall asks, looking shaken.

Pollux blinks at Tamsin, almost as if she doesn't recognize her, then looks to Niall. "I'm not hurt," she answers weakly.

Raina thinks she detects a hint of irritation in her voice. "What's that on your hands?"

"N-nothing," Pollux sputters.

Raina peels back Pollux's sleeve, then tips Pollux's head to one side and looks at her neck. Pollux is covered in hives. "It's gotten worse. It's not nothing."

"It's only…it doesn't matter."

Pollux focuses on Raina, but her eyes still don't quite clear. Instead, they dart around the room like she's expecting the creature to jump out at any moment. "When this is over," Raina says, "you really need to get that looked at. It doesn't look good." When Raina reaches up to wipe a smudge of blood from Pollux's eyes, she flinches.

"Where are the others?" Morven asks.

"I ran," Pollux whispers. "No choice. I left them." She swats Raina's hand away, digs her fingernails into her neck, scratching violently, then shoves Tamsin to the side.

"You left them?" Morven's shout clears Pollux's eyes instantly.

Raina is glad when the sergeant's jaw clenches. She's coming back from wherever her mind has gone. For once, Morven's abrasiveness is working for Pollux instead of against.

"Where'd you leave them?" Niall asks.

"No. You can't help them. *It* got them," Pollux says.

"Don't say that," Tamsin whimpers.

The sergeant sits up from her slumped position and hands the water tubing back to Raina, who then passes it off to Avram. He reaches above and reconnects the tubing to the network overhead. "It killed them," Pollux whispers. "Blood everywhere. Nothing I could do. It won't die."

"They could only be wounded," Morven says.

She shakes her head. "No. They're gone. I ran. Valda told me to. He called me chica."

"Where did this happen?" The intensity of Morven's words sound more like a command than words from a concerned colleague.

Worry clouds Raina's consciousness. She can see it now. He's going to run off and avenge them and get killed. Or worse, get them all killed. Or worse yet, he's going to argue with Pollux about how he should stay in command even now she's back. Or, defying all logic, he could decide not to go after any surviving officers in hopes that thing ate them, and he'll keep his newly established control.

All these options leave Raina's blood running cold. She hates herself for thinking this of him, but the look on his face as his hand hovered over the door control panel is etched into her memory. He actually thought about it.

"M-mid-deck," Pollux says. "Can't kill it. Can't crush it. Lasers don't wound it."

"What if we upped the wattage?" Avram suggests.

"Tried that. Doesn't work. The rifles only burn out."

Tamsin slides and leans her back against the door control panel. She looks sick. "Valda?"

Pollux nods slowly. "Osric, and Gayla too."

Raina feels a tug on her gut. "What about the flight crew?"

"And Sorrel?" Niall adds.

"All dead," Pollux confirms.

Raina catches Morven's eye. It's what she feared. Sometimes, she hates it when she's right. She wonders if he's relieved to hear the news.

Tamsin bursts into sobs and whispers, "And Kris."

"I came down here," Pollux says, gaining a little strength. "To get a weapon. But I heard movement inside and thought...."

"It's just us."

"You sure?"

"Well, us and the other spore, which we put in the airlock," Avram says and sniffs.

"Spore?"

"It's where the foreign biological came from," Raina explains. "We picked it up on Kepler 22b. Two of them. They were classified as seed spores. One hatched. The other hasn't yet, so we were going to release it out into space using the airlock. But we can't override the bay door controls from here."

"The red trees," Pollux says, and Raina blinks at her.

"What?"

"Think you can lead us up there, to the flight deck?" Niall asks, and Morven's face clenches.

Raina catches it out of the corner of her eye. His expression speaks volumes. There it is. He's no longer in command. Not with Pollux here. His face reddens and the vein on his forehead pulses. This isn't a good sign, and her suspicions about his true intentions surge.

Pollux nods, although she looks terrified. "I can lead you up. We'll need different weapons."

"There aren't any weapons in the greenhouse," Morven says sternly.

She shakes her head. "Not true. A mattock, or a hand axe. I was hoping for a bolo, or a machete."

"You serious?" He scoffs like she's lost her mind.

Raina wonders if they both have.

"Deadly serious," Pollux says. "Time to put your hand-to-hand combat training to good use. The biological is lethal. It has metal-like claws and the hide is just as thick."

"So what good is a machete going to be against it?" Morven asks.

A flash of anger crosses her eyes and Pollux bites her lower lip. She looks like she's about to cry. "I don't know!" she says. "Do I look like I know everything? Jesus Christ, Morven, I'm only trying to help!"

"All right!" he barks back, jerking his head. "Fuck!"

"A machete's got to be better than a rifle," Pollux says. "Those did nothing! Barely singed the fur and it's too fast to shoot."

"We saw. It came at Raina in the galley," Avram says.

"How'd you get away?" Pollux looks to Raina, dumbfounded, her eyes wide.

Raina hasn't a clue. "Just lucky, I guess."

"It helps that she's faster than a jackrabbit," Morven says, and Raina is so suspicious at the compliment her mouth actually drops open.

"We're going to need some luck," Pollux says, reaching her hand out to Raina so she can get to her feet. She digs at her neck and steps forward. "And some body armor couldn't hurt. But since we don't have that, we'll have to make do."

CHAPTER THIRTEEN

Back through the greenhouse aisles, Raina and the others follow Pollux as she leads them toward the tool locker, located in the back, on the opposite side from the laboratory. After a few meters navigating the labyrinth of plants, Pollux gains some strength, and picks up the pace. The others straggle behind. Raina can't help but watch them with mounting concern.

Ever since Tamsin heard confirmation that the other officers were killed, she hasn't stopped bawling. Her eyes are red and swollen and she's dripping snot and tears like a faucet. Raina can't imagine she's going to be much help with a sharp implement.

Avram's face is slowly gaining color with the increased pace, but he still sniffs and sneezes on occasion, and every now and then he wheezes.

In the past, when he had done that, Tamsin would act the attentive nurse, reloading the epi-injector and shooting Avram with medications, but she's currently too consumed with sobbing to be of any help to him now.

Behind Tamsin walks Niall, who has a permanent scowl on his face and a determination Raina hadn't noticed before. Maybe it's because he's no longer the sole officer. Maybe it's because he's no longer in charge. Either way, he looks fierce enough to take on an entire race of foreign biologicals by himself, and this troubles Raina more than she'd like to admit.

How old is he really?

Something bumps her elbow and she looks over to see Morven walking beside her. His fiery eyes search her face. For what, she doesn't know.

If they were alone, she's sure there's much he'd say to her, and she to him, but a part of her is glad they aren't alone, in that case. He looks like a pent-up balloon filled to near bursting, and she isn't sure hand-to-hand combat is in his best interest, either. He's reckless when he's like this.

After a brief walk, they reach the tool locker. Pollux fumbles around and mumbles to herself. Something about which weapon would be the most damaging. Raina can't be sure.

Then Pollux sets about distributing bladed weapons to the others. There are only three machetes, so they also take a hand axe, a sledgehammer, a pointed spade, and long, sharp hedge clippers.

Raina ends up with the axe and a sharp pair of pruning shears, which she snaps into her tool belt. She notices Morven takes a machete for himself.

When Pollux is finished handing out the weapons, she turns away from the toolshed, scratches her arm, then mumbles one more comment under her breath, and marches back through the greenhouse toward the door.

"What'd she say?" Raina asks.

Morven, who trudges in the back of the group looking angry, shakes his head and whispers, "She said, 'Bad odds'."

Her stomach turns over and she instinctively reaches for her rifle, but then realizes she left it with the others beside the toolshed. Thinking more clearly, she re-grips the wooden handle of the axe in her right hand and tests its weight.

Nice and solid. It should do the trick, if she can get close enough to the Kepler, if she has the chance.

Raina has to admit Pollux is right.

Bad odds, indeed.

★   ★   ★

Six Months Ago....

"What happened? What did Pollux and the captain say?" Morven demands.

Raina swallows and sits on the cot in his sleep chamber. From the looks of the room, he's been on a rampage. All the contents of his storage locker have been scattered across the room. She'd better handle this carefully. "He asked if I wanted to press charges, but I said no."

"Charges for what?"

"Exactly. I said no and he left. That's all."

"But that's not what Pollux wanted?"

She pauses. She hesitates to mention what Pollux said.

"I don't think you understand what's happening, Raina. Don't you see what he's doing? You're playing with fire and you're going to get burned."

"I can handle him."

"That was handling him? This is classic abusive behavior. It's only going to get worse. You know that, right?"

"I'm not sure what Pollux wanted," Raina lies. "I think she's just overly sensitive."

"Sensitive to what?"

"She *heard* you yelling at me."

"So now couples aren't allowed to argue? What the fuck is her problem?"

"Yes, well," Raina says, trying to lighten the mood, "that's a whole other kettle of fish."

It doesn't work. He punches the air and swings around to face her. "I swear, Pollux has had it in for me since day one. Doesn't trust me as far as she can throw me. Pisses me off. She won't be happy until I'm a fucking gardener on some far-off colony. And now she's trying to use you against me too?" He grabs Raina by the shoulders and lifts her off the cot into a tight embrace. "You can't let her do that, Rain. You can't let her twist your mind against me. You know I love you, right? You know I would never hurt you. She's just putting ideas into your head." He kisses the top of her crown and squeezes her to him. She can almost smell his desperation.

Every muscle in her body constricts.

Is Pollux playing with her head? Or, more accurately, is she just calling attention to what she already knows?

It certainly does feel warm and comforting with his arms around her. But she knows it won't last. It never does. One slipup and he'll be twisting her arm, shouting in her face, and calling her names, and then falling all over himself to apologize. She knows the pattern too well now.

Pulling back, she slips out of his arms as gently as she can and puts her back to the door. "Maybe we should take a break, back off a little. Let the captain and Pollux calm down about it," she suggests.

"What?" He looks aghast at her words.

He looks so devastated she almost takes it back, but doesn't. "Just for a little while."

"How can you—? I don't—! No."

"We have been going pretty hot and heavy for a long time, Moe. Maybe it's time to slow it down. The mission's almost over. Only six months left. What's going to happen to us when it ends? You'll get shipped off to some science detail as an officer, and I'll probably have to go back to the Academy to repeat courses, if Osric has anything to say about it. Don't look so upset. This was how it was going to end all along, but if we part as friends now, it'll be easier at the end of the mission, and it'll smooth things over with the captain and Pollux. Don't you think?"

"You're leaving me?"

"No, I'm not leaving you. How can I leave? We're on the same ship! I just think we should be friends from now on. That's all. Just not spend so much time together. To make it easier later."

"You want us to go our separate ways while still on board the same ship? That's stupid, Raina. Even for you."

"You know what I mean."

"No," he says, his face reddening, "I don't know what you mean. This doesn't make any sense – at all. You let them get to you. You listened to Pollux's bullshit and now you're leaving me?"

"Moe…."

"Don't call me that!" he spits, his temper erupting. "You don't get to call me that anymore."

She takes a deep breath, trying to control her racing heart, but she's losing that battle as well as this one. "I'm sorry."

"Fuck your sorry. And fuck you."

"Okay. I see how this is going to play out, so I think I should just go until you calm down."

"No!" He slams his fist against the wall, cracking the mirror over his sink. Her fear freezes her feet to the floor.

"You don't get to spew shit like that and walk away!" He bounds to her, wrenching her by the arm with such force she lurches and almost falls.

"Ow! Morven! Wait – let's talk about—"

"You don't have the right to play games with me!" he screams in her face, shaking her back and forth so hard her teeth crack together. "To fuck me for almost two years – two years! And make me *love* you – to just walk away the moment some bitch opens her mouth and tells you to? You can't give up like that. You can't! You're a coward. Nothing but a fucking coward!"

"Stop it, Morven. Let me go!" She swings wide with her free arm, hoping to catch his shoulder, but she overcompensates for her height, and without meaning to, slaps him square in the jaw.

His response is fast and fierce. He releases her, pushing her slightly forward. Then, quick as a flash, he punches her clean across the cheek, sending her careening to the floor face-first.

The room darkens and her head swims. She's on the floor but she doesn't know how she got there. She tries to get up, but a fist punches her, this time on the arm. It sends shockwaves of pain down to her fingertips. Instinctively, she curls into a ball.

Morven stands over her, bellowing between choked sobs. "You coward! You fucking coward!"

She feels his hot tears hitting her face in between more punches to her head, arms, and legs. When a punch to her back arches her open, he kicks her ribs with his boot.

She screams.

The last thing she remembers is the taste of blood.

★ ★ ★

Demeter
30.8.2231 AD
1632 hours

Pollux's legs feel loose and her head floats someplace above her neck, but she marches through the greenhouse pretending she knows what the fuck she's doing. She can't allow the shock and terror she's seen these past few hours to cloud her judgment, but it's hard to focus. She swears she can hear her mother shouting in her ear.

Quit acting like such a girl!

She shakes her head. God, it's hot. Every inch of her body itches like mad, and she has to stop herself from scratching off her skin.

Despite everything, it feels good to have people around her again, even if the thought feels like a weakness and fills her with enough self-hatred to collapse a black hole.

They're only a band of untrained ensigns, and a cook who should have retired long ago, but it's better than being alone, isn't it? Honestly, she's not sure. Half of her is glad they're here, and the other half wants to bury her machete in their skulls for being such morons and not staying in the galley like she ordered.

She uses the throbbing pain in her skull to pull her focus back from the brink.

It's up to her – again. As always. These ensigns might be stupid as fuck, but she can't fail them like she did the others and run away again like a child. She can't believe she left Valda bleeding out on mid-deck, alone to get eaten alive.

Her mother screams in her ear.

You loser!

She also can't believe she's been trying to find the courage to go back to mid-deck, and use the escape pod – which is what she was doing when the ensigns found her. What the hell is the matter with her?

A part of her is glad she hadn't moved forward with that plan yet. Another part of her wishes she had. The good news is that these ensigns have worked together and come up with a plan – sort of. It's pointless, she supposes. But it's better than crying in the corner like a chickenshit.

Morven, regularly an entitled asswipe, seems to have taken charge of the group – and this fills Pollux with a mixture of gratitude and hatred. Of course, he's taken charge. What else would that jackass do?

But, if worse comes to worst, she'll at least be able to count on him to protect the others. He looks ready to kill the creature by himself. Maybe she's judged him too harshly in the past. Maybe his nasty temper and control-freak habits are serving him well. He seems the least panicked of the group, including herself. Even so, he's still an insufferable asshole she'd like to slap upside the head.

They reach the greenhouse door, pop it open, and crowd around the ladder leading to mid-deck, jockeying for position in the small access shaft.

Morven's machete clinks against the wall as he moves toward the ladder. Avram sneezes once and wipes his nose on his sleeve. She wonders why he looks so sick.

"Up we go," Pollux says.

Morven motions for Raina to go first, but Pollux watches as Niall plows through the ensigns and beats them to it. He labors up, grunting along the way. He's probably eager to get this over with. Avram is just behind Niall, so Pollux tells him to go next.

As she stands in the back of the group, by the open greenhouse door, she taps Tamsin on the shoulder. Pollux can feel the kid trembling with fear. "Pull yourself together, Ensign. It's up to you now. You can open the bay doors from the flight deck, right?"

Tamsin nods. "Yes, ma'am. Page three hundred and twenty-two of the navigations manual. Paragraph two."

"Okay, whatever." Her mind is at work. She only hopes the girl can pull it together and get the job done when it's time. "You next," she says to her, dragging her nails up and down her arm and groaning with satisfaction.

Raina keeps staring at her, watching her scratch.

"What are you looking at?" Pollux snaps.

"Are you all right, Sarge?" Raina asks.

"Just get up the ladder."

Tamsin grasps the rungs of the access ladder in her hands, and Pollux's gaze flits across the wall, up and back, and around again.

Fuck, she hates this ship. This whole mission was the worst idea she's ever had in her life and she deserves to die for being so stupid.

Didn't I tell you? her mother shouts. *You never listen to me.*

Pollux's eyes catch something. There's a hole in the electrical conduit she hadn't noticed before. Then she sees it.

On her left, the foreign biological is latched to the wall next to the access shaft, right beside them. Four yellow eyes stare at her.

Raina spots it too. "What the—!"

"Get up! Get the fuck up!" Pollux barks. "Hurry up!" She positions herself between the group and the creature, and shoves Raina toward the ladder. "Move!"

Pollux slashes the machete with wide strokes, hoping to hold the beast back. Her other hand clasps sharp, pointed clippers that jab the air like a saber. The biological turns its head to one side but doesn't move, as if sizing up this new form of weaponry.

Pollux thrusts forward. Her machete connects with the Kepler's front left flank and slices a thin purple cut across its side. The beast shrieks, then retreats a foot, growling deep in its throat.

"Yes!" she cheers.

Finally! She can wound it!

The creature turns its attention toward the ensigns on the ladder.

She waves her arms in the air, drawing its attention back. "Go!" she yelps at the others. *"Go! For fuck's sake!"*

On the access ladder, Raina hesitates.

Pollux slashes the air again. The creature bares its teeth but remains frozen on the wall.

"That's right, motherfucker," Pollux says to the creature. "Now I can bite back." She glances over her shoulder to check on the ensigns' progress. They haven't moved in the last few seconds. "What're you waiting for?" Then she turns to get a better look.

Tamsin, the youngest one, is stuck in place in the middle of the access shaft, shaking like a child and holding up the others' escape.

"Tam, move!" Raina shouts. "Tam!"

The others call her name and try and coax her up, but the petrified girl doesn't budge.

"Goddamnit! Get a move on, kid!" Pollux bellows. "That's an order!"

Ensign Raina pushes her shoulder up and into Tamsin's ass. The kid's gasping sobs continue, and she slowly inches one foot off a rung and climbs, bringing her closer to the top.

"Somebody smack that idiot!" Pollux bellows.

She catches a glimpse of Niall's hands reaching down the shaft. He lifts Tamsin by her uniform collar. Her feet scramble quickly upward. This clears the way for Ensign Raina to scurry up the access shaft behind, leaving behind Pollux and Morven.

Pollux turns her attention back to the biological. It's moved closer to her while she was looking away. It growls and inches forward again, making her take a step back. Any fear the beast may have felt about the machete seems to have evaporated. The fucker is coming straight at her.

She shoots a quick glance at the access shaft. They'd better get a move on, or this will be over before it starts. Maneuvering herself between the door to the greenhouse and the creature, she hopes to distract it long enough to give the others a chance to make it up.

Plans formulate in her head. She can herd it into the greenhouse and trap it inside. That'll hold it long enough for them to make it to the flight deck and then to the escape pod.

It's a defeat, fleeing the ship like a bunch of weaklings, but given what that thing has done to the others, she doesn't think the ensigns have a chance in hell. And she'll be damned if she lets them down. At least this way, they'll survive, even if they don't deserve it.

The beast inches closer again and a realization hits her.

Where the hell is Morven?

Out of the corner of her eye, Pollux spots him. He's standing at the base of the ladder, guarding Raina's escape. But instead of climbing, Raina watches.

Morven shouts at her, "Get up the ladder!" He shoves her up so hard she almost loses her grip.

Raina holds tight, then extends her hand past Morven to Pollux. "Come on, Sergeant!"

"Get up there!" Pollux says. "We're right behind you."

Her shouting has drawn the thing's attention to her again. She inches backward toward the greenhouse door and the creature follows. "Morven," she calls, "push it toward me. We'll trap it in the greenhouse."

The biological stalks her every move. It hops off the wall and lands low to the ground, slithering from side to side across the floor – straight for her. It can't be more than a few meters away. She swishes her blade again, trying to keep some distance between them. The creature slows its approach.

Morven remains under the access ladder, doing nothing, while Raina climbs up.

"Morven – help her!" Raina shouts. In response, he shoves her farther up the shaft.

Pollux's machete slices another purple crescent across the Kepler's approaching leg. It retreats, crouching low as if it's about to pounce. "Morven!" she bellows. "Come up from behind it!"

But he only stands there.

"Morven!" she shouts again.

What the fuck is he doing?

She reaches behind her with one hand and searches blindly for the door control panel. Finding it, she opens the greenhouse door and attempts to lure the beast into it, but it only follows her. Seeing no other choice, she backs through the greenhouse door.

"Morven, get ready to shut the door when I'm out. Okay?" Her eyes flick up to meet his. He inches forward, following a few feet behind the creature. There's a strange look on his face. He's either scared to death or feels nothing. But at least he's engaged, which fills Pollux with hope that her plan might actually work.

The humidity of the greenhouse saturates her skin as she backs through the door. The biological slowly slithers toward her. Once she and the creature are both inside, she slides to the left of the aisle, hoping to get on the other side of it, when suddenly, the greenhouse door closes.

There's a click as the door locks from the outside.

She peers over her shoulder at the window. Morven stands on the other side, looking in. "Morven!" she shouts. "Morven?"

What the fuck?

The biological approaches. She slashes again and edges toward the door, her heart racing so fast it feels like it might burst. She tries the control panel, but it's locked.

You idiot! her mother screams.

When she looks to the window again, it's empty. Morven's abandoned her. Worse yet, he's deserted her with the creature.

Her hands slap the controls again and again. It's useless.

As the beast approaches, she chokes on her tears and raises her machete, swishing once, twice, a third time.

The biological lifts off the ground and extends its talons. Pollux sucks in her tears and braces for impact.

Quit acting like such a sissy! her mother shouts.

CHAPTER FOURTEEN

Demeter
30.8.2231 AD
1635 hours

On mid-deck, Raina, Niall, Tamsin, and a wheezing Avram crouch by the access shaft opening, waiting for the others to ascend.

Morven arrives after a few moments and grunts, "Up to upper deck. Come on."

"What about Pollux?" Raina breathes, looking back down the shaft. "We can't leave her."

"She gave you an order," Morven says, and Avram shoots him a dirty look. "She's covering us. Don't waste it. Get up the ladder."

Raina, shocked at Morven's insistence, grasps the first rung of the access ladder leading back down to the greenhouse, but thick fingers close around her arm and stop her descent. "I'm not leaving her!" she shouts.

His red fingers squeeze her arm so tightly she feels it bruise. "Get up the ladder," he commands her, and tosses her body across the access shaft as if she weighs nothing.

She just manages to protect her face from crashing into the metal rungs of the ladder.

"Get up, now!" he screams at her.

Avram coughs and sneezes.

"But what about Pollux?" Tamsin cries.

"Go!" he shouts fiercely.

"She gave an order?" Niall asks Raina.

Her heart beats so hard it presses against her ribs. She wants desperately to explain to the others what she suspects is happening, but she's so stark raving furious at Morven, she can't tell what's the right thing to do.

It's quite possible she wants to do the exact opposite of what he says, just because he's the one who says it. It's either that, or she's paranoid. It would be hard to believe he'd leave Pollux down there to die just so he can reassume command of the ship. That would be crazy! Wouldn't it?

"Did she give an order?" Niall demands, and Raina reluctantly nods. "She did."

"Then go or we're all dead," Niall says.

She had given an order, she remembers. Morven is right. She could be messing everything up by waiting for Pollux to catch up, if she ever does.

Raina reaches across the ladder, grabs Tamsin's hand and practically drags her up to the next level. She may lose Pollux, but she'll be damned if she'll lose Tamsin.

When they reach upper deck, she hears Niall and Avram shouting after Pollux, but after only a few seconds, they arrive on upper deck alone.

A lump clogs her throat. "She didn't make it?"

"She's still covering us," Morven says, and even as the words come out of his mouth, she feels their inadequacies. "Keep moving." He motions toward the access ladder leading up to the flight deck and nudges Raina to start climbing.

"Come on, Pollux!" Niall shouts down the access ladder again. "Hurry up!"

"She can't hear you. She ran into the greenhouse. The Kepler followed her," Morven says.

Raina watches his face but can't read how he feels about it. "How do you know that?"

Niall is stricken but holds it together. "She led it away?"

Morven nods. He looks directly at her as he says it. "It followed her into the greenhouse. She closed the door behind them. I didn't want to tell you until later, but the more you keep shouting, the quicker the Kepler will find us."

Tamsin chokes back new sobs. "She's so brave," she whimpers.

Avram clears his throat. "She's made it this far on her own. I'm sure she'll kick its ass."

Tamsin nods but Raina can tell Avram doesn't believe that.

"You saw this?" Raina asks Morven again.

He narrows his eyes at her and sets his jaw. "That's what I said."

She doesn't know what to think. Unlike Avram, Morven is a good liar.

With no other avenue to pursue, she moves to the access ladder leading up to the flight deck. A puddle of vomit and blood at the base of the ladder catches her attention.

Morven doesn't seem to notice. "The flight deck is designed for four people," he says. "We aren't all going to fit up there."

Avram sniffs and nods. "Take Tamsin. I'll stay here."

"Me too," Niall says. "And take Raina, too. In case the consoles need repairs."

Morven shoves her toward the stairs. "Move it."

She has to grab the rungs to keep from being pushed over. As she holds the ladder, standing in a puddle of vomit and blood, Raina's head swims. She looks back at Morven and the others.

Does anybody else see what's happening?

She swallows the bile in the back of her throat. Forcing herself up the shaft as quickly as possible, she is nowhere near prepared for the sight above.

Bodies, blood, vomit, severed limbs, the open hollow eyes of her captain and former crewmates…Kris's head.

The sight almost makes her lose consciousness. If it weren't for Tamsin crying just behind her on the ladder, Raina would turn back around.

"Tam?" she calls. "It's bad."

"What's bad?" she asks from down the shaft.

"The flight deck. Just be prepared."

"What do you mean?" Tamsin whimpers.

Raina steps onto the deck and maneuvers around the corpses, doing her best to keep from tripping. She nudges a body out of the way with her boot and pokes her head down the shaft, facing Tamsin eye to eye.

"Just keep looking at me," Raina coaxes. "Don't look at anything else."

But the moment Tamsin's head emerges from the access shaft and her eyes dart across the carnage, she knows Tamsin is a lost cause. If it weren't for Morven being directly behind her in the shaft, she might have fallen. He practically carries her up the remainder of the way.

Once they're all on the flight deck, Tamsin deteriorates into wails. "Oh my god!" she bellows. "Oh my god!"

"We know! Shut up!" Morven says.

"Tamsin, look at me," Raina tries.

Her wails give way to uncontrollable sobs and she collapses onto the bloody flight deck floor, unable to move. "No. No. No. No. No. No. No."

"Tam?" she says. "Tam, the controls. Just look at the controls. They're right in front of you."

Morven moves to the payload console and flicks a switch to activate it. "Where's the bay door release?" He eyes Tamsin on the floor and groans.

"Tam?" Raina prods again, but she doesn't budge.

"What the hell?" he grumbles. "We don't have time for this."

"I know!" Raina says, and cups her palm under Tamsin's arm to help her stand.

Her legs buckle under the pressure, and she's on the floor again without having ever reached her feet. Her sobs worsen. "I can't. I can't. I can't."

Raina plants her face in front of Tamsin's and tries to talk sense. "All you have to do is tell us. Just tell me what to do, and I'll do it. Don't look at the bodies. Look at me. Just tell me how to open the bay doors."

Tamsin's red and swollen eyes shift about the flight deck and scan the pile of bodies and severed limbs and her mouth hangs open. "So much blood."

"Come on, honey. The controls are ready. Do I use the crane? Can I force the doors open using the crane?"

When she still doesn't answer, Morven pounds his fists against the payload console's chair, and the noise causes Tamsin to shudder and cower further into herself.

Now she's clutching her knees to her chest and rocking back and forth.

"Damn it!" he bellows, which only makes her weep louder.

"Tamsin, come on," Raina says. "You don't have to worry. I'm here to protect you while you use the controls. Just stand up."

She shakes her head like a rebellious toddler and a dribble of snot cascades down her lip. "Can't. Can't. Can't. Can't."

"We need you to tell us how to activate the bay doors," Raina says. "Can I override the safety protocol from here?"

Tamsin doesn't respond. Her sobs echo off the flight deck walls.

Morven's boots pound the floor as he crosses to her. With an open palm, he slaps Tamsin across the face with a loud crack of skin on skin. "Get it together!"

"Morven!" Raina shrieks, and without thinking she snatches the pruning shears from her tool belt and slashes the air at him, causes him to swing backward.

"What the fuck!" he shouts.

"Don't *touch* her! Don't you lay a finger on her!"

Tamsin doesn't hesitate. She's halfway back down the access ladder before Raina can stop her. As she disappears down the ladder, her hands shake so badly Raina isn't sure how she doesn't lose her grip and fall.

"What the hell is the matter with you?" he says.

"What's the matter with me?" she asks. "What the hell is the matter with *you*?"

He watches her panic in confusion. "Don't go all psycho on me," he snarls, scratching his palm against his thigh. "Someone needed to slap some sense into her."

An anger so fierce grips her, she literally sees red. "You left Pollux on purpose," she blurts out. She knows it's a mistake the moment it comes off her lips.

His expression is somewhere between fury and hurt. "She gave us an order."

"I thought you only followed orders that make sense."

"Yeah, well staying behind and dying doesn't make much sense to me. The biological was stalking her, you saw it. She was a goner. If we stayed behind, we'd all be dead. Now, come on, focus – in case you haven't figured it out yet, we just lost our way of opening the bay doors." He turns his back on her and faces the payload console.

"You shouldn't have hit her," she says. "Why do you have to do that? Why are you such an asshole?" If she didn't know any better, she'd swear she just hurt his feelings.

He turns back to her with a wounded glare. "If you're supposed to be so smart, then what do we do now?"

She swallows hard and snaps the pruning shears back into her tool belt. The best way to get away from him is to just get it done and get back to the others. She hates that she's alone with him when he's like this, but there isn't any way around it.

She crosses the flight deck to assess the payload control panel, careful not to turn her back on Morven, who stands beside her on the left. "We can hardwire it," she says after a moment.

"Won't that render the controls useless afterward?"

"Yes, but what choice do we have? Back up. You're crowding me."

He takes a step backward and leans against the pilot's chair. "The doors will burn up when we reenter the Earth's atmosphere if they're open," he says.

"You mean *if* we reenter Earth's atmosphere."

He nods. "Fine. Do it." As if he were back in command.

Raina puts her paranoia aside for a moment and rummages in her tool belt, coming up with her screwdriver. Within minutes she has the payload console apart and in pieces. She takes wires from one circuit board and runs them to another, shamelessly cutting and reattaching without concern for how she'll put them back.

He watches her silently. She talks to herself while she's doing it, mentally laying the power source from the crane joystick to the bay door controls, and then using the payload console motherboard to activate the lock release.

Sweat pours from her brow, and the smell of blood, vomit, and rotting bodies fills her nostrils, but she does her best to put that from her mind as she concentrates, trying to ignore how hot it's gotten and how having Morven staring her down makes her feel.

When she's ready, the console is a jumble of stretched and patched wires, broken and jerry-rigged processing cards, and she uses almost an entire roll of electrical bonding tape, but once satisfied, she looks to Morven when she's done.

"Are you finished yet?" He leans against the back of the pilot's chair, his arms across his broad chest. His shoulders slump slightly.

"I think so." Her finger lingers over the switch.

"Just do it."

"All right!" Her finger snaps the green switch.

There's a humming and a loud whirring noise that brings Morven around the pilot's chair. He stands on the seat and cranes his body and neck around, trying to catch a glimpse of the doors outside and behind the observation windows.

"Is it working?" she asks.

"Can't tell," he says. "Wait, I see something."

The grinding is so loud inside the flight deck she wonders if her bypass of the bay door locks didn't deactivate, but then a large *crack* shakes the entire room, and the familiar sound of the bay doors trudging open causes them both to smile.

"I see it!" he shouts over the noise.

Raina abandons her post in front of the destroyed payload console and climbs into the pilot's chair to stand on the seat, crushing her body next to his for a glimpse out the window.

Sure enough, the tips of the doors can be seen separating, and then the unmistakable sight of the seed spore cascades directly above the observation window.

It floats away from the *Demeter* like a loose balloon.

Raina cheers, flinging her arms into the air. She teeters backward.

Morven's large hands encircle her waist to keep them both from tipping and she's suddenly aware of how closely they stand together.

She can feel the heat from his chest behind her, and before she can clamber out of the way, his nose brushes against her neck and his lips tickle her ear. "Good job," he moans.

A tingle surges across her skin. "Don't." She quickly scrambles away and into the center of the flight deck. She trips over a leg and shudders.

When she looks up, Morven's face has a familiar look of intensity as he watches her. She can feel the weight of his expression. He scratches one hand with the other.

"God," he breathes, and she's suddenly afraid of what he will say. "You stink."

She sighs, having imagined worse. "What's wrong with your hands?"

"What?" He stops scratching. "Nothing."

"You keep rubbing them."

"I do not."

"Morven, *look* at your hands."

He glances down. When he holds them up Raina finally gets a good look at them. They're scarlet red to the tips, even under his fingernails.

"Fuck," he breathes. "They itch like crazy."

"Just like Pollux. Do you have welts?"

He pulls them closer to his face. "Little tiny white dots?"

"Something's wrong," Raina says. "There's been a contamination." She studies her own hands but they look perfectly normal. "I don't get it. Something from the greenhouse maybe?"

"Probably," he says, dropping his hand and absently scratching his shoulder.

"Stop scratching!"

"I'm not scratching! Jesus, Raina, you're a fucking nag. It's just a rash. Shit like this happens all the time down there."

"But if Pollux had it too—? What about the spore? That clear stuff...."

"Would you leave it alone? We have bigger fish to fry than a stupid rash. Fuck."

"If you don't get that treated it could get worse and possibly send you into anaphylactic shock and kill you. I'm only trying to help. You don't have to be such an asshole about it."

For once, he doesn't argue. "I have an idea." He hops over the pilot's chair and crawls over the bodies to the command station. "Let's send the distress signal."

A glimmer of doubt descends on her. For a man who seems hell-bent on retaining command of the ship, why would he call for help? The other ship's captain would immediately outrank him and assume command. "Niall says we aren't authorized to do that," she says.

"Think I give a fuck what Niall says?" He types on the captain's console. "I'm trying to save our skins. I'm not sure what the hell he's trying to do."

She makes note of his pronoun. *Our* skins.

Has she read him wrong? Maybe he hadn't contemplated leaving her alone with Pollux, after all. Maybe he was just anxious to shut the door behind them as they entered. And maybe he was only following Pollux's orders when he left her alone with the Kepler? If he's sending a distress signal now, it would certainly appear so.

She supposes it's entirely possible her personal distrust and anger for him clouded her judgment. Or, maybe he's sending the distress signal to put her off his track?

No. That doesn't make sense.

She's almost certain that the moment she stops being suspicious, he'll prove her paranoia correct. There's nothing worse than thinking the worst of someone, then convincing yourself you were wrong, only to be proven right. With all this crowding her mind she can only manage to say, "Never thought I'd hear you say that."

"I'm full of surprises." He finishes typing then transmits the code. "There."

She can't imagine there's another vessel anywhere in the sector, especially considering they are so far from their own galaxy. But it's worth a shot. "Suppose they'll come for us?"

"They'll come for the plants, at least."

The realization that the Space Corps would come to rescue the plants, and not the crew, has never occurred to her, but now that he says it, it makes sense. Crew members are a dime a dozen. But alien plant life? That's invaluable.

"Best keep this to ourselves, though," he says, and her suspicions once again awaken. "We'll just pretend the captain transmitted the code, in case anyone asks."

She tries to keep her face empty, but it takes effort. "I thought you said you didn't care what Niall thought."

"True. But I don't want his panties in a wad. He's trouble enough."

She raises an eyebrow. "He's trouble?"

"All right then, come on." He climbs back over the bodies and is the first to start down the access ladder. "Time to kill an alien."

She watches him descend and disappear from view. Doubt haunts her mind. Doubt of her doubt comes right after.

Truth be told, she doesn't know what to think anymore.

CHAPTER FIFTEEN

When they reach the others, Raina can't help but feel relieved. Safety in numbers, right?

Niall looks at them expectantly. "Well?"

"It worked," she says. "It's out. We saw it float away."

Avram crouches on the floor beside Tamsin, who has curled into the fetal position. "What happened up there? Why is she like this?"

"The bodies freaked her out," Morven says and shrugs, conveniently leaving out the part when he slapped her.

Raina's anger resurges but she lets it go, not wanting to upset the others. When the time comes....

She steps over to Tamsin and sits on the floor beside her. Together they curl into each other like scared puppies. Raina strokes her hair. The poor girl is shaking violently. When this is all over, she's going to make this up to her. She promises.

"What's next?" Niall asks and Morven's face reddens.

"We hunt down and kill the fucker," he says, but Avram shakes his head.

"That's what got the officers waxed. We should trap it. Maybe get it into the escape pod and then chuck it out into space?"

"And blow any chance we have of using the pod?" Morven asks.

Avram wipes his nose on his sleeve. "You got a better idea, Einstein?"

"The airlock," Raina suggests.

"Don't be an idiot," Morven says. "The airlock doors are too slow. It'd jump out before we could get them closed."

"The freighter pod?" Avram asks.

"Internal controls," Raina says.

"We've been over this before," Morven says.

"What about the main room in the sleep chamber?" Niall offers, rubbing his hands down his wrinkled face.

"What about it?" Morven scratches his elbow.

Avram nods at Niall. "There's not much equipment inside except the door to the sleep compartments, so it won't damage the ship. There's only one air vent in that room, so if we close that off it can't escape. And Raina here can rig the doors for rapid release."

"I can?"

Avram raises his eyebrow. "That's how you got the bay doors to open, right? I'm assuming Tamsin wasn't much help, and heaven knows muscle man over there didn't know what to do."

Morven opens his mouth to protest but Niall interrupts. "Why doesn't she just rig the airlock doors?"

Raina shakes her head. "Can't work around the decompression. Plus, the sleep chamber has double reinforced walls. It's a good idea."

"It's the emergency isolation chamber," Avram says. "The doors have dual plates in case of a hull breach. It's supposed to be for when we cross the asteroid field, but the captain never enforced using it."

"We should just kill the damned thing," Morven objects, but no one listens.

"I'll need some time to rig the doors," Raina says, and Avram taps the pickaxe on his waistband.

"We've got your back."

They nod to one another and Avram helps Raina get Tamsin to her feet.

"It'll be okay, Tam," Raina whispers. "We're going to trap the foreign biological in the sleep chamber."

Her eyes dart around like a bouncing ball. "Then where will we sleep?" she whimpers and Morven scoffs.

"This idea is stupid. We should just kill it," he mutters.

Raina shushes him and he stalks off ahead, checking both ways down the hall.

"It's clear," he says, and the rest follow slowly behind.

When they reach the sleep chamber door, Raina leans Tamsin against Avram and brushes by Morven to get to the front of the group.

"Wish me luck," she says to no one in particular.

"Sure," he says. "Good luck."

She can't help but notice he doesn't sound like he means it.

★   ★   ★

Raina works for the next half hour on rigging the sleep chamber door. She tests it multiple times but is never quite satisfied with the speed. She keeps at it.

Morven grumbles and complains the entire time, distracting her from her task, but she does her best to ignore him. Although it's not easy.

Avram uses the time to try and calm Tamsin down. He gets her talking about her family, the ranch where she grew up, and her love of horses – which Raina had not known about.

When Raina is finally content with her reconfiguration, she tests the remote from across the hall to gauge the range. But no matter how she tries, she can't extend the reach beyond four meters. It's a little too close for comfort.

"We'll have to be in the next chamber," Raina tells the others.

Tamsin and Niall both look stricken.

The next chamber is the spacewalk preparation room and the bathroom. But seeing as how it's less than three meters away, and the next chamber after that, the galley, is four and a half meters down the hall, the remote runs the risk of not working when needed. There will only be a split-second window to click the remote and close the doors on the Kepler. The last thing they need is to be out of range, even by an inch, and blow the whole plan.

Morven doesn't seem fazed. "Prep room it is."

Avram wipes his nose on his sleeve. "How do we draw it there?"

An uncomfortable silence ripples across them.

Raina's first thought is to volunteer as bait. If she lures it there and then jumps out the chamber door and clicks the remote, she can lock the beast inside without incident.

Hadn't Morven said she was faster than a jackrabbit?

But there are too many things that can go wrong with that plan, and she realizes the risk is too high. Besides, isn't that how Pollux died? It would also mean Morven and the others were in charge of helping her escape, and Morven might actually work against that, and then she's as good as dead. So, instead of volunteering, she stares at the sleep chamber door and does her best to think.

"We need bait," Morven says.

She shakes her head. "It's too risky."

"Too risky if we're alive," he says, and Avram glares at him because Tamsin has begun to whimper again.

"Kinda goes against the whole idea of trapping it if we're dead," Avram quips.

"What about the ones who aren't alive?" Morven suggests.

Raina hates to admit she knows where he's going with this plan. "The bodies on the flight deck."

Tamsin cries again. "Ooohh nooo."

"What are you suggesting?" Niall asks. "I'll not have you desecrate the bodies of my friends for some cockamamie idea."

"I hate to break it to you," Morven says, "but the Kepler did the desecration already. They're like empty shells up there. It ate out the insides."

"Morven, zip it," Avram says and points to Tamsin, who is back to sobbing.

"So, if it ate out all the insides already, why would the Kepler come back for them?" Niall points out.

"He's got a point," Raina says and Morven frowns at her.

"I have a better idea," Niall offers.

"Yeah?" Morven asks. "And what's that?"

Niall nods out the door toward the galley. "Spam."

*　　*　　*

Nine Months Ago....

"I saw you with them this morning," Morven says. His face is stiff. "What were you talking about?"

She shrugs and screws in the last piece of the wall console on the greenhouse deck. "I don't know, stuff. Nothing important."

He sets his jaw and tilts his head with a quick jerk. "Didn't look like nothing."

"Well it was." She wants to tell him to relax, but knows that'll just set him off again. Honestly, she's so sick of living in a minefield these last few months, she almost says it just to get it over with. Ever since he heard about his father, Morven's been an absolute beast to deal with. Between him and Osric always ordering her around, she wonders why she doesn't just set him off like a bomb. It'd be a relief to finally be blown to bits.

"What did Avram want anyway?" he presses.

"Nothing. He just wanted to see what my plans were tonight." *Ah, shit.* She shouldn't have said it like that. "He, Tam, and Kris are trying to put together a party," she adds hastily. "For the whole crew – for the captain's birthday."

"The whole crew, huh? Funny. He didn't mention it to me." He crosses his muscular arms across his chest and rests his fingers on his elbows.

"I'm sure he'll get around to you later." She puts her screwdriver back into her belt and rubs her fingerprints off the console with the sleeve of her uniform.

He scoffs in an exaggerated way that she knows is meant to get under her skin. It's working. "I'm sure."

"It's no big deal. We don't have to go if you don't want to," she says.

He raises an eyebrow. "Why wouldn't we go?"

"Oh, I don't know. I thought maybe you'd want to stay in?"

"You know what I think?"

She's afraid to ask, so she just stands there, mute. It's like watching a comet plummeting straight into a planet's atmosphere. She knows it's coming, but can't do anything to stop it.

When she doesn't answer he continues, just like she knew he would. "I think you've been talking about me with them, and you don't want me to go so I don't hear what you've been saying about me."

"Do you even hear yourself?"

He steps forward, getting in her face. "That's it then, isn't it? What have you been saying?"

She steps back, eyeing him quizzically. What's his deal? "I haven't said anything. Why would I?"

"You told them about my father, didn't you?"

"You know I would never do that."

"They've been giving me looks, Rain. They obviously know something."

Her blood curdles to the point of boiling. This is such *bullshit*. She's had it up to her eyeballs with this guy but still isn't sure how to end this conversation, or this whole fucking affair, without things getting out of control. Her back is pressed to the ladder of the access shaft and in a fit of rage she lashes out. "Maybe they're giving you looks because you're an asshole!"

He presses into her face. Nose to nose, he talks through clenched teeth. "Oh, so now I'm an asshole?"

"If the uniform fits…."

"You think this is funny?" he shouts, making Raina step back again. She can't move. There's nowhere for her to go.

She's tempted to make a run for it, or to knee him in the nuts, but he's blocking the doorway to the greenhouse and there's nowhere for her to go but up the access shaft, and she won't get far. He'd grab her by the ankle and drag her back down to his level in an instant. She wouldn't put anything past him.

"You think my father's a joke?" he sneers. "Ha. Ha. Poor Morven. His dad is a *coward*."

"No. I would never—"

"I bet that's exactly what you said," he spits, pointing a finger in her face. "I bet you and Avram were laughing like a pack of fucking hyenas about it."

"No, Moe…I would never—"

"Is there a problem here?" a voice interrupts. Pollux comes from inside the greenhouse and stands behind Morven.

She looks fiercely angry. There's dirt under her fingernails and all over her fingers, plus a smudge of soil on her cheek. She must have been working on the greenery just inside, and overheard.

Part of Raina is relieved at this. Another part of her is petrified. He's pissed enough already, and Pollux could make this a hell of a lot worse.

Morven takes a step back and away from her, and Raina's stomach untwists. She didn't even realize she was cowering in the corner like a rabbit, but she grabs hold of the ladder and takes a step up. She's hoping to use the interruption and make an exit. He's gotten so much worse over the last few months, she can't even take a shit without getting the third degree from him, and the only solution she sees is to remove herself until he calms down.

"Don't move, Raina," Pollux orders, and she stops on the second rung. *Damn.*

"No, there's not a problem here," Morven says. "Is there something you need help with, Sergeant Pollux?"

Pollux's face doesn't move a muscle. She stares at him like she's just seen him for the first time, and maybe she has. Her eyes trail up and meet Raina's, and despite her best effort, Raina knows she's not hiding her fear very well. He's got that look in his eye now, like a rabid dog. A cold sweat has already broken out down the small of her back and her palms feel slick. She takes it back. His blowups are never worth it.

"Raina?" Pollux asks. "You all right?"

"Of course she's all right," Morven answers.

In a flash Pollux's calmness evaporates. "I wasn't talking to you!" she shouts. "Ensign Morven, you will confine yourself to quarters until you hear otherwise from me. Is that understood?"

"What the fuck? I didn't do anything wrong!" Morven says but he stops when Pollux whips her hand out and taps the control panel beside her.

"Captain, this is Technical Sergeant Pollux, I request your presence in the greenhouse immediately."

There's a brief squeal and a burst of static from the intercom before the captain answers. "What's the matter, Pollux? We have contamination again?"

"Negative, sir. Personnel issues. Get down here on the double," Pollux answers.

There's an audible sigh of impatience from the captain that is heard throughout the ship on the intercom. "On my way." And then the transmission cuts off.

Raina's cold sweat drips from her hairline and down to her chin.

Jesus Christ, they're just making it worse!

They have no idea what she's going to have to do to calm him down.

"I said to quarters, Ensign Morven. Now," Pollux says.

"This is bullshit," he blurts, pushing Raina out of the way and barreling up the access shaft, almost stepping on her fingers as he goes. "Fucking bullshit!"

Pollux doesn't answer.

Raina watches Morven move up the ladder then looks back at Pollux.

"You okay?" she asks. Her face softens.

Raina nods, thunderstruck.

Morven's going to kill me for this.

CHAPTER SIXTEEN

Demeter
30.8.2231
1736 hours

Niall's idea isn't astrophysics, but it's not bad either. Inside the galley cooling unit, he hands the group cans of meat substitute. Several loads later they trudge back to the sleep chamber, seal off the air ventilation shaft using the doors off the lockers, and then set about opening the cans of meat.

The smell is horrendous.

After piling the opened cans into the far corner of the chamber, they go back to the space prep/bathroom and crack the door, just wide enough so Raina can see the opening to the sleep chamber.

"This is the stupidest idea I've ever heard in my life," Morven mutters, and Avram scratches his palm, glaring at him.

"I'm open to suggestions," Niall grumbles. He settles in a corner of the room on the floor.

No one has any.

Much to Raina's chagrin, Morven's doubts prove correct. Minutes pass, and she finds herself in the uncomfortable position of wondering if her ex is right, again. This may very well be a huge waste of time, and succeeding in nothing but putting them all on edge.

Morven only paces – back and forth, back and forth. It's irritating as hell. Even good-natured Avram looks dejected, slumped by the bathroom and scratching his palms against his thighs. Then there's Niall and Tamsin. Underneath a row of empty space suits that hang on the wall, Tam is curled up beside the cook on the floor, sleeping with her head in his lap.

How she's managing to sleep is beyond Raina's understanding, but it's obvious Niall isn't happy about it.

Although, Raina hates to admit, she's glad – the break from Tam's continual sobbing has been nice.

"What the hell is taking so long?" Avram asks.

From her position by the door, Raina rubs her stiff neck with her palm. "Maybe the Kepler doesn't like meat substitute."

"Who does?" He vigorously scratches his palm with his other hand. "I can't even breathe and *I* can tell how ripe it is."

Niall eyes the clock on the wall and sighs. Raina cranes her eyes away from the crack in the sliding door and blinks a few times. It's been only a few hours since this whole thing started, yet if feels like days.

"Why don't you try and get some sleep too, Niall," Raina suggests. He looks a hundred years older than he did the day before.

He frowns at her. "We can sleep when we're dead."

"Nice," mumbles Morven, and he crouches down behind Raina at the door. He's not looking much better. In fact, he's so flushed there's a rosy blotch of skin on his neck. He digs at it absently with a pink hand.

"It's spread to your neck," she says.

"This whole situation is making me itch," he growls, and glares at her with enough venom she looks away.

She does her best to keep her face expressionless. None of them have eaten in hours or cleaned themselves up, even after their trek onto the bloody, vomitous flight deck. They're all sweaty, flushed, and smelly. It's no wonder they're cranky.

But, given the way Morven's digging at his neck, it won't be long before he breaks skin. She reaches up to grab his hand and get a better look, but he jerks away like she's poisonous.

"Don't touch me!" he snaps.

"All right. Jesus."

"Play nice, children," Avram says. His usual smirk has been replaced with a grimace. He's still pale, but at least he's not wheezing anymore. "Honestly, I'd love a nap," he adds, "but don't think I could sleep, even if I tried."

"We're not going to be much help against the Kepler if we're exhausted," Raina says.

"I don't think a nap is going to solve this," Morven says.

"It couldn't hurt."

"You want a break, princess?" he asks sharply. "Maybe you can take a shower and do your hair while we wait. How's that?"

"I wasn't suggesting—"

"Just shut up and keep your eyes on that door," he says. "It won't be much longer."

"That's what you said an hour ago," Avram whines.

"Nobody asked you."

"Please," Niall groans. "For the love of all things holy, will you three *shut up*?"

"Is that an order? Or are you just making a helpful suggestion?" Morven asks.

Avram rolls his bloodshot eyes. "For fuck's sake, not this again."

"For the last time," Niall growls. "Until I know beyond a shadow of a doubt that Technical Sergeant Pollux is dead, *she* is in command."

"Nice way to pass the buck. I'm so reassured to know we're under the command of a corpse in the greenhouse."

"Morven!" shouts Raina, but he just opens his eyes wide and points at the door.

She turns back to her position and stares through the crack again. The sleep chamber door across the hall sits wide open and unchanged, just like it has for the past hour. She's been staring at it for so long it feels like she's watching a screen.

The lights above flicker for the tenth time since they've sat down.

Avram frowns at the ceiling. "Anybody know a mechanic? Oh, wait." He looks to her, a hint of sarcasm and truth laced in his face. He scratches his arm again. "Never mind."

"That's gotta be the biological ripping apart the ship," Morven grunts. "We're wasting time with this idiotic plan."

"Maybe we should just send the distress signal?" This is the millionth time Avram suggests this.

Raina turns from the door to look at Morven, but his eyes stay transfixed on his feet.

"If you want to risk your life by going back to the flight deck before we capture this thing – by all means," Niall sighs. "There's the door."

"I knew we should have sent it while they were up there," Avram grumbles.

"Only officers are allowed to activate the distress signal," Niall explains again. "And that's only *after* containment."

Morven eyes Raina and shakes his head.

The only reason she can think why he doesn't want to come clean about sending the Mayday is for fear he'll get reprimanded and possibly discharged from the United Space Corps if he's found out. Although under the circumstances she hardly thinks that would happen. But she also wonders if there's another reason why he won't speak up – some motive that's much worse. Another thought occurs to her.

"Will you two stop it? It's already been sent," she says.

Morven shoots her a look of panic, but she doesn't look at him for fear she'll lose her nerve.

"I sent a distress signal when I was up there," she says.

Niall looks appalled, but Avram sighs with relief. "You could have mentioned that before."

"I was trying to avoid…" Raina starts.

"Why did you do that?" Niall asks. "You have no authorization!"

"…that," she finishes.

"Oh, whatever," Avram says, rubbing his arm. "I'm glad you did. It might just save our asses."

Morven cusses under his breath, but she cuts him off.

"I don't care if I have authorization," Raina nips back at Niall. "Write me up. Discharge me. Whatever. After this is over I could care less if I ever have another commission aboard a United Space Corps vessel again. Seriously."

"What if they send a rescue ship and board us?" Niall asks in panic. "That *thing* could end up killing the entire other crew!"

"That doesn't seem to be an issue, seeing as how I sent the transmission over an hour ago, and we've gotten no reply," she reasons.

"You don't know that. The response could be waiting up at the command station," Niall seethes. "We're supposed to wait until it's contained!"

"And what if we're all too dead to do that?" Avram asks, coughing once.

"Then all the more reason why no other ship should come." Niall stands, rustling Tamsin from her sleep. "It's procedure."

"Fuck procedure," growls Morven. He's gotten to his feet as well.

"Did we catch it yet?" Tamsin asks sleepily.

"Oh, shut up," Morven barks at her.

"Following procedure is what got the other officers eaten," Avram says again.

"Besides, we need backup," Raina adds.

"We won't need backup if we catch it!" Niall continues.

"It'd be better odds," Morven says.

"Better odds?" Niall asks. "Better odds you'll survive if that thing has other officers to kill, you mean?"

"That's not what I meant, and you know it."

"I'm not sure what you want," Niall argues, and Morven's temper shows on his flushed face.

"The good news is that once the other ship arrives there won't be any question about who's in command," Avram offers, scratching his arm harder.

"What's wrong with your hands?" Tamsin asks him.

He stops itching for a moment and looks at them. They're so red and flushed Raina wonders how he's not in pain. "I don't know. They itch like crazy. It's driving me nuts."

"You too, Morven," Tamsin says, pointing. "Your whole neck is pink just like Pollux's was. Are you feeling okay?"

"Shut the hell up," says Morven, scratching. Then, noticing what he's doing, he stops.

"No, really," Raina agrees. "The two of you won't stop scratching."

"It's probably just my allergies," Avram volunteers, rubbing his palms against his legs.

"That doesn't explain Morven and Pollux, though," Tamsin adds. "All the botanists have been contaminated."

Raina nods. "I said that earlier."

"But contaminated by what?" Avram asks.

"It doesn't matter if that thing eats us first," Morven says, reddening more. "So just drop it."

"It's starting to piss me off," Avram says, banging the back of his head against the wall behind him. "I could seriously punch something."

Tamsin scoots away with a dubious expression. "You better hope the rash doesn't get infected."

Raina nods. "You have any more antihistamine in that med kit, Tam?"

She shakes her head. "I used it all, but there's another kit on the flight deck, I think."

"No one's in a hurry to go back there at the moment," Raina says. "I guess you two will have to wait until the cavalry comes. If you don't scratch yourselves to death first."

Avram grimaces, angrily digging at his shoulder. "No shit."

Turning back to her post of peering through the cracked door, Raina shifts on the floor and comes nose to nose with the snarling, drooling, and razor-sharp jaws of the Kepler.

With a shriek she skids backward on all fours, scrambling for her life.

Over her shoulder, a machete slices downward and narrowly misses her as it connects with the Kepler's face. It imbeds directly between its eyes. The thing squeals and recoils, but Morven can't get the machete out.

He yanks the blade, pulls it back and swings again.

Raina jerks quickly out of the way as a chunk of the Kepler's face slices off and drops to the floor from Morven's second blow.

She can barely think from Tamsin's screaming and Morven's shouting. Her eyes stay transfixed on the beast as it attempts to squeeze through the inch opening in the sliding door. It rams its head repeatedly with deafening crashes.

She can smell its breath in her nostrils.

When the biological finally appears to give up, disappearing from the door, Avram, who stands at the inside controls, wheezing horribly, clicks the panel and the door seals shut the remainder of the way.

"We're trapped," Niall whispers.

Raina gets to her feet and scans the room. There's only one way out of the space prep room, and a man-eating biological now blocks it. "What do we do?"

There's a crash at the door. The metal sliders bend inward.

Tamsin screams again.

"Shut her up!" Morven barks, and he rips the weighted space suits off the wall and uses them to barricade the door. "Help me!"

Morven and Niall pile space suits, ventilators, planetary gravity-assist boots and every moveable, weighted object in the room at the door.

Tamsin, petrified beyond hope, is curled into a ball in the corner, weeping and screaming at the top of her lungs.

It isn't until Raina looks to Avram that she realizes he's in trouble.

Doubled over with his lips blue, he's bent in half by the door controls, wheezing louder than ever, and coughing violently.

Raina sees the source of his anguish, the shred of Kepler flesh at his feet.

"Tamsin! The injector!" Raina cries, and she snatches the bloodied piece of purple flesh in her bare hands and enters the water closet.

Inside the small bathroom is a tiny sink and a toilet. Raina tosses the slab of Kepler into the toilet bowl and pulls the lever to empty the basin. But the chunk is too large and it takes two tries before it disappears out of sight.

When she comes back out, the situation has worsened.

The door crashes again, bending farther. Morven and Niall brace their backs against the pile of debris in front of the door. Niall is nearly knocked off his feet from the force of the next crash. If the creature keeps banging at that pace, the door won't last much longer.

With each crash, Tamsin sobs louder, wailing in the corner in horror.

Avram still lies on the floor by the door panel. His face has gone purple. Raina goes to him and tries to sit him up, but he's too tall, and she doesn't have the strength to move him.

"Tamsin!" Raina cries. "The injector!" When she doesn't move, Raina leaves Avram on the floor, and goes to her. "Give me the injector! Give it!" She attempts to pry the medical kit from around Tamsin's neck. But the strap is tight against the girl's body and she fights her off like a cornered cat. Raina reels back, then slaps her on the shoulder. "Tamsin! Stop! Tam!"

The door crashes again. This time Niall hits the floor. One side of the sliding door is so bent the metal looks ready to rupture.

Morven adjusts his position into the center of the door and presses his back against it again. "Raina!" he cries. "Help me!"

Getting desperate, Raina whips the pruning shears from her tool belt and slices the shoulder strap off Tamsin's flailing body. The girl screams louder.

The medical kit in her hands, Raina crosses the room, almost tripping over Niall as he struggles back to his feet on his way to help hold the door.

Finally reaching Avram, she dumps the medical kit onto the floor, fills the injector with the first vial she can find without even checking the label, and hits Avram in the neck with the needle. It hisses with release.

There's no improvement. He lies on the floor, rigid, his hands clenched, his face puffed and swollen. His lips are no longer blue but bright purple.

When she hits him again using another random vial, his eyes glass over.

The door crashes again.

"Rain!" Morven screams.

The door splits open.

A Kepler claw slides through the opening and slashes the air not an inch from Niall's head as he presses his back against the door and debris.

The old man drops to his knees and bellows with frustration as the pile of stuff topples over him.

Dropping the vials, Raina scrambles to her feet, and with one swing of her hand axe, she dives over Niall's crouched body and chops off the Kepler's paw. The blade buries itself into the pile of debris, getting stuck.

There's a blood-curdling squeal from the hall.

The bloodied Kepler leg trips down the pile of space suits and equipment and tumbles like a time bomb at Avram's face.

Tamsin's screams echo off the walls at an ear-splitting decibel.

The crashing stops but Morven's back stays firmly pressed against the door, as if he's too afraid to let go.

Raina leaves her axe buried in the pile and slides down, making her way over Niall and back to Avram. But she's too late.

The whites of his vacant eyes have gone red with burst blood vessels. He no longer breathes.

"Avram!" she cries. She rolls him onto his back and straddles his abdomen. She starts chest compressions, but then thinks better of it and dives for the medical kit. Her fingers dig through the shards of broken and empty vials and comes up bloodied. She must have stepped on the bag when she dived with the axe. Giving that up, she returns to Avram's still body and tries chest compressions again.

"Come on, Ave! Come on!"

"Raina, we have to go," Niall says. He's digging out the door with Morven's help.

Tamsin's screams have abated to wails of sorrow, but she doesn't move from her corner.

Raina pumps Avram's chest again and attempts to blow air into his mouth, but his tongue is so thick it blocks his windpipe and his nose is so swollen on the inside both nostrils are closed tight.

"Let's so, Raina!" Morven shouts. "It'll come back. We have to get out of here!"

"There's nothing you can do," Niall says. "Raina!"

"Come on!" Morven bellows again, and he tosses her bloodied axe at her feet.

It knocks Avram in the head.

"Stop it!" she screams back, but Morven keeps digging out the door.

"We gotta go!" Niall shouts. "Now!"

Morven pushes back one side of the sliding door and steps away from the opening, waiting for the Kepler to burst back in.

When nothing happens, he reaches with his free hand toward Raina and points out the door with the arm holding the machete. "Now, Raina!"

She sits atop Avram and tears of anger and frustration burn her eyes. "No! I just need a minute. He's not dead. He's not!" She pumps two more times. She knows it's hopeless. She drops her head to Avram's quiet chest and weeps.

Not Avram! Not Avram!

By the time Raina looks up, Morven is already out into the hallway and Niall is halfway through the door.

She runs her palm across Avram's eyelids, closing them.

"Raina!" someone shrieks.

She climbs off Avram's limp body and stumbles across the room. Taking Tamsin by the arm, she drags her behind.

With one last look at Avram's body, they leave together.

CHAPTER SEVENTEEN

Out in the hallway of upper deck, Raina drags Tamsin after her. Droplets of purplish blood leave a twisted trail across the floor. Ahead, Raina can see Niall and Morven, running along the trail in hot pursuit.

"Morven, get back here!" Niall shouts. "I order you to get back here!"

"It's wounded! Now's our chance!" he yells back, and he's running down upper deck like a comet.

"Morven!" Niall gives chase, but he's no match for the ensign's speed.

A few paces behind, Raina clasps Tamsin's hand and drags her along. The girl continues to sob and gasp for air, but at least she's moving. In between sobs Raina hears her whisper Avram's name, but there's nothing to be done about that right now.

She checks over her shoulder. She and Tamsin have fallen dangerously behind. Ahead, Niall has all but given up chasing after Morven. He's stopped, grasping his knees and gasping for breath. She knows if they get separated, they're all as good as dead.

When they finally catch up to him, Niall points in the direction Morven went. "I can't..." he gasps, "...keep up."

"Where's he going?" she asks.

He shakes his head. "Ran after the Kepler."

"Ran after it?"

"To kill it."

"It'll slice him to shreds!"

Niall swallows thickly and nods, unable to speak further.

A man's yell echoes off the hallway walls.

After shoving Tamsin into Niall's arms, Raina takes off running toward it.

Her boots pound the floor like anvils, yet she books down the hallway at lightning speed. When she rounds a corner, she skids to a stop.

Morven stands in front of the workstation by the galley. As she runs toward him, he slumps and collapses, hitting the floor hard, face-first.

"No!"

In a flash she's to him. She kneels and rolls him over onto his back. Four slashes mark across his chest. "Oh no! Moe, can you hear me? Moe?"

He groans once, and his eyes flutter open. He moves his arm into the air and winces. It drops to his side.

Her initial instinct is to cover his wounds with her hands, but she stops herself. Leaning in close, she realizes the slashes aren't too deep and his breathing is steady, although there's a good amount of blood. It must have just swiped at him.

Did he faint? she wonders. Why did these shallow wounds make him fall?

"Rain," he whispers, and her heart flips once. "It hurts."

"Oh Moe – get up. Get up, we have to get you out of here."

"Rain," he whispers, his eyes growing larger.

She leans in close, putting her ear to his mouth. "What? What is it?"

His hot whisper tickles her earlobe.

"Behind you."

She whips around. Her eyes scan the wall and around in circles. "I can't see it!"

"Purple," Morven whispers.

She looks harder. The wall appears unscathed except for small droplets of purplish blood that splatter upward. Then she sees it. The spots of purplish blood are *on* the Kepler. It hangs on the wall just below the air vent shaft, invisible and wounded. A bloody stump dangles limply from its body where a leg used to be. The droplets ripple off the stump and hit the floor with tiny splats.

Scrambling to grasp her hand axe from her tool belt, Raina doesn't take her eyes off the creature.

It growls once; the starkness of its teeth sends ripples of fear down her spine. The beast is as still as a statue, watching her. The four beady eyes squint at the axe in her hand, and the biological snarls. The creature slithers backward silently into the air vent and disappears from view, dripping a trail of purplish blood behind it.

Raina stares after it a moment, her heart pounding in her chest so hard it hurts. Then, using her free arm, she helps Morven to his feet. "Come on, we gotta go."

"You could have had it," he whimpers. "Why didn't you kill it?"

"Are you kidding me?" It's difficult to help him stand. He's twice her size and wounded, but he manages to get up. "You're lucky to be alive."

With one arm draped over her shoulders, and another gripping his bleeding chest, they hobble down the hallway, back toward where she left Niall and Tamsin.

Morven tips his head to the side and rests it on top of hers. "Thought I could take it. It's wounded."

"Shh, quiet. We have to get you patched up."

"But it's wounded. That could have been our only chance, and I fucked it up. Why didn't you just chop off its head?"

"Like I could get close enough."

"*I* could have. I almost had it," he breathes. "But it swiped once then ran away from me."

"Lucky for you it did! Look what it did to you. It certainly wasn't one of your brightest ideas."

"Damnit, Raina."

"What do you want me to say?"

They round the corner and find Niall and Tamsin just where she left them. They're gripping each other and looking every bit as helpless as they are.

"What happened?" Niall asks.

"Just a scratch, but we need to get him cleaned up," Raina says.

"This way." Niall helps her by taking Morven by the other arm. "To the sleeping chamber. We can use the smell of the synthetic meat to hide us."

Tamsin groans in between sobs. "What about Avram?" she asks. "Are we just going to leave him in the bathroom?"

"Nothing we can do for him now," Niall says. "Let's save who we can, and then get the hell off this ship."

★ ★ ★

Inside the sleep chamber, Niall helps Raina drop Morven into his compartment cot, then gives her the remains of the medical bag. He mumbles something about not leaving Tamsin alone as he departs.

She helps Morven lie down on his bunk, then slowly and carefully undoes the clasps on the shirt of his uniform. The blood from the cuts has already begun to crust around the edges, and with each tug of his shirt, the slash marks bleed anew. The rash on his hands has spread too – tiny white spots and red skin run up his arms and across his chest, aggravating the wound. She has to slap his hands away three times to stop him from scratching.

She snatches a towel from the clasp by his sink and uses it to absorb the blood. He groans in protest, but she doesn't stop.

The familiar action of opening his shirt and moving about his chamber stirs conflicting emotions through her. She's done this a million times. When he sits up and pulls the shirt off his muscular shoulders, she almost doesn't notice when her fingers shake.

He reaches up and clamps his large hand on top of hers. His fingers are so hot, it warms her down to her bones. She can tell he has a fever. The rash has got to be infected. This is the last thing they need. She has the sudden and uncontrollable urge to cry.

He takes one look at her and frowns. "Stop blubbering," he says, and he lets go of her hand. He drops back onto the bunk with a groan.

The warmth inside her fades. This is a familiar feeling as well.

He never did like when she showed any weakness.

She nods, unable to speak with tears clogging her throat. This isn't the time for feelings.

She sets back to work, absorbing the blood with the towel. His chest moves up and down with the labored breathing of a man in pain.

She reaches toward the medical bag at her feet and searches it for antibiotics. There aren't any. Instead, she pulls out some medicated swabs. It's not much, but it'll have to do. She's halfway through wiping down the first of the four slash marks when he gasps in pain and her hands freeze in place.

"No, it's fine," he grunts. "Just get it done."

"Sorry," she whispers, and turns the swab over, to use the other side.

He flinches again and she stops.

"Sorry," she says again.

"Stop saying that."

"Sorry."

He lets out a noise that's some cross between a scoff and a laugh. "Now you're saying you're sorry for saying you're sorry. I said stop it."

She rolls her eyes and sets back to cleaning his wounds. It takes almost all the medical swabs, and a good ten minutes. During this, and for just a moment, Raina realizes she could easily forget where they are, and what they are doing. It's oddly comforting, hiding in Morven's bedchamber, together, with her taking care of him.

If she didn't know any better, she'd think he's enjoying it too.

She reaches up for another swipe at his wound and his hand catches her wrist.

The rest happens so fast she barely has time to react.

With a grunt of pain he sits up, grasps the back of her neck in his other hand, and brings her face to his as if it were second nature.

His lips cover hers and she's immediately lifted onto the bunk, her body entwined in his, her legs wrapped around him, her hands in his hair.

She forgets everything. Anything that's happened between them before is washed away as his tongue delves into the warmth of her mouth. She involuntarily presses her hips into him and moans. Then suddenly, his lips lift off hers with a smack and her body is unceremoniously dumped onto the floor beside the bunk.

She lands on her back with a grunt. "Ow!"

"Damnit!" he shouts, scratching his neck.

She pushes off her hands to sit up. Looking down, she notices their little tryst has smeared Morven's blood on the front of her uniform. "Don't scratch! You're making it worse."

He's on his feet. He angrily snatches up the remains of his shirt, slides one arm into a sleeve, and winces from having moved so fast. "Fuck you."

"You were the one—!"

"I can't do this again, I can't," he says.

"But you were the one—!"

"Just get out, I can't think with you here."

"What about your cuts? And the rash? You have a fever, you know."

"I'm fine. Just get out."

"Fine." She gets to her feet. She's almost to the door when....

"Wait."

For some unknown reason, her feet have turned to stone. Here it comes. A tiny saddened part of her knows it's sick and twisted, even after everything, but she's actually glad it's coming.

She doesn't answer, but twists her head to see the look on his face, and there it is. She knew it would be there, that same look. She wants it to be there and hates herself for missing it.

It's a comfort, really, to know that look is still hidden underneath everything else. That vulnerable, sad, hurt, confused look that he always gets whenever he is overcome with emotions he can't process. His confusion manifests into all sorts of angry words and violent threats but it always boils down to that look.

Her Achilles' heel.

The look could melt glass.

"I'm sorry," he whispers, and her tears threaten to return. "I'm so sorry."

It's the first time he's ever apologized to her for anything, at least sincerely. The words hit her with such force, her fingers tighten in her palm. "Forget it," she says, because a part of her wants to. "Just forget it."

"Rain—" he starts, but she cuts him off.

"There's more medicated swabs in the bag over there. You should finish cleaning that last cut."

She turns to leave. His hand catches her arm. For a second she lets it linger. He rubs his thumb against a bruise that's formed where he grabbed her previously. His touch is gentle this time, soft and warm, but the bruise still hurts.

The look that passes between them says more than anything they can verbalize. It says yes. It says no. It says maybe, and probably not. After a moment, she gently pulls her arm out of his hand. He lets her go.

"Oh Moe," she sighs, and is almost stricken to see the pained look in his eyes. "I can't do this again either."

His breath lets out with an audible hiss.

She closes the chamber door behind her.

★   ★   ★

Twelve Months Ago....

Morven lies beside her and touches her hair with his palm, running it down her neck, shoulder, back. He then grabs her bare ass a little too firmly. There's possessiveness in his touch that didn't used to be there.

She shifts, trying to pull out of his grip, but he only clutches tighter. "Ow."

"Oh, shut up," he teases, nuzzling into her hair. "You love it."

She doesn't move after that. She doesn't dare. She'd love to escape, to get some space, but he was so upset over his father's death, and she still doesn't know how it happened.

"You ready to talk about it?" she probes gently.

He sighs, finally releasing his hold on her. He lies on his back. She doesn't move, so he snags hold of her arm and pulls her over to him.

"He was stationed on a combat vessel in the Omega galaxy," he says. "There was confusion during a battle."

"What do you mean?"

"For some reason, he disengaged."

She rolls over to face him. He looks so deflated, vulnerable, confused. She's never seen him like this. He's always so tough and abrasive, with a tinge of sweetness hidden underneath. It's part of the reason she likes him. He's complex – like a circuit board in need of a few new connectors.

"They say he left his post," Morven says softly, his voice clenching with emotion. "They're calling him a coward, but I can't believe that. There's no way. He's the bravest man I know."

She can hardly find the right words. How do you respond to information like this – something so private, so embarrassing? "Maybe there's some sort of mistake?" she manages.

"It's not a mistake!" he says, tossing his hand up and slapping the wall beside the bed. "He's dead. Almost his whole unit. Dead. There's records, Rain. Computer data."

The slap to the wall makes her jump but she holds her position beside him. "I mean about his leaving his post?" she tries to clarify.

He grips his hands to his hair, losing all control. His face contorts with grief and he sobs, and sobs, and sobs.

He melts into her, clinging on for dear life, soaking her shoulder with his tears. In the tangle of bodies his lips find hers, and before she knows it, he's holding her down with ferocious and terrifying passion.

★　　★　　★

Demeter
30.8.2231
1755 hours

Back in the main sleeping chamber, with the stinking meat substitute still rotting in the corner, Tamsin and Niall sit huddled on the opposite side.

Raina enters from the sleep compartment and runs her hand over her ponytail. That was a close call. How easily she falls into old habits. It's frightening.

"Is he okay?" Niall asks, and Raina nods.

"Eh. The cuts aren't deep, but his rash has spread and I think he has a fever."

Tamsin surveys her. "What happened to you? There's more blood on your uniform."

"He's bleeding a lot but it seems to have stopped."

"You're all flushed. Do you have a rash too?"

She checks her palms and hands. They're clear. "No, I'm fine," she says. Making every attempt to change the topic, she turns her back to them and clears her throat. "So, what's the plan, Niall?"

"You don't look fine to me. Did something happen?" Tamsin stops when Raina turns around and gives her the evil eye. "Oh. Okay. You look great."

"The plan?" Niall says. "There is no plan. How about 'don't die'. That sounds like a solid plan."

"Oh Niall," Tamsin whines, and starts to cry again.

"We can't stay here in the sleep chamber. The air vents are blocked, and we're going to run out of oxygen if we stay too long," Raina says. "The first part of the plan has to involve getting out of here, to someplace safe."

"I'm open to suggestions," Niall says.

"What about the escape pod?" Tamsin whispers. "Can't we just leave?"

"I'm inclined to agree with her," Raina says. "Screw the plants. I want to live, and as far as I can see, there's no way we can kill that thing."

"I think you're right," he says. "But the pod is on mid-deck, and I'm still not sure if Pollux is alive."

"Really, Niall? Really?" It's Morven. He stands in the doorway of his sleeping chamber, looking haggard but alive. He wears his sliced uniform shirt, but must have splashed cold water on his head, because his hair and reddened face are drenched and dripping.

"I don't want to abandon her," Niall adds.

"That's bullshit," Morven says, and he steps into the room. "You're just too chickenshit to leave, that's all. You're too scared to climb down a ladder onto mid-deck and cross the platform to the escape pod. If it were up to you, we'd stay in here and hide with the rest of the meat until we suffocate."

"Don't be absurd, of course we can't stay," he says. "I just don't want to leave Pollux."

"Pollux is dead," Morven blurts out.

"We don't know that," Niall says. It's almost a whisper.

"You know it. Raina knows it. I know it. Damn, even Tamsin knows it, don't you?"

Tamsin nods.

"See? I saw the Kepler follow her into the greenhouse, she's dead. Just like the rest of them. And if we don't kill that damned thing, we'll be dead too."

"Now's our chance," Raina says. "We can get to the escape pod while it's wounded. We should grab some supplies and get out now."

"Negative," Morven says. "We're not running away from battle. We kill it. Plain and simple."

"We can't kill it," she argues. "You saw what it did to—"

"I saw what *you* did to it. I nearly had it myself," he says. "Between you and me, and those two over there, if we surround the thing, get it trapped in a confined space...."

"We already tried to trap it and it didn't work," says Tamsin.

"The four of us can take it," he insists. "It's wounded. Slower. And now that it's bleeding purple sludge all over, it's easier to see."

"Not going to happen," Niall says, and he gets to his feet. "Raina's right. We should head to the escape pod now."

"Negative," Morven says again. "We kill it. We can't give up. Especially when we're so close."

"We're not close," Niall insists. "You're delusional if you think we can win."

"Niall's right," Raina says to Morven.

"Nobody asked you," he says. "And if you recall, you backed me up as commander of this vessel. I'm in command, and I say we stay and fight."

Niall's face has grown red. "I'm senior officer. I say we use the escape pod."

"You're not in command. There was a vote in the greenhouse," Morven corrects him.

A cloud covers the old man's expression. "You mean your ill-fated attempt at a mutiny?" It doesn't escape Raina's notice that he rests his palm on the handle of his weapon, which is tucked into the belt of his uniform. "That plan was shot to shit the moment Pollux showed up, and you know it. I'm in command. Besides which, even if you were, Raina and Tamsin agree with me. If you want to stay and fight the Kepler, be our guest. But we're abandoning ship, and you bet your ass when I reach headquarters, I'll tell them everything you've done."

"What the hell is that supposed to mean?" Morven's spotted hands drop to his sides. "We wouldn't have lasted this long if it weren't for me."

Niall doesn't flinch. "Bullshit. If we'd abandoned ship instead of trying to trap it, Avram would still be alive."

"You all voted to trap it, not me! This is *your* fault, old man." Morven steps forward and Niall's hand grabs at his pickaxe.

He sees it and stops. "Are you threatening me?"

Niall swallows, his pale face going paler. "You want to try me?"

"Stop it!" Tamsin cries. "Stop it!"

Morven smirks. "Careful, Grandpa, you're making the baby cry."

"That's enough!" Raina shouts, and both men turn their attention to her. "This is ridiculous. Both of you knock it off!"

"I don't know why you're siding with him," Morven challenges her. "You were on my side before."

Her heart pumps in her throat. Anger rises up so far from her gut she can taste it on her tongue. "If you recall, I agreed to your plan if Niall agreed to it, and if you had some other plan than 'let's go kill it'. And so far, that's all I'm hearing from you."

"Thank you, Raina," Niall says, and she reels on him next.

"But I don't think running away is the answer either," she says. "If a rescue ship shows up after we've jettisoned and comes aboard with no further communication from us, they'll get slaughtered. We have to go to the flight deck first, send a warning, *then* we escape through the pod."

"That's the stupidest idea you've had yet," Morven moans.

"Not as stupid as the Spam," Tamsin adds, crinkling her nose and wiping tears off her cheeks.

"All right, that's enough!" Niall says. "I'm senior officer, I say we get to the escape pod, send a communication *from there* and get the hell off this death trap. Understood?"

"I'm good with that," Raina says. "Tam?"

Tamsin frowns, but nods.

The only one left is Morven. His arms are crossed, his face is splotchy and clenched, and a vein visibly bulges in his temple. His eyes dart angrily to her, and Raina knows he blames her for siding with Niall, but what choice does she have? He's flat-out wrong.

"Chickens," Morven spits out.

Niall accepts this as his consent and turns to the exit. "Yeah. I'm okay with that. Let's go."

Tamsin scrambles to her feet, but Raina just stares at Morven.

A gnawing worry edges its way through her, tugging at her heart, and melting in her gut like rock tossed into a molten volcano.

Morven stomps off after Niall and Tamsin, as they crowd around the door leading back out into the hall, but Raina hesitates.

He gave up command rather easily. She has a hard time believing he's just going to run away with his tail between his legs. That doesn't sound like him at all.

CHAPTER EIGHTEEN

Twelve Months Ago….

"Where were you?"

"What?"

Morven glowers at Raina so hard, she actually takes a step back.

He's at the door of her sleep chamber, looking livid and leaning up against the wall with a forced nonchalance.

"Where. Were. You?" he repeats.

"In the galley," she says, immediately aware of how her defenses rise. He's worse than her mother sometimes.

Not again. Please don't start this again.

"With who?"

"Morven," Raina says, trying to deflect, but it's too late, she can tell from the look in his eye. His jaw is clenched and his hands flex and unflex like he's squeezing an invisible balloon. "With Avram, Kris, and Tamsin." There's no sense in lying, he'll know the truth with one check of the ship's camera system.

The invisible balloons pop as he squeezes his fingers closed against his palms. Turning red, he hardly looks as if he's breathing. He stalks up and back inside her sleep chamber and puts his fists to his scalp. "Did you stop and think for a moment about letting me know?"

"I didn't realize I needed your permission to eat," she snaps back, but instantly regrets it.

He stops in his tracks and glares at her with the heat of a thousand stars. "I *waited* for you."

"You could have come up to the galley and looked for me. It's not like it's a big ship. Or better yet, call me on the intercom."

"You know I can't do that," he says.

"Okay, fine. But really, what's the big deal? I'm sorry you waited. I didn't think we had plans tonight."

"We've been together every night after duty for nine months straight, and you wonder if we had plans? Are you fucking kidding me?"

She knows full well that they've been with each other every night for months. Her throbbing crotch is proof of that. Truth is, she's a bit burned-out on the whole arrangement, but she's not sure how to slow it down. He's like a runaway freighter, barreling toward a supernova. There's no stopping him once the momentum gets going.

In fact, he's gone as far as showing up at her workstation when she's on duty. Getting in her way, trying to talk and have meaningful conversations when she's got a shit ton of work to do, and Osric always breathing down her neck.

Morven's hot, and an animal in the sack, and my god, he's the best time she's ever had – but he's fucking clingy and she just wanted to have a nice, fun meal with Tamsin, Kris, and Avram for a change.

They don't judge her every movement, or comment about how great her ass looks in her uniform, or pressure her to make commitments about the future she can't keep. They're just fun – Avram with his quick jokes, Kris and her slicing sarcasm, and Tamsin with her heart of gold. They make her laugh.

She misses that.

Laughing.

Aren't relationships supposed to be fun?

Honestly, she's not even sure that Morven is worth the amount of work she has to put in – all that reassuring, all that constant ego-stroking and fucking. Endless amounts of fucking. God, what she wouldn't give for a break.

"Look, Moe. We need to talk," she begins.

"My father is dead," he says, dropping to his knees right there in the middle of her chamber.

"Oh my god," she gasps. Forgetting all else she kneels beside him and pulls his enormous frame into her tiny arms. "I'm so sorry."

He shakes in her arms with silent sobs.

"What happened to him?" she asks gently. "Was there an attack on his ship?"

He doesn't answer, he just clings to her, gripping her so tightly she can scarcely breathe. Finally, he whispers, "I needed you. Where were you? I *needed* you."

"I'm so sorry," she answers. "I didn't— I'm so sorry."

His hands slide from her arms and grab hold of her uniform, pulling the fabric. In a fumble of fingers and gasps he yanks at the clasps on her chest, popping them open with fierce intensity. His mouth finds hers and she tastes tears and salt, and his tongue dives toward hers.

He's all over her, pulling off her clothes, grabbing at her body and tasting every inch of her skin. He's desperate, unflinching. She tries to pull away, but he bats her hands aside.

"Morven," she says, attempting to pry herself loose, but he won't let her go.

"I needed you," he growls, rolling on top of her and grabbing at her pants as she lies supine beneath him.

"Morven, no…." she cries, as the weight of him crushes her to the floor. "Not like this. I said no!"

He ignores her words.

★   ★   ★

Demeter
30.8.2231 AD
1800 hours

Outside the sleep chamber, and into the hall, the survivors walk stiffly. Packed closely with the others, yet feeling meters apart, Raina can't help but be ill at ease.

Something isn't right – other than the fact that most of the crew is dead, there's a killer foreign biological on board, and she's covered in blood and vomit. She's not sure how to put words to it. But something else is off.

Morven's cooperation, for one.

He's walking beside Niall, his machete in hand, his eyes darting around the corridor, alert. He even goes so far as to look back and check on her and Tamsin, who walks behind the men. But his eyes are molten. His hands are white-hot.

If the others knew him as well as she does, they'd sense it too. But it's too subtle. They're too distracted.

She'd like the opportunity to take him aside and have a conversation — get a sense of where he's at. But they're on a mission to save themselves and now isn't the time. Even aboard the escape pod they won't be alone. The time might never come. She's just going to have to watch him.

When they reach the access ladder leading down to mid-deck, Morven steps aside to allow the women to go first, but Niall stops them.

"I'll go, then Tamsin. Then Raina, then you," Niall says to Morven.

Morven clenches his jaw and nods.

This sets her even more on edge. The Morven she knows argues at every turn. He never wordlessly follows anyone. She almost questions him about it but stops herself.

Not now. He could blow his top and they can't afford to waste time.

They climb down the shaft without incident and fall back into formation on mid-deck. The escape pod is on the other side of the floor, down two hallways and past the mechanics workstation.

They're silent, afraid to make a noise, and too uncertain of each other to risk communication. The only sound that is unavoidable is the clunking of their boots as they pound the grated hall floor.

They pass Gayla's body without comment. But when they round the second corner, they stop short. Two more bloodied bodies crowd the hallway.

Tamsin gasps and then whimpers. She buries her face into Raina's shoulder, wrapping her arms around her.

Raina can't help but stare at the remains: it's Osric and Valda.

Niall and Morven both hesitate. There's only one way around, and that's through the blood and carnage. They'll have to step over the bodies to make their way to the escape pod.

Niall puts his hands on his hips and shifts to one side as he forces himself to look. He coughs once, as if suppressing a gag.

Raina has to look away to stop the bile churning in the pit of her stomach.

While Niall debates how best to pass the corpses, Morven plows straight through. His boots make a wet and sticky noise as he steps over Valda. He scoots past the slices of what used to be Osric, then waits on the other side of the hall. Although his eyes do not meet those of anyone else, he waves them through.

"Come on," he urges. "It's best to just get it over with."

Raina reaches up and grabs Tamsin's hands, with the intent of pulling her along. But Tamsin somehow already has a grasp of her palm. She looks as pale as the man on the moon. Raina brings them both forward.

The first body is easiest to recognize. For the most part, it's fully intact. The only thing missing is the insides of the torso. It's Valda, and Tamsin gasps. He's face down in a pool of his own blood. His eyes are open and his mouth hangs wide as if he were trying to tell them something.

Raina steps around the next body, pulling Tamsin along. It isn't as easy to discern the identity of the second figure, but by process of elimination, Raina can guess who it is. As they pass, she recognizes the sleek dome of the head. It had to have been Osric. Now, he's a pile of bloody dough. As much as she hated her boss, seeing him shredded to pieces is enough to break her heart.

After Raina leads Tamsin over the last of the remains, Niall brings up the rear. He barely looks and slips once on the puddle of blood near Valda's abdomen.

When they are together again on the other side, Niall takes the lead and the rest follow him down the hallway and around the last corner.

No one speaks. No one utters a word. There aren't any.

Around the bend, Raina sees the escape pod entrance and the door control panel that opens it. They're within view across the hall, and she sighs heavily with relief.

Finally, this will all be over. She wasn't sure they were going to survive. Her mind flicks to Avram and Pollux but she shoves the images away.

It's not until she hears Tamsin scream that she sees it. The Kepler sits on the floor just in front of them. They had all been looking down the hall at the escape pod controls, and didn't notice the creature, right at their feet.

The beast's purple bloody stump has scabbed over with a thin layer of clear slime, and thin strips of purple flesh are visible where it has been previously wounded. But it looks otherwise healthy, and angry. It bares its teeth, growls in the back of its throat, and launches immediately into the air, straight toward them all.

The four of them peel off, scattering in different directions like shards of a dropped glass.

Raina dives to the side, hitting the floor. She slides on her ribs until her back smashes up against the wall. She almost cries out with relief to see just above her head is the door control panel for the escape pod. She scrambles up, taps the panel, but the door doesn't open. Instead, the screen above requests an access code.

"Motherfucker…!" Raina starts.

Behind her, Tamsin screams.

She turns.

The girl is directly across the hall, screaming her head off. Tamsin watches Morven and Niall. They have the Kepler backed into a corner; both hold their weapons in their hands. With their backs facing Raina, she can't see much. She notices that only Morven is swinging his weapons at the creature.

On Morven's right, Niall stands still. His pickaxe and hedge clippers slip from his limp fingers and rattle as they hit the floor.

What is he doing?

As Morven takes another stab at the Kepler, it maneuvers across the wall toward Raina.

Niall's body has gone rigid. He falls stiffly to his knees, then pitches forward, face down. He lands with a splat. A pool of bright red blood collects under Niall's throat.

"No!" Raina shouts.

Tamsin screams again.

Raina reaches above. Her hand pounds on the control panel to the escape pod. "Open, damn you! Open!" It's no use. The door refuses to cooperate, and with Niall dead, the only person who would have had the access code is gone.

She snatches her magnetic screwdriver from her tool belt and manages to remove the front panel covering. She'll override the access code request by hand if she has to, but a blade swishes downward in front of her, catching her screwdriver, and the panel. The tool is knocked from her fingers and clatters to the floor. The blade from above imbeds into the panel with a cascade of sparks. She instinctively falls backward, covering her face with her arms to shield it from the spray of electricity.

Lying on her back, she pulls her arms away from her face and looks up. She's nose to nose with the Kepler. It dangles upside down from the ceiling, hanging over her like a noose. The beast's muscular back two legs grip the ceiling, holding it there, and its front three remaining claws swipe at her face.

A scream bursts from her lips and she rolls to the side, crashing up against the shins of someone's large boots.

The claws narrowly miss her. She feels the wind as they swish across her back.

The boots she's mashed against belong to Morven. From above her, and in front of the escape pod door, he yanks at his machete blade. It's stuck inside the remains of the escape pod control panel. With a grunt, he wrenches the machete free. As it swishes through the air in the other direction, Raina realizes it was his weapon that had knocked the screwdriver from her hands.

The blade breezes by her and catches the Kepler on the chin. The creature jumps backward. Morven brings his arm back around for another slice. All Raina can do is stay out of the way.

The machete slashes continue. With another thrust, Morven misses the Kepler entirely and buries the blade again into the pieces of the escape pod control panel that dangle from the wall.

More sparks fly.

The Kepler squeals an ear-piercing shriek. It pulls its body up by its back legs and re-grips the ceiling with all five claws. It then scampers backward across the ceiling. Sparks from the control panel pop and spray across the hallway. The beast recoils with another shrill shriek, then runs away to an open air vent grate down the hallway.

Tamsin screams again.

Raina jerks upright. She turns to face her and sees that her friend is not screaming in the direction from where the Kepler went, but instead, at Morven.

"You killed him!" Tamsin cries. "You killed him!"

Raina gets to her feet. She snatches her dented screwdriver off the floor while she's at it. Maybe she can still fix the escape pod door panel, but the moment she sees it she knows it's impossible. Several of the boards are cut in half. "Damnit, Morven. Could your aim be any worse?" She won't be able to repair any of it. At least, not without a few replacement boards from the mechanics workstation. It's only one door down.

"You killed him," Tamsin cries again. She's consumed with hysterics and backs away from Morven as if he were the monster. "You killed him!"

"Tam?" Raina calls to her, but she won't take her eyes from Morven's face. "Can you get me a new processing board from the mechanics room?"

Raina's eyes follow Tamsin's. Morven looks panicked. His eyes dart to hers and then back to Tamsin. What just happened? Did the Kepler reappear, and she can't see it?

"Tam?" Raina calls to her friend.

"Niall," Tamsin whispers. She looks across the hall to the old man's body and Raina's eyes follow.

She can tell from the stillness that he's dead. His body lies face down a few meters away. She wants to go to him, to roll him over and start chest compressions like she did with Avram, but another part of her is so tired. So very tired of looking into the faces of her dead shipmates. She remains where she is, one eye on Niall's corpse, and another watching Tamsin deteriorate into a heap of sobs.

She should go to her. She should get up and comfort her friend. But she has no energy for that either. She's more irritated that Tamsin won't get her a new processing circuit board.

"I know, Tam," she says as softly as she can manage. "I know. He's dead. It's horrible. But there's nothing we can do for him. Just get me the processing board, and we can get off the ship." She turns back to the broken pieces of the escape pod control panel and pulls out a few singed wires. "Come on, Tam! Get to the mechanics workstation."

"Forget the pod!" Morven says. "I got at least two good slices into the Kepler. Come on. We should go after it and finish it off."

Raina turns away from her work, momentarily stunned into stillness. She looks over at Tamsin, who bawls incessantly, then back at Morven, who points down the hallway toward where the Kepler escaped. "You're kidding," she says to him. "Right? We're leaving. That's the plan."

Tamsin lifts one finger and points at Morven in complete incapacitating horror. "You killed him," she whispers.

"Raina!" he exclaims. "The Kepler. Come on! Let's finish this." He starts down the hallway toward the open air vent, but stops when he realizes she won't follow.

She can't keep her eyes from watching the beleaguered Tamsin. "What do you mean, Tam?"

The girl's eyes search for Raina in her hysteria. "He killed him. I saw. He killed him."

"Tamsin?" she says calmly. "The Kepler killed Niall. Is that what you're talking about?"

"Him," Tamsin cries, pointing again at Morven. "He killed Niall. Not the Kepler. I saw."

"He *what?*"

"Don't be stupid," Morven says. "The Kepler killed him. Sliced Niall right across the throat. I was standing right beside him. Now come on, let's go get it!"

Tamsin shakes her head. "I saw."

"You did not!" he says. "You've gone off your rocker. And besides, how could you even see that – you were too busy cowering in the corner." He turns toward Raina. "Raina, come on, the Kepler's done for. We've got it! Let's go!"

Raina's eyes dart back and forth from Tamsin to Morven, and back again. Her heart flutters so hard it's hard to catch her breath.

He wouldn't.

She can't believe it. It's impossible. Wordlessly, her gaze drops to the pieces of the sliced circuit boards in her fingers.

He didn't. Did he?

Would he cut the escape pod control panel to stop them from leaving? Would he murder Niall so he could be in command? Is he so determined to be the hero and kill the Kepler he'd resort to murder?

Raina lets the broken boards slip from her fingers. She walks across the hallway to Niall's bleeding corpse.

"Come on!" Morven shrieks. "Let's go get it!"

"You killed him!" Tamsin cries. She's backing up and away from them both, lost in madness. She's almost halfway down the hall.

Raina bends at the knees beside Niall, reaches across his body, and with one great heave, she rolls him over. His eyes remain open. They stare at the ceiling, unblinking and cold.

Tamsin squeals in agony and Morven once again barks at Raina to hurry, that they are missing their chance to finally kill the Kepler.

All she can see is the truth. It's sliced across Niall's throat. Once.

One slice. Not four.

Tamsin's past words echo through her memory. "Four striations," she'd said.

She remembers Morven's hand when he clawed down the air across her face. "It's a talon mark!" he'd shouted at her.

Another image: Raina peels off Morven's shirt in his bedchamber and cleans four thinly sliced wounds across his heaving and chiseled chest.

Four. Not one.

Her eyes fill with tears of terror as she realizes what this means. "Oh my god."

Movement behind her causes her to look up. Morven stands just above her. He's come down the hall and stands right next to her. His rash-covered face looks blank. In fact, he looks calmer than he has since this whole thing has started. His red fingers adjust their hold on the weapons in his hands.

Raina's eyes trail down his large arm to his fingers and farther, to the tip of his blade. Red blood drips from the machete. Not purple.

Red.

"No," she whispers. Her chest aches with breath she can't catch. "No." She's frozen in place. Disbelief and shock have trapped her to the floor. "How…. How…?"

Memories flash: Morven's hand hovering over the door control panel in the greenhouse as Raina helps Pollux stagger inside.

He shuts the galley door in her face. "You made it," he had said, sounding disappointed.

In the hallway, beside Niall's body, Raina's vision comes back into focus. She looks into Morven's eyes, and all she can say is, "Oh Moe."

A wave of hatred smears across his face. He pulls back the arm holding his machete as if to swing. "Don't call me that!"

Tamsin's screams shatter her fog. "Raina – *watch out!*"

She feels it before she understands what happens. From behind, she's knocked to the floor. She tips over sideways, crushed under someone's body. She knows it's Tam because beaded necklaces cascade over her face.

The wind knocked from her lungs, she lies on her side on the grated floor, Tamsin on top of her. She instinctively plants a palm on the ground to push up. But Tamsin shoves her down, and the next thing she sees is the machete barreling down from above. The tip pierces the air and slices directly into the small of Tamsin's back.

They both scream.

Tamsin's back arches, and she rolls to the side, taking the machete with her as she slips off Raina and hits the floor beside her.

Raina's screams echo in her own ears. It sounds like someone else's voice. Someone else's pain and horror. Her eyes finally focus on a trickle of blood as it drips from Tamsin's mouth. Her soft brown eyes find Raina's. They lie, facing each other. Raina's hands grip Tamsin's sagging shoulders.

Before the life escapes her eyes, Tamsin whispers, "That hurt…." And then she slumps, the tip of the machete poking out of her stomach. Blood spilling from her like a spigot.

"No!" Raina's hands shake her shoulders. "Tam! Tam, no!"

With a wrench, the machete is yanked backward from Tamsin's spine.

Raina looks up just in time to see Morven holding the blade in his hands once again.

Shock renders her speechless, but instinct prevails. She knows she has only a few seconds before another blow will come from above. She lets go of Tamsin's shoulders, and crawling on hands and knees, she scrambles to get up.

Morven looks crazed with fury, splotchy red on every inch of skin that shows, and he heaves like a bull in a ring. The machete climbs, ready to strike again.

Thinking quickly, she whips her legs forward and slides on her hip, straight at him. Before he can move aside, Raina plants the weight of her boot directly into his right kneecap. It snaps and bends backward. He bellows, collapsing forward. The machete hits the floor.

Taking the opportunity, Raina gets to her feet and sprints to the nearest door. It's the mechanics workstation. She scrambles through and locks the door from the inside.

She can hear Morven's groans of pain in the hall. Twisting around, she scans the room, hoping to find something, anything, useful.

She tries to think, but she's too busy panicking. Tamsin's blood is still on her shaking hands. The sight of it chokes her with sobs.

What is she going to do?

She's trapped! There's nowhere to run. There's nowhere to hide. She can't block the air vents to prevent the Kepler, or she'll suffocate, and she can't go outside, or Morven will murder her.

How did it come to this? Was he planning this all along?

How could she have not seen what he was capable of?

She has to get away. Another solar system isn't far enough.

Maybe she can get to the escape pod control panel and fix it, and then jettison into open space, but seeing as how Morven is just outside the mechanics room door, she doesn't see how that's possible.

She's got to get out of this!

Ideas!

She needs ideas!

She crosses the room to her workbench, and rummages around the pile of junk, searching for something. Any clue.

"Please!" she gasps, as she tosses scraps aside. "Think!"

She hears a clatter and her eyes go to the air grate in the corner of the room. The sight of it sends a whole new level of panic though her.

The Kepler is still out there.

A new thought occurs to her: she could break through the wall, maybe go through and crawl out a hole, run. But surely Morven will hear what she's doing and meet her on the other side.

She's fucked. She's royally fucked.

Raina rummages through her workstation again, tossing circuit boards, rolls of wire, tools.

"Come on, come on! Think!"

Her hands settle on a small rectangular electrical coil and she suddenly knows exactly what she has to do.

CHAPTER NINETEEN

Fourteen Months Ago....

Morven cups her face in his hands and kisses her so tenderly, she feels as if her legs might give out. It's a good thing she's already lying down.

He breaks away and sits back, resting against the wall of her cot. "Tell me about your day," he says.

Raina snuggles into the crook of his arm and sighs. "Osric really is the biggest cocksucker I've ever met. I hate him. I really, really do."

He laughs, his body shaking her gently with his movement. "Shall I murder him for you?"

She smiles. "Ha, ha."

"Why's he a cocksucker?"

"You should hear the shit he said to me today. He called me worthless, and stupid, and made me dismantle all the improvements I did to the ventilation system. Did you know there are no filters in between decks? I just don't understand it. If there's a contamination in the greenhouse, the whole ship gets tainted, but if he'd just let me build a filter, we could protect the other floors."

"Doesn't a filter like that already exist?"

"Sure." She nods. "On the newer freighters. But none are manufactured for this bucket of bolts, and Osric won't let me make one unless it's approved by the Space Corps Maintenance Committee. Can you believe that?"

"That's crazy."

"I totally agree."

"We should kill him in his sleep."

"Very funny."

"No, really."

Raina shakes her head. "Sometimes your sense of humor is really sick, you know that?"

"Who says I'm joking?" he asks, his voice sounding cold all of a sudden.

She leans up to look into his eyes and blinks at him. He's staring straight ahead with a weird smile on his face, like he's imagining just what murdering Osric would be like. "Quit messing around," she says, shoving him slightly. "Don't get my hopes up."

She was trying to lighten his mood, but he just keeps staring at the wall, unblinking.

It's unsettling. A chill runs up her spine.

★　　★　　★

Demeter
30.8.2231 AD
1825 hours

Raina's hands work feverishly, digging through the parts on her workbench.

"Where is it?" she whispers harshly. "Come on!"

A memory comes to mind. It's of the Kepler, and its shrieking away from the sparks as they burst from the escape pod control panel when Morven chops it with his machete.

She finds what she's looking for and snags a capacitor. She reaches across the table and with a flick of a switch, she heats her soldering iron.

"Damnit, Raina!" Morven shouts through the door, making her jump. He bangs twice. "Why'd you have to do that? I wasn't going to hurt *you*."

She ignores him. What she should have done is plant her axe between his eyes, instead of just her boot into his kneecap. But she knows herself well enough to realize she's not truly capable of that.

Images of Tamsin's dead eyes make her reconsider that thought. Maybe next time.

Raina's hands come up off the workbench with the casing of a broken flashlight. She inspects the inside, rummages around her bench again, and then drops the power cell from a laser rifle inside the casing.

"Raina!" Morven yells. "Come on, let me in. We'll have to work together to kill the Kepler."

"Go away!" she shouts at him but concentrates on her work. She connects the battery and checks the snap switch on the flashlight casing to make sure it's working. It is.

Satisfied, she grabs a pair of bolts and secures them in a vise. After tightening them up, she snags a laser cutter and lobs off the bolt heads.

"Please!" he pleads. "Let me explain. Just open the door."

"Go to hell!"

She takes the heated soldering iron and, turning on her overhead magnifier work light, she leans in close and secures the bolts with soldering metal to the rectangular electrical coil. She then attaches them all to the capacitor.

Smoke from the soldering iron trickles up and around her face. It's a familiar sensation, and one that reminds her of the many hours she spent at home, making contraption after contraption, gadget upon gadget. She's sure if she counted the hours she spent building electronics as a kid, she'd have years of accumulated time. It's why she joined the Space Corps to begin with. Not just to get a moment's peace from her crazy family, and not just because her parents had been so proud of her brother when he joined, but because Raina had had visions of creating all sorts of electronic designs for the Space Corps, of bettering the world with her creative intellect. It wasn't until she failed her first electronics exam at the Academy that she realized the Space Corps wasn't interested in advancement. They just wanted cadets who could repair a circuit board the same way they've always been repaired.

Raina puts the soldering iron down for a second while she blinks back tears.

Suck it up.

"You will get home," she whispers at herself. "Come on, now."

"You don't understand!" Morven shouts through the door again. He pounds mercilessly. "Niall was going to report us to headquarters for mutiny. I didn't have a choice! Do you know what they do to mutineers? We'd be sent to a penal planet or farmed out as colony slave labor. I did it for us! Just let me in and I'll explain."

Raina's hands stop in place.

Sick bastard.

Is that really the excuse he's trying to use?

There's no way in hell she'd ever truly believe murdering Niall and Tamsin is justified. Does he really think that after she saw what he did, that she'd run into his arms and thank him?

He does.

Just goes to prove he never really knew her. Either that, or he doesn't think she'll buy it, and he's just blowing sunshine so she'll open the door and then he'll slice her across the throat just like he did Niall.

No matter if he believes it or not; either way, she can't live with the outcome. She suspects he has the same idea.

She sets back to work building her RC network, squinting through the magnifier, and trying to concentrate.

"Come on, Rain! Open up! You know I didn't have a choice. Tamsin saw the whole thing!"

This stops her again. Her hands shake with rage. Poor, sweet Tamsin. Without her diving in the way, Raina would be dead right now. She's not blind. She knows full well he was going to kill her if Tamsin hadn't pushed her down.

"Don't you see? I didn't have a choice. I did it because I love you."

This is the last straw. "Shut the fuck up, you fucking lunatic!" Raina shouts back, and then leans over her workbench to finish.

Now she *knows* he's messing with her.

"Crazy fucker," she says, and once again she tries to concentrate on her work.

For the next few minutes she succeeds in shutting out Morven's cries. She's almost done. She snatches another transistor from her bench and integrates it into the network. As she works, she can hear Osric belittle her over her shoulder like he had so many times before. She uses it to drown out Morven's pounding fists just outside the door.

"Stop wasting your time," Osric would say. "You and those fucking gadgets. You'll never be a full-fledged mechanics specialist, not with your attitude. You'll be lucky to graduate from the ensign program. Maybe you should apply for a job as a chef's assistant. I hear Niall needs help peeling potatoes. You could handle that. Maybe."

She shakes her head as images of Osric's dead body cloud her memory.

She wraps the device one time around with electrical bonding tape, bites off the tape with her teeth, then snaps another laser rifle power cell into her tool belt.

It's now or never. She hits the switch on the device. It powers up with an electrical squeal.

Osric's words come back to mind. "You could handle that," he said.

"Maybe," she answers aloud.

The silence suddenly bothers her. Where did Morven go? Why is he so quiet? She's not sure when he stopped banging on the door. She was too busy working and, as usual, lost track of time.

She'd like to open the door and work on the escape pod control panel, but knows she'd be a fool to do so. He could be just outside. He could be waiting for her to open the door so he can slice *her* open. Or, he could be sitting there, hoping she'll come out and understand why he did what he did.

Not going to happen.

Her eyes scan the wall of the workstation and settle on the air vent across the room. She swallows thickly. So screwed.

She takes a moment and rummages around the station again, picking up various tools and circuit boards, in case she needs a quick repair later on.

She has to get off the *Demeter*. That much is true. But she's still not sure how. With the Kepler and Morven both stalking her, she's not sure how she'll have the time to repair the pod panel. Maybe if she rebuilds the circuit board here in the mechanics station, then all she will have to do is cut the existing broken boards off the panel and attach a new board. She can rig the new panel with a fingerprint identification power switch, so only she can activate it.

But first, she'll use the RC network on Morven, then she'll repair the pod control panel and get off the ship. It's not foolproof, but it's a plan.

She sets back to work. After gathering a pile of supplies from her bench and from the other workstations in the room, Raina gets halfway through constructing the replacement panel for the escape pod before her plans are derailed.

She hears it. It's there, in the air vent, rattling around in the metal shaft. It scrapes against the walls, loping along on five limbs. The Kepler. Just on the other side of that wall. Any moment now, the beast will appear in the air vent.

Time's up.

She drops her tools and takes her axe in one hand, the RC unit in the other.

Suddenly, she has an idea.

Snapping the axe back into her tool belt, she moves forward, rests her thumb on the switch on the RC unit, and waits just under the air vent opening. She works hard to control her breathing, feeling lightheaded with panic. If this doesn't work, she's going to have to get out of that room fast, and she still doesn't know if Morven is waiting outside, machete at the ready.

Then it comes.

She hears the snuffling of the biological's breath first, then she sees the tip of its nose. It smacks the grate of the air vent with a paw and the grate cover falls.

The corner of it lands tip down into her scalp, catching her off guard. As she suppresses the pain, she jumps upward, the hand holding her RC unit extended. With a flick of her thumb, the unit sparks to life. Electric volts shoot through the coil and bolts, and the homemade taser gun zaps the Kepler directly under the chin.

The stench of singed fur permeates the air, and the beast squeals and recoils, disappearing back inside the air vent.

She just has time to pop out the spent laser rifle battery from the flashlight casing and replace it with another when she hears the beast growl.

It wasn't enough. The charge only stung it, but the taser didn't render it unconscious.

Raina grasps for the axe and backs away from the air vent. She crosses the room backward, a beast in front of her, a killer behind her.

With no choice but to run, she reaches behind and turns. To her left is the door control panel. Back at the air vent, she can just see the Kepler's four yellow eyes peering out of the darkness. It looks slightly dazed, but very much conscious.

Let's do this.

She uses the handle of the axe and reaches for the door controls. The door hisses open behind her and she swishes once with the blade as she runs through the door, trying to clear a path.

Just on the right, Morven stands propped up against the wall. His leg is bound with strips from his shirt and held stiffly with a splint he's constructed with poles of metal. Raina recognizes them as support beams for the space suit lockers. It occurs to her that he left her alone, working inside the mechanics workstation, so he could fashion himself a splint, and she could have escaped while he was gone, but she's got the Kepler at her back and she doesn't have time to lament that now.

Morven bends back, dodging her axe swing, but then bounds forward, calling her name. "Wait! Just let me explain!"

He catches her arm in his hand as she bolts to the left. She jerks to a stop. Lifting her fingers, she compresses the button on the RC taser and zaps Morven in the wrist.

He seizes and releases her arm as he loses consciousness. His eyes roll back and he drops like a rock. On his way down, the bulk of his meaty arm knocks the RC device from her hands. It clatters to the floor and skids a meter away. She doesn't move to retrieve it.

Instead, she twists around and shuts the door to the mechanics workstation, just as the Kepler leaps from the air vent straight at her.

The door closes with a hiss and the creature bangs into it on the other side. The door bulges with the force of its jump but holds.

She jumps backward, away from the door and Morven's unconscious body, nearly losing her footing. Then, she steps over him and sprints as fast as she can.

* * *

Demeter
30.8.2231 AD
1800 hours

Pollux rolls over onto her side and pushes herself up off the floor.

The walls spin.

She's surrounded by colors and covered in dirt. Plant life is everywhere, but the hues are off. The green is too bright. The red is too piercing. There are leaves, and stalks, and stems, and flowers – but it's not any kind of plant life she recognizes. She presses her eyelids closed then opens them again and the walls warp for a second time, making her nauseous.

Her mother stands beside her, wearing that horrible house dress that's always looked more like a bathrobe than an item of presentable clothing.

Get off the floor, you lazy lout! her mother bellows. *What the hell's the matter with you? Quit acting like such a baby.*

Pollux fumbles to her feet, her head throbbing. Every inch of her skin shrieks with an unbearable itch and her head pounds. There's evidence of a fight all around her. Pots are knocked over, one shelf looks sliced in half, and there's a machete with some sort of purple goop on it at her feet.

Why is she wearing Space Corps boots at home?

Just look at the mess you've made, her mother says.

Pollux bends over to right a tipped pot, but her head swims and she finds herself back on her hands and knees, sweat dripping from her scalp and stinging her eyes.

It's got to be over a hundred and ten degrees, yet it still feels dry. Why has her mother set the thermostat so high?

Wait.

It comes back to her slowly, and in pieces. Pollux is keenly aware there are holes.

There was a monster. Yes. A fucking vicious one. She fought it with the machete. And it was about to eat her, but it didn't. It knocked her down, and sniffed her, then turned away. She watched while it climbed into the air vent. She watched until it was gone, but then she must have passed out.

What is her mother doing here?

You know, if your brothers were here, they'd have killed that thing already.

"Shut up, Mama, I'm trying to think."

Mama doesn't answer but taps her foot.

Pollux gets back up and her eyes focus. How'd she get in the greenhouse? Has it always smelled like shit in here?

Like a flood, every scrap of memory returns. A tsunami of images rushes at her, knocking her back to her knees.

Overcome, Pollux clasps the nearest shelf to keep from hitting the floor. She's locked in from the outside, thanks to that asshole, so there's no escaping the greenhouse until someone lets her out. She's a sitting duck. Her first order of business should be to find a safe place and devise a plan.

You know what you need to do, right?

Pollux shakes her head. It's throbbing so hard it feels as if it's pushing out her eyeballs. She digs her fingernails into her scalp and scratches at her skin until her fingertips are wet with blood. Every inch of her body screams for similar treatment.

The first thing you need to do is kill that monster, her mother says. *And I'm not talking about the Kepler.*

"Yes, Mama."

*   *   *

Demeter
30.8.2231 AD
1838 hours

Climbing up the ladder, Raina plows hand over hand, foot over foot. Her boots slip once as she rushes. Reaching upper deck, she hops off the ladder and jumps across the access shaft onto the one leading up to the flight deck. There's a patch of vomit on the floor, but she steps over it and grabs hold of the ladder.

When she reaches the top, she bypasses the bodies of the flight crew and plops down into the command chair. She snaps a switch on the console, activating the keypad. Automatically, she pulls up the activity log from the past twenty-four hours to verify the original Mayday, and the deepest sadness stops her cold and plunges through to her core.

There is no record of a distress signal ever having been sent. No record at all. Not from the flight crew, and not from Morven. He never sent one.

All that drama about him not wanting her to tell anybody he sent it, and he never did it in the first place. But that doesn't make any sense. Why would he do that? When it comes, the answer baffles her.

It could mean only one thing. That he never meant to save her, or any of them. It means that he'd been pretending as far back as their trip to the flight deck, together, when they released the spore into space through the bay doors. He'd wanted command since then. He'd been planning to kill them all along.

Then why pretend to send the distress signal?

Her throat clogs with emotion. He tricked her. He wanted her on his side, against Niall. And now that Niall is gone, and Tamsin, the only obstacle left between Morven being the hero, the sole survivor, and receiving all of the accolades for valor and bravery, and in killing the Kepler – the only person in his way, is Raina.

Heat gushes through to her ears.

She has to wonder: at what point did Morven turn into the monster?

★   ★   ★

For a moment or two, she types on the command console keyboard. Her fingers fly with little effort. It's a comfort, this keypad – this feeling of familiarity, of doing something normal.

When she's done typing she reads over what she has written and with a click, sends it out into the cosmos. It reads:

MAYDAY, DEMETER IN DISTRESS. HOSTILE FOREIGN BIOLOGICAL ABOARD. MUTINY. SEND REINFORCEMENTS.

Now, there is little else to be done. She's left with only one other course of action: reactivating the autopilot. If she does, the ship will automatically fire the boosters, and begin the slow advance back toward Earth. They are light-years away, and the journey will take almost two weeks of traveling at a high velocity.

Still, it won't solve the issue of how she will dock the ship once she reaches port. Without the pilot or the captain there's no way to do it. Or if, heaven forbid, the ship should come up against some previously undocumented ship, a comet, nebula, or asteroid. How will the autopilot accommodate for those? She's sorry to admit, she doesn't know.

In order to monitor the ship's voyage, she'll have to remain on the flight deck. She'll need to give it her full attention, and as of that moment, with the Kepler and Morven still aboard, she knows she doesn't have the attention to give.

Activating the autopilot could lead to a crash, and then, what good would it have done? Her fingers linger over the autopilot switch, but don't move beyond that. After. She'll have to do it afterwards. After the other ship comes to rescue her. After they contain the Kepler, and Morven. After she's safe.

Although, she has to wonder if she'll ever feel safe in her life again.

CHAPTER TWENTY

Demeter
30.8.2231 AD
1825 hours

Raina takes only a few minutes at the command console to send the distress signal, but the moment she hears movement behind her, she knows she's taken too long.

She stills her breath to better hear. But strain as she might, she cannot determine what it is. It's a low-level thumping, which could easily be a man with a metal splint climbing up the ladder, or an animal crawling up an air vent. Either way, she's stuck.

There's only one way off the flight deck, and that's down the access shaft, and since she's unsure if the noise she's hearing is coming from the shaft itself, or the air vent beside it, she has nowhere to run.

She could take a minute and check the navigations controls to find out what's causing the noise, but she's not sure how to pull up the information and doesn't want to waste any time figuring it out. Instead, she gets up from the command chair and surveys the flight deck for a hiding place. At first glance, there isn't one. There's nothing but the chairs, the controls, and the bodies.

Her heart skips a beat as she hears another rustle of noise approaching. Feverishly, she looks around again. The only option that comes to mind leaves her sick to her stomach. But a banging noise beneath her feet convinces her to act on it. Whatever is coming, comes now. She has no choice.

Move!

Behind the command chair, and between the navigation controls, lie the bodies of Kris and the captain. Raina suppresses a gag and reaches under the captain's armpits, pulling his remains over to the headless corpse of the Navigations Ensign. He's literally dead weight, and hardly budges.

After tugging him three times and only moving the body an inch or two, Raina reconsiders her plan. She steps over his torso, reaches down to the captain's feet, and while resting one hand on his thigh, unbuckles his boots with the other. Free from the added weight, the captain's body is slightly less heavy, and more moveable.

Raina reaches back under his arms and yanks, dragging his bloody and hollowed corpse toward the empty space behind the command station. She grunts once with effort and stifles a whimper. It's a vile and disgusting experience and takes a colossal effort on her part not to vomit.

Once she has the body in the desired position, she takes the boots, and shoves them back onto his feet. She doesn't bother with the buckles.

Then, reaching over to the navigations console, Raina does the same to Kris's body, propping it up against the captain on the other side. Luckily, Kris isn't nearly as difficult to move.

The bodies now sit shoulder to shoulder in the corner – a grotesque display. The irony of having two corpses next to each other in such a casual manner is not lost on Raina. If she didn't know any better, and Kris wasn't missing her head, it could appear as if they were having a casual chat.

Raina swallows down the lump in her throat and forces herself ahead. She slips in between and behind the two bodies and shimmies her tiny frame into the middle of the tower, just behind each of their torsos, or, what's left of their torsos. Then she huddles on the floor of the flight deck against the wall, curling up as small as her frame allows. As she crouches down on the floor behind them, she tugs on the captain's arms, pulling his body up and over her head.

His body weighs her down like a pile of rock. She grunts once as the smell of rotting flesh fills her nostrils. She can only pray that this will work. Whatever comes up that shaft or vent, she's hoping it won't realize that the bodies have been moved, or that an actual living person is hiding behind them, breathless, gagging, and on the verge of tears.

Whatever comes, it better hurry. She's not sure how long she can take hiding in this position. The thought of what she has done is enough to make her scream in agony, but she holds it in, catching her breath.

She'd like nothing more than to shift her position and move the captain's heavy body off her, but the source of the noise has arrived, and she's suddenly frozen in terror.

She hears a growl and knows. It's the Kepler.

From her position under the bodies, she squints to see. With one eye, she can just catch a glimpse of the beast. It slithers with the silence of a serpent, over bodies, across the floor. It sniffs the air. Fur ripples across the beast's torso, and as the animal stalks back around the flight deck, the fur rests on a soft beige color one could almost call pretty. Then, the Kepler reaches the captain's body.

Raina holds her breath and watches the animal as she cowers beneath the captain's corpse. She feels her body begin to tremble with terror and almost gasps aloud in fright. The creature is only inches away.

Inspecting the captain's remains, it turns its head to the side, looking intently at the heap of flesh with its four yellow eyes. Then, it shakes like a wet dog and grunts, relaxing its posture. Leaning forward, it sniffs Kris's legs, just where Raina had grabbed them to move them into position.

The biological snorts, shaking its head. A droplet of slobber flies from the animal's mouth and splats on the captain's uniform. It is all Raina can do not to cry out.

After just a moment, the Kepler peels off. With a flick of its back end, it slithers across the flight deck and down the air vent, disappearing from view.

Raina releases her breath with a hiss. She cannot help but feel as if she is the luckiest person in all of outer space. That was a fortunate break, if there ever was one. She almost laughs with relief.

Instead, she pushes with her feet and shoves the captain's corpse off her. Tentatively, she stands, and steps over his body and into the middle of the crowded flight deck. She needs another plan, and fast.

It's too bad that there isn't some sort of way she could up the volts on her homemade taser gun. Clearly, the Kepler doesn't like electricity. It's the only weakness she's been able to pinpoint, except the blade of her axe, but she'd rather not get within arm's length of it again. Still, with the animal having such a thick hide, there isn't enough power to zap it hard enough with the taser to do any real damage, and no other battery source than the laser rifle cartridge comes to mind.

As far as she can tell, there is no way to kill it, and she doesn't see how she'll be able to bring herself to kill Morven, unless, of course, it's in self-defense – which, truth be told, it is. But she can't stomach the thought of hunting him down either, or of even looking at him in the eye one more time. She just wants out. She wants the comfort of being alone. She wants to go home – no, anywhere, just anywhere but here. And the only way to get that is through the escape pod – which is right where she left Morven, unconscious.

Has Morven regained consciousness after being hit with the taser? Or did the Kepler eat him while he was knocked out? Her skins crawls. She has to check. A part of her has to know if he's still alive.

And if so, has he moved on to another part of the ship? With any luck, that'll allow her the chance to get back into the mechanics workstation and finish the replacement control panel she started before the Kepler so rudely interrupted. Then, she'll be able to repair the panel without incident, attach it to the pod controls, and finally be free.

It's not much of a plan. But, at least it's something.

She looks around at the bodies of the flight crew and shudders. Time to go. There's nothing here but death.

Back down two access shafts, past Gayla, Osric, and Valda, and halfway down the mid-deck hall, she hears something. Tools? Metal? The sound of metal on metal? It's not until it sounds again that she understands what it is. It's boots, scraping across the grated floor of the hallway, and headed straight for her.

Morven is coming.

Unsure if she should duck into the mechanics workstation behind her and wait for him to pass, or to make a run for it, she hesitates, thinking feverishly.

Poking her eyes around the corner of the hall, she spots him. He's right there, limping toward her and scratching at his arm. His eyes lift. He sees her. She doesn't wait around to chat.

Bursting into motion, she zips down the mid-deck hallway in the other direction, past the armory and the other workstation. She reaches the access shaft within seconds. Knowing it will take more time to climb up than to fall down, she slides down like a fireman, using the arches of her boots like a rail on the sides of the ladder.

She thumps to the bottom, and just as she looks up, Morven's splotchy face appears at the top of the shaft.

"Stop running!" he says. "Will you just stop and listen to me?"

She doesn't answer. She takes off at full sprint, but it's a quick trip. The only place to go on lower deck is the greenhouse, and the doorway is just a few meters away.

Morven calls after her again. "Wait, stop this and listen to me. Let me explain!"

She runs. She doesn't want him to explain. She understands perfectly.

Morven's limps gallop behind her.

She twists around and stumbles toward the greenhouse entrance. Tapping the control panel beside the door, she realizes the exterior lock has been activated.

The *exterior* lock?

Suddenly she remembers Morven's words from the last time they were here. "I saw the Kepler follow Pollux into the greenhouse," he had said. "She's dead."

It would have been impossible for Pollux to lock the door from the outside if she were inside the greenhouse. Raina's stomach lurches and she deactivates the lock, just as Morven's boots pound the floor behind her. She's barely able to slip into the greenhouse and close the door before he reaches her. She feels the breeze of his grasp on her shoulder as she lurches inside.

Morven's panicking face pops into the door window and Raina shrieks. She activates the interior lock and backs away.

"Rain!" he shouts through the glass. "Stop running. You've got to listen to me!"

"You wanted to lock the door!" she yells at him through the window. "I saw you. Here in the greenhouse with Pollux – you wanted to lock us both out. I saw your hand!"

"Would you listen to yourself? You sound nuts! Now come on. Just let me in and I'll explain!"

"No! You locked Pollux in here with the Kepler. You murdered Niall and Tamsin!"

"Please – you don't understand. I didn't have a choice!"

"You're crazy! Go away!"

"Fine. You know you can't stay in there." He's not shouting anymore. In fact, his face isn't even in the window. His head pops in and out, and he's looking down and to his right. It's the control panel. He's trying to override the lock.

"There's still a foreign biological on the ship," he says. "We have to work together, or we're both dead."

"I'll take my chances with the Kepler before I trust you again."

"Just listen to me! There's no way out of the greenhouse. You're trapped in there. The airlock is up at the bay doors, remember? There's no access shaft inside. What if the Kepler comes down the air vent? Aren't you worried about that?"

"Not if it gets you first," she answers, and her eyes scan the greenhouse, searching for an idea, any idea that could save her life. But her mind is consumed with panic, her heart is broken into shards, and all she can do is feel the pressure of a thousand Kepler claws eating away at her soul.

He wanted her dead all along. He murdered Pollux. He would have killed Raina too, but he'd needed her to outvote Niall. He was aiming for her with the machete, and Tamsin saved her.

Raina's face flushes at the memory of his hands when he touched her after she had bandaged his wounds. He had never loved her. Not like any normal person loves. What the hell had she been thinking? There was never any Moe. That was just a game he played to get her to do what he wanted. She was a fool, a full-blown ignorant stupid fool, a total moron. Osric was right.

Anything that she felt for Morven was a twisted lie, a manipulation on his part. He used her. The whole entire time they were together he had just been using her.

Hot tears burn Raina's eyes as she continues to scan the greenhouse for an idea. Her eyes just hitch on the sprinkler system on the ceiling when she hears a click behind her.

Morven's undone the lock. The door slides open.

She runs for her life.

CHAPTER TWENTY-ONE

She breaks left. Then right.

Morven was correct about one thing: she's trapped. Her boots pound the aisles of the greenhouse with quick and heavy steps as she runs.

There's no way out, not unless she can get him behind her, and then she can make for the door. She can lock him in just like he did Pollux. She can jam the control panel so he can't reconfigure his way out. But first, she has to get away. She has to find some way of outsmarting him.

He's still shouting at her from behind. If he doesn't shut up, he'll attract the Kepler, but she's not about to stop and tell him that.

"Wait! Just wait!" he bellows. "Jesus, girl! Will you hold on for just a minute? You really fucked up my knee."

She breaks left again and stops cold.

Plants, leaves, and dirt are scattered everywhere as if there's been a brawl. It must have been where Pollux died, but her body is nowhere in sight.

Raina frantically scans the greenhouse. She'd love nothing more than to call out to the sergeant, but there's no time to waste. She doesn't even know where she's going.

Raina can hear Morven's labored gait behind her, a few aisles over. She's got one thing working for her, and that's her speed. Now, if only she can double back and get around him from the other side, she might be able to escape, but she's never been this far inside the greenhouse except for when she's done repairs and when the group of them were here earlier that day, and with the pressure of a murderous ex-boyfriend behind her she's losing track of where she's been, and where she's going. There's nothing but plants, aisle after aisle. The cascade of odd alien colors leaves her mind in a blur. She's good and lost now.

From somewhere else in the greenhouse, Morven shouts. "Raina! Please! You're being ridiculous."

This only infuriates her further. Then, to the left she spots the glass enclosure where the foreign biological seed spore came from. The door is still open.

She runs inside. There's just enough space on the shelf where the pods once were for a small girl like her to squeeze through. She swings one leg over the shelf, sits on her behind, then swings the other leg over.

Between the shelf and the wall, there are blue vines that grow up and over the ceiling. She crouches down, climbs in between the vines and flowers, and ducks just underneath the shelf. She has no idea if she can be seen from the other side, but she's hoping, since her hiding place above on the flight deck had fooled the Kepler, maybe she'll get lucky twice.

Her breaths are jagged. Her lungs burn. A thick layer of sweat pours from her body as she roasts in the greenhouse humidity. Angry tears once again threaten her concentration, but she sucks them back. She doesn't move. All she can do is wait.

There's a thumping noise on her left. Here he comes. That didn't take long at all.

"Raina? You in here?" he asks, limping into the enclosure.

As if she'd answer. She holds her breath as he ambles by.

Long drag, short step. Long drag, short step.

It's a miracle he's standing, given the way his knee looks when he limps by. She might have broken his knee in half. It's twice the size it's supposed to be and lumpy, and swollen. It stretches the seams of his uniform to near bursting.

Good. She hopes it pops his skin wide open.

He passes her and checks around the enclosure, but then gives up and turns around. When he limps by her again, she almost cries with relief. How she's pulled that off again, she'll never know. She's never been so glad she's short.

Around the other side of the enclosure, she watches through the glass as Morven limps and stops at the toolshed. "Raina, come on!" he shouts. "This is getting ridiculous. I just want to talk to you!"

From her hiding place, she can see his legs by the shed. He's leaning his back against the glass enclosure and bending over, reaching for something. When he comes back up and she sees what's in his hands, she can't stop herself from gasping.

He's taken a laser rifle. One of the five they'd left by the shed after Pollux told them they weren't any good against the Kepler. He knows they're useless against the foreign biological, so there is only one reason why he'd take a laser rifle. For her.

"Please come out!" he fake begs. "Just listen to me for a minute, then if you don't like what I have to say, we can figure something else out."

She scoffs silently. He's unreal. He's holding a murder weapon in one hand and lying through his teeth. She'd like nothing more than to tell him to go to hell, but not until she's clear of the greenhouse.

Morven turns then and limps off in the other direction. She just has time to make out the top of his head as he rounds the corner. If she can stay behind him, she'll be able to track where he's going, and when the time is right, she can make a run for the door – there's no way he'll be able to catch her with that knee.

After slipping from her hiding spot, she climbs back over the empty shelf and drops to her feet. She quietly makes her way out of the enclosure.

To the left and past the toolshed, she follows the sound of his clunky limp as he walks deeper and deeper into the greenhouse. As he goes, he continues to call for her. With each increasing word, his voice grates on her patience.

"Rain, come on now. Let's talk this through."

He's made his way to the dehumidifying room and computer lab.

Raina, a few rows over, sees her chance. Change of plans.

She watches as Morven hesitates in front of the door. He places a hand on his hip, shifts his weight, then grunts in pain and shifts back. He must be wondering whether or not she's hiding in there.

She wishes there were a way to telepathically suggest that he go inside, but there's nothing she can do but wait and watch. She casts a glance over her shoulder in the direction of the greenhouse door.

Patience. Just wait. Almost.

When she looks back at him, he hasn't moved. Finally, he slings the rifle strap over his shoulder and then taps the door control with his other hand.

The dehumidifying door hisses slowly open. He enters, then taps the controls behind him.

Raina hears him call her name again. "You in here?" he asks. He powers up the laser rifle.

She inches forward, rounding the corner from where she crouched, watching, and waits for the dehumidifying process to complete so he can enter the laboratory workstation. Her patience pays off. The internal dehumidifying doors hiss open, and Morven limps inside the control room, tapping the panel again to close the door.

Just one more second. She tries to calm herself. Almost there. When the dehumidifying doors close, she's up like a shot.

Morven catches movement out of the corner of his eye and whips around. "Raina!" he shouts. "Thank god you're all right! What the hell are you doing? We should be going after the Kepler together. Raina?"

She doesn't answer. She's on her knees in front of the dehumidifying external door. In a flash she has her bent screwdriver in her hands, fast at work.

"Raina?" He taps the controls to the internal dehumidifying door and waits for them to amble open. "What are you doing?"

She plucks the last screw from the door control panel and pops off the cover. In seconds she has the circuit boards out of the casing and dangling from wires. She yanks twice, removing both circuit boards completely.

"Stop that! What the hell?" He pounds on the other side of the dehumidifying door and shouts through the glass window.

Knowing full well that the door is impenetrable, Raina doesn't flinch. She rips out the last circuit board from the door control panel with a yank and steps back when she's through.

"You've just killed me!" he yells. "Now I'm trapped! What if the Kepler comes down here?"

She once again eyes the sprinkler system snaking across the greenhouse ceiling. Wiping sweat from her face with the back of her hand, she says, "I'm counting on it."

The panicked look on Morven's face gives her pleasure. Then he turns to stone. He swings the laser rifle off his shoulder, aims at the window, and fires twice. Black dots appear on the singed glass, but it doesn't break.

Raina jumps back at the shots but then realizes her mistake. Even if he shoots out the window, which he can't since they're triple-reinforced diamond glass, the window is too small for him to crawl through, and the door is broken. Thanks to her, there aren't any circuit boards to operate it and it's too heavy to open by hand. He's trapped whether he likes it or not.

"Raina – what the fuck?" He's furious. Through the glass she sees his infamous blood vessel of rage surging in his temple.

"Listen, you asshole." She tries not to seem smug but can't help it; this is a long time coming. "I have a plan to kill the foreign biological, but I can't have murderous lunatics stalking my every move. So just stay there like a good little prick—" she wags her pinkie finger for emphasis, "—and let me do what I need to do."

In response, he shoots the window again with the laser rifle. It gets him nowhere.

"Just sit tight," she finishes and spins her screwdriver into her tool belt like she's holstering a six-shooter. It rests next to her axe. "After I kill the Kepler, I'll get up to the flight deck and check to see if there's a response to the distress signal I sent – yes, I actually sent one, unlike you."

Losing all control, Morven pounds the window like a lunatic, cursing and wailing. Raina quickly loses interest. Instead, she looks away from the laboratory window and Morven's purple expression, and her eyes train up to the ceiling again. Back in the corner of the greenhouse she knows the air vent sits, wide open, and ready for the Kepler to crawl through.

She'll have to work fast. But she has a plan. The ultimate tinker. The mother of all jerry-rigs. Osric would have hated it.

The thought makes her smile.

*　　*　　*

Twenty Months Ago....

Morven pushes her against the wall of his sleep chamber, his hands pinning her wrists, his tongue tracing her jaw.

She lets out an involuntary moan and flexes her hips, which only serves to encourage him.

She should put a stop to this. It's too fast. They've really only been dating a few weeks. She should pull away. She should tell him to knock it off. Slow down.

Before the words form in her mouth, she's tasting his tongue. He's powerful, demanding. He bites her lip playfully and she breaks away, gasping for air and aching for more.

"We should.... We should...." she breathes.

His large hands slide down her arms and unclasp the front of her uniform with lightning speed. He pushes up her bra and cups her breasts, squeezing and running his thumbs across her nipples and....

"Aw, fuck it," she moans.

Her hands dive for his trousers and in a matter of moments they're both naked and up against the wall with such strength she feels like she's floating.

Hard. Fast. Powerful. He's deftly skilled and full of stamina and before she knows what's hit her, she's clutching his shoulders, digging her nails into his skin, and howling.

Every bone in her body clenches as they writhe and pulse in unison. She orgasms once. Twice. Three times in rapid succession. She's bent over him, her toes scrunched tight in spasm. He's a machine and she's holding on for dear life.

Finally, after she's raw and her cries are mixed with pain, he releases inside her, seizing her hips to him so tightly she thinks she might bruise.

Afterwards, he bends down, putting her feet to the floor. They stand entwined, panting, sweating.

"Fuck, Raina," he whispers coarsely between gasps.

"I believe we just did."

He doesn't smile. "No, I mean. Did you feel that?"

"I think the whole ship knows I did."

"No. That was, that was different. That was...." He pauses, looking into Raina's eyes with such confusion, she wonders whether she somehow read the signals wrong. She thought it was the best lay she'd ever had in her entire life, but he's looking at her like she's some sort of alien, out to possess him and devour him whole.

"That was what?" she asks, afraid of how he'll respond.

"That was electric," he says, grabbing her face and kissing her fiercely. "That was amazing. How did you do that?"

Her fears release and she talks against his mouth. "How did I do what? You did most of the work."

"No, I mean it." He pulls away slightly, searching her face with deep intensity.

Her stomach twists impulsively.

"How did you do that to me?" he asks again. "Why do you feel so good?"

Heat fills her face and Raina runs her hand against his chest. She has no idea what to say, or even what he's talking about. He almost looks angry with her. Like she's somehow bewitched him, and now he's pissed about it, while loving it at the same time.

Sure. Let him think that. Let him think she's the most amazing thing aboard this ship. This could be what she's been searching for – something hot and liquid to fill the cold parts of her sad life aboard. Maybe that's what she's been missing all this time – a partner, someone to trust and confide in. Working with Osric has made her life on board hell, but this, this would make it easier to bear. Morven's the key. He's solid. Real. Intense.

And it *was* a good fuck. A great one, even. Plus, given his expression, it looks like his experience may have been a religious one.

It'll be nice to be worshipped for once.

What's the harm in that?

CHAPTER TWENTY-TWO

Demeter
30.8.2231 AD
1908 hours

The first thing Raina does is search around the perimeter of the greenhouse to locate the main water valve. When she locates it, over by the toolshed, she stops. The shed door is open, wide. It looks like the closet's been ransacked. There are empty clips and missing tools; a couple lie on the floor at Raina's feet. She doesn't remember Pollux leaving the shed in such a mess when she was handing out tools, but then again, Raina had been distracted by Morven's odd demeanor, and rightly so. Confused, but not distracted from her mission, Raina leaves the mess and moves to the water valve, cranks it closed, and continues with her plan.

Secondly, she heads over to the front greenhouse door panel, and sits on the floor beside it. Around her are the circuit boards she's taken from the dehumidifying door, which sealed Morven inside like a caged lion.

It feels good, but she can't rest on her laurels. The Kepler is still out there, and she doubts her lucky streak of hiding will be able to save her a third time. Now, she's got to think bigger.

After taking the circuit boards apart, and using some spare parts in her tool belt she snagged from the mechanics workstation, she assembles a small remote control, then sets it to the frequency of the greenhouse door.

She tests it twice, clicking the remote. It works. Now, she'll be able to open the greenhouse door from four meters away. It'll save her time when she has to make a run for it.

After that part is finished, Raina stands from the floor to work on the door panel itself. Taking some of the wires from the extra boards, she strips off their plastic protective coating and strings them along until they reach as far up the wall as they can. She uses a staple gun to secure them in place. She then splays the ends of the wires and fans out the edges so they resemble the tail of a comet.

Stepping back, she puts her tools back into her belt, then flicks the switch on her homemade remote control. She grins as sparks shower from the door control panel. At the same time, the door slides open.

"Perfect," she says to herself. She clicks the remote again, closing the door. The sparks stop.

Step one, done. Now for step two.

She starts right where she's standing. She steps up onto the lowest shelf, climbs to the top, then stands beside the alien plants as she reaches above her head and disconnects the tubing that waters the plants.

Driblets of liquid trickle from the plumbing as she does her job, but since the main water line has been closed at the valve by the toolshed, only her arms and hands get wet.

It takes longer than she would like.

Each plant has its own sprinkler, and if her memory is correct, Avram mentioned there were over fifteen hundred plants in this room. She disconnects each one, leaving none untouched. Aisle by aisle. Row by row.

Sweat beads on her brow, and her arms tire. Her back and legs have begun to shake as she climbs up and down on the many greenhouse shelves.

At one point, she loses concentration and can't remember if she's done the connections on the other side of the aisle. Another time she thinks she hears rustling behind her, but then it stops, so she keeps going.

Exhaustion and the humidity sap her. Eventually, she gets so dizzy, she has to rest for a minute. It feels like the longest minute of her life.

During all this, she hears crashes coming from the dehumidifying chamber. She guesses that Morven is attempting to smash his way through the door. Let him try. It's impossible. Maybe he'll get tuckered out and take a nap like a good boy. She has to admit, the idea of a nap is appealing. She's beyond exhausted.

Setting back to work, she finally completes the task of unattaching each and every sprinkler head. Then she makes her way to the air vent in the far right of the greenhouse and attaches a wire straight across the opening, securing it with staples, and connects the ringer from the front door intercom board. If anything attempts to get through, the ringer will sound, alerting her.

With tired and aching bones, she walks back through the greenhouse and by the chamber where Morven continues to pound. She ignores him as she shuffles by, making her way back to the toolshed.

"Hey!" he shouts at her. He stops pounding for a moment and presses his swollen face to the door window. Every inch of him is covered in the rash, from his lips to his eyelids. He looks about ready to pop. "Raina! What are you doing? What's with the sprinklers? Will you please tell me what's going on?"

She shuffles to a stop. "Just stay there and you'll be safe," she says. "I'll deactivate the trap when help arrives. I'll let them deal with you."

"You built a trap? What kind of trap?"

"Just stay there," she warns him again, and moves away.

"You'll need my help!" he yells after her. "I can help you. We'll trap the Kepler together. You can't do it by yourself, you can't! Your trap could fail! Your other one didn't work. Remember? Then what will you do? You'll need someone to bail you out like always. Let me out. Please! I'll help you trap it. Come on, you know you need me. After all, you're just a mechanic."

Raina's feet stop moving.

Just a mechanic.

She *is* just a mechanic, and a failed one at that. She's a flunky, a rule breaker, a useless ensign who wouldn't know a regulation repair if it bit her on the ass. Two years' worth of Osric's abuse comes crowding through her mind. She rehears every word. She feels every defeat anew. She is *just* a mechanic.

Raina sucks back tears of hurt and anger and she turns to face Morven. She looks at him intently, taking in every detail of his desperate eyes and large meaty hands pressed up against the glass window. His face looks engorged and contorted.

"Rain," he calls to her, his swollen eyes pleading.

Something snaps within her.

Just a mechanic, huh?

She sets her jaw and squares her shoulders.

Pollux, she reminds herself. *Niall. Tamsin.*

Me.

She raises the middle finger of her right hand and glowers at him as his eyes go wide. "Go fuck yourself," she says, then she shuffles off toward the toolshed.

Something in him breaks. Like a crazed switch, he goes from insincere calm to ballistic in two seconds flat. He shouts obscenities and screams at the top of his lungs, hammering the door with his fists and then slamming the bulk of his weight against it like a sledgehammer – he's lost all control.

Raina watches him lose his mind, but she's immune now. Let him.

Just a mechanic. Just a mechanic, my ass. If I'm such a mess of an ensign, why the hell am I the only one left?

It's not just because Morven left her to the last.

She's the one who outsmarted the Kepler on the flight deck. She's the one who got the bay doors open and released the other pod into outer space. She's the one who rigged the sleep chamber door for rapid release. If the others hadn't been shouting at each other over a fake distress signal, the trap could have worked. She's the one who chopped off the Kepler's leg. She's the one who managed to hide from a serial killer and trap him so he wouldn't be able to hurt anyone else. She did that. Just a mechanic.

If Morven is so great, and managed to get outwitted by 'just a mechanic', what does that make him? *Less* than a mechanic.

Raina reaches the toolshed and pulls a step stool over to the main water valve. She sits on the stool, rests her head against the wall, and tries to imagine what a welcome she'll receive when she finally reaches civilization again. She'll have a shitload of explaining to do. And if her plan works, she may have hell to pay. But she can't worry about that. She must go ahead, she must stay focused.

Raina grips the remote control in her sweaty palm, casts her eyes at the main water valve and closes her eyelids.

Just for a moment.

She'll rest for only a second. She needs to gather strength for when the Kepler comes. She'll need all the energy she can muster, if her plan works.

Just for a minute.

Her eyes flicker. She slumps against the wall, slipping into an exhausted slumber.

★   ★   ★

Twenty-Two Months Ago....

Raina squints at Osric. She finds if she peers at him through slit lids, she can almost tolerate the look of him.

"And what chapter of the repair manual details how to fuck up a propulsion system to this magnitude?" he asks.

"Is that a rhetorical question?"

He raises his hand like he's about to slap her and Raina's eyes pop open.

"Don't talk to your superior officer like that!" he barks.

"Okay, sorry."

"Sorry what, Ensign?"

She blinks at him. "Um, sorry, sir."

He bristles with obvious satisfaction. "I've been around this galaxy three times over, and I haven't lost a ship yet. I'm not about to let some second-rate ensign fuck up *my* ship and ruin my reputation. You got me? I don't even know what you did here. This is such a fucking pile of shit, I can't even recognize what you ate."

"Well, obviously whoever designed this propulsion system didn't know the difference between an injector nozzle and a nosecone. How is this supposed to stabilize combustion?" She laughs at her own joke, then taps the coupling, but the look on Osric's face stops her cold.

He's turned a violent shade of purple. "It's stabilized combustion just fine for ten years before you came aboard."

"Yes, but that's my entire point...." She stops mid-sentence and grimaces.

Oh my god, Raina. Shut up!

"While you are aboard my ship, *Ensign*," Osric says, shaking so badly he looks as if he might explode like a geyser of stinky flesh, "you will refrain from unregulated alterations. You will follow the systems manual to the tee. Am I making myself clear? This…" he steams, waving his stubby arm around like a saber and pointing at Raina's work, "…is subpar and inadequate, just like you. You are nothing. You hear me? Noth. Ing. And I am writing you up in the official report for insubordination and unregulated repairs. Now, put that back the way it was, and see that this *never* happens again."

He turns then, stomping away from the workstation with exaggerated footsteps, which only makes him look comical, given his oversized boots.

Raina's not sure whether she should laugh or cry. She's been on board only two months, and she's already getting written up? It's going to be a long two years if Osric is like this the whole time. Maybe he's just nervous because they're about to reach their first destination? Who knows. She turns back to the panel and sighs.

"What the fuck is his problem?" a voice asks.

Morven stands in the doorway. He's looking as sharp as ever. In fact, he's not shaved in a couple days and the stubble gives him an even more rugged, sexy appeal.

Damn him.

"I got creative," Raina explains. "Guess that's not allowed."

"Well, fuck him. I'd much rather have an upgraded ship than an antiquated pile of space junk."

"I thought the same thing, but I should have figured. They were pretty strict back at the Academy about this too. Apparently, it's the same here."

"So much for innovation," Morven says, leaning against the wall beside her and looking a bit too comfortable.

Raina turns back to the nozzle and grabs her wrench, but stops when Morven doesn't move. "You going to watch me?"

"I like watching. Don't you?" He's got a smirk on his face, which makes it pretty clear he's not talking about the ship anymore.

She stands, still gripping the wrench in her hands. Whether or not he's too forward, she still finds herself grinning back at him like an idiot. "You've got a mouth on you, don't you?"

"I certainly do. Would you like to taste it?"

"Morven!"

He chuckles and tosses his head back. The muscles in his jaw clench and damn it if Raina doesn't feel her knees weaken.

"What time is your chow break?" he asks, looking smug and charming all at the same time.

"I'm done in two hours."

"Great. Then it's a date."

"Now hold on. It isn't a date. You heard the captain. No fraternization. I'm in enough trouble already."

"Yeah, I heard him. But I also know you're a creative type who doesn't like following regulations and wouldn't mind getting into a little trouble. Am I wrong?"

She doesn't exactly like that he's figured her out so quickly. What's with this guy? He's coming on awfully strong, but she must confess – she kind of likes it.

"Just chow. No hanky-panky," she says, and re-grips the wrench in her hand.

He nods and then smirks again. She doesn't know whether to clock that smile off his face or lick it off.

"For now," he says, and then saunters away, leaving her alone in the workstation.

She watches him leave, enjoying the view, then looks back at the coupling. She knows full well where chow will lead but doesn't want to stop it.

Raina drops down to her knees and sets back to work, laughing at herself.

You're your own worst enemy, girl.

*　　*　　*

Demeter
30.8.2231 AD
1946 hours

Raina jars awake with a snap. What happened? Did she fall asleep? How long has she been out? Her gaze scatters over every inch around her, taking in her surroundings. What woke her up? Something did, but she doesn't know what.

The overhead lights that hang just above the ceiling sprinkler system look the same. The plants all around the toolshed look untouched. Nothing's moved.

She reaches up and wipes sweat and hair from her face, and realizes her hands are empty. She must have dropped the remote when she fell asleep. She checks and finds it at her feet. She picks it up and inspects it for damage. It appears unscathed, but she can't know for sure. It would be a costly mistake if it doesn't work when needed. A deadly one.

A shred of panic festers in her gullet. She debates if she should go back to the greenhouse door and test it again. It's put together with a portable soldering iron and electrical tape, so the contraption is flimsy at best. If she hurries, perhaps she'll have time to fix the remote before the creature shows up. If it shows. She's beginning to wonder if it ever will. If it takes too long to arrive, she could die of starvation first. Or worse, fall asleep again and wake up when it's too late.

She gets to her feet.

It's eerily quiet. There's no more shouting or banging coming from the dehumidifying chamber anymore. Morven's probably curled up in a comfortable air-conditioned ball having himself a nice snooze.

The palm of an alien plant rustles to her left, and Raina darts to the main water valve, ready to crank it open.

But what comes out of the bushes is much worse. It's the barrel of a laser rifle.

"Hello darling," Morven says.

CHAPTER TWENTY-THREE

"Ah, hell," Raina swears as Morven limps out of the bushes. "How'd you get out?"

"Aren't you glad to see me?" he sneers. Swollen, crimson on every inch of showing skin, and wild-eyed, he looks god-awful, limping forward then stopping with a grunt. "I got out using brute strength, *bitch*. I used one of the chairs in the control room to pry the door open. I'm so glad you're finally up. For a while there I thought you'd died."

"You've been watching me sleep?"

"Only for a few seconds," he admits with a shrug of his massive shoulders. "But, now that you're up, tell me about this trap of yours. What's with the sprinklers?"

She eyes the laser rifle in his hands and doesn't bother to hide her scowl. "Why would I tell you?"

"Because if you don't, I'm going to shoot you."

"And if I do, you'll shoot me anyway."

He raises a pus-covered eyebrow. "Give the girl a prize."

"So why don't you get it over with?"

He looks like he's considering it. "You know, I actually did like you."

They both know full well he more than liked her, but she doesn't figure pissing him off now will help her any. "Says the man with a rifle pointed at my head."

"I'm serious. You were fun. You helped time go by quickly on this fucking ship. I'm going to miss you. Well, parts of you, anyway."

Raina rolls her eyes, but her mind is elsewhere. She's formulating a new plan. If she can get the axe out, she can chop off the end of the laser rifle, or at least bend it. That could give her enough time to run away. But he's watching her every move, measuring her like she's some alien plant specimen, and she's not sure she's quick enough. She's fast. But faster than a laser? Not so much.

"I really am sorry," he says, a trickle of sincerity playing at the corners of his mouth.

"I doubt that."

"Give me that thing in your hand," he says.

He reaches out his puffy, red palm, as if she would voluntarily hand over the remote, the only chance she has to survive. With the other rash-ridden hand he grips the laser rifle.

Her breath catches.

Come on, think!

"And tell me," he adds, "what's with the ringer?"

This gets her full attention. "What?"

"The air vent," he says. "I don't get it. That alarm that went off. And that thing in your hand – what is that? A remote? And the sprinklers, and the air vent? What's the trap? It's so bad I can't figure it out."

"I attached a ringer to the air vent grate to warn me when the Kepler arrives," she whispers. The palm of her free hand goes to her axe handle. "It's in here with us."

Morven's eyes flash with surprise. "Bah! You're full of shit. You're messing with me."

"Shhh!" she hisses at him. Her eyes dart around the greenhouse, up and down, every inch of the toolshed, the aisle leading off to the glass enclosure, the path leading to the front door. They all look clear. Then her eye catches: four yellow eyes and a purple stump.

"Morven," she whispers as she bends into a crouch, "it's right behind you, on the left."

"Bullshit," he says. "You just want me to turn around so you can plant that hand axe into the back of my skull."

"I'm not kidding!" she whispers harshly. "Move a little to your right. Just move."

"Fuck you."

"It's going to pounce on your head! But you know what? On second thoughts, stay right where you are."

"All right!" he says, using the full volume of his deep voice. "This is ridiculous. I'm so over you." Using both his hands, he grips the laser rifle and pulls the butt up to his shoulder, ready to fire. "It's been fun. Bye, Rain."

Just as his finger squeezes the trigger on the laser rifle, Raina dives to the side and grasps her empty hand around the circular lever of the main water valve. As she falls to the floor, her left hand twists, turning on the sprinklers above. In a matter of seconds there's a downpour. With all the sprinkler heads having been disconnected, water pours everywhere, all over the greenhouse, hitting the plants, the walls, the metal shelves, the grated floor, and drenching Raina, Morven, and the Kepler.

Raina hits the ground outside the toolshed and slides on her side. She just has time to see Morven shove aside the Kepler mid-flight, using the tip of his rifle to keep the beast at arm's length.

The Kepler roars as it's tossed and crashes into a shelf of tall fernlike plants, knocking them all to the floor. But the beast recovers quickly, despite still missing its front limb. It turns on Morven again.

This is her chance. She scrambles to her feet, slips behind Morven as he whips the machete from his utility belt, and runs as fast as she can down the aisle that leads to the greenhouse door.

"Raina!" he calls to her, as if asking for help, as if he hadn't just tried to shoot her thirty seconds before.

She doesn't stop. Her boots pound the floor as her right hand grips the remote control with a hold so tight, she's half-afraid she's already triggered it. But that can't be. They'd all be dead if she had.

From behind she hears the unmistakable crashing of the Kepler. It smashes and bounds after her, from aisle to aisle, row to row, in hot pursuit. She casts a glance over her shoulder and spots it, slicing its way through the alien plants as if they were air.

Where's Morven? Did he get away?

With a burst of speed she rounds another corner.

Water gushes everywhere, blinding her eyes, and covering the entire greenhouse with a thick, dense fog.

Almost there. Almost....

She sprints down a straight aisle. Her legs tire and her body fights against this burst of energy. Suddenly, a rush of searing hot pain shoots through her leg, knocking it right out from under her. She hits the ground with a crash and skids in the water. A wave of liquid splashes her face.

Her free hand flies to her thigh. She's been shot. The pain is almost blinding. Luckily for her, she's been hit in the meaty part of her leg, and since she was shot with a laser, the heat from the blast cauterized it immediately.

Sheets of water cascade from the ceiling and pour into the wound, expanding the pain tenfold. But she's not dead, or mortally wounded. She can still make it, if she can get up.

She struggles to get on her feet, but her leg gives out, sending her back down. Another laser shot rings out and sears the floor an inch from her head.

There's only one explanation: Morven's trying to stop her from using the trap. He knows what she's doing. He's figured it out. He knows he'll die too, if she sets it off.

Crawling on hands and knees, she reaches for the floor in front of her, one hand at a time. Stretching and clawing like an animal, she moves across the ground, desperate. The greenhouse door is just ahead, only meters away.

Another shot near misses. She flinches. This time she can feel the heat as it burns a hole in the ground beside her.

She claws on. She can still hear the Kepler approaching. The floor shakes as it bounds from shelf to shelf, slicing from aisle to aisle as it nears.

She looks up at the door. Still so far to go. She's never going to make it at this speed. She tries to get up again and then someone screams.

But it's not Morven.

Confused, Raina turns to look.

Pollux is there, bellowing with rage and flying through the air as if in slow motion. Above her head she holds a mattock – a flat-headed pickaxe – and she's aiming straight at Morven's head.

Caught by surprise, he raises his hands, trying to fend her off, but Pollux descends with a crazed vengeance. Swollen and red, she screams at the top of her lungs. Using her full body weight, she slams the mattock straight through the top of Morven's skull, cracking it open like a melon. In a heap, he collapses. On his way down, Pollux yanks the mattock out of his head, and hits him again, crushing his head flat. Blood, and chunks of scalp and brain, splatter and mix with the gushing water, painting the entire area scarlet. But Pollux doesn't let up. She continues to hack with the mattock, again and again, screaming, until Raina can no longer stand the sight and is forced to look away, dazed and in utter shock.

The sound of the approaching Kepler awakens her. Raina looks around and spots it. Twisting back, she stumbles to her feet and toward the door. She trips once and falls, but quickly gets up again.

The Kepler jumps from the shelf and lands on the ground behind her. Just as its front leg swipes for her, a mattock flies through the air, catching the creature square in the spine. The beast rears up, squealing and flailing.

Pollux runs up the aisle, straight for the creature, wrenches her mattock free, and hacks it in the face again, imbedding the blade between its eyes.

The biological howls and swipes but misses Pollux. She scrambles out of the way and sprints toward the greenhouse door.

Raina can hardly believe her eyes. In desperation, she dives, hits the floor, and slides across the slippery greenhouse grates. Flicking the remote switch in her palm, she activates the door. Sparks shoot everywhere.

As she slides, Raina feels the burning jolts and heat from the electricity as it conducts through the cascading water into the greenhouse and courses through her body.

Still slipping forward with the help of the water, her wails of agony mix with Pollux's as they skid through the door.

Raina smashes into the hallway wall just on the other side. The force of the blow opens her palm, and the remote scatters from her hands. It slides from view. She scrambles on all four limbs, diving at the exterior door controls. But Pollux gets there first. She slaps it with the tip of her swollen middle finger.

The greenhouse doors hiss closed.

Raina and Pollux are left on the other side.

★   ★   ★

Two Years Ago....

Captain Cabano walks down the line of crew, inspecting each of them with an air of suspicion. As far as Raina can tell, there are seven officers, plus the captain, and five ensigns, which seems like a huge crew for such a tiny ship.

When the captain's eyes pass over her, she feels her stomach take a nosedive.

What if he hates her? What if he thinks she's the biggest idiot in the universe?

This is possible. There were plenty of instructors at the Academy who told her as much. But thank god, that's all behind her now. This is a new beginning. Her fresh and well deserved start. She's going to take this crew and show them just what she's made of. She can hardly wait.

"On this two-year mission," the captain says, pausing for a split second in front of her, then walking on, "we are tasked with collecting plant life from the multiple habitable planets identified by the Planetary Habitations Committee. We will have little to no contact with any other humans than those aboard this ship during this time frame. I expect professionalism, courtesy, and absolutely no fraternization of any kind. Am I making myself clear?"

An older, slick, short-haired female officer at the end of the row stares straight ahead, but nods. "Sir. Yes, sir."

Raina watches her from her peripheral vision. She looks downright fierce. Raina knows she's a science officer of some kind, but the captain hasn't gone over names yet. She wonders if the officer is that severe all the time. Or if she's only like that when the captain is around? Only time will tell.

She just hopes her own superior officer is a little more relaxed.

"Ensigns will report directly to their departmental superiors," the captain continues, "and maintain decorum on and off duty. I can and will jettison you from this ship in an escape pod if you annoy me."

There's a snort of laughter from the super-tall and skinny ensign beside Raina. His Adam's apple bobs up and down and his unibrow scrunches together. She can only guess he's fighting to stop himself from snickering, although she's not sure why. The captain doesn't seem the type to make false threats.

Luckily, he ignores the ensign's laugh and spins on his heel in the other direction. "Despite my expectation of professionalism I do want this crew to operate like a tightly knit family, therefore we'll be referring to each other by our first names – except for myself, of course. Do your job. Do it well. Be good to one another, and these two years should fly by. Now, ensigns, report to your departmental workstations to receive your orders. Officers, we depart in three hours. Dismissed!"

The captain stomps away and the tension in the room visibly relaxes.

Down the single row of crew members, Raina takes a second to inspect the officers, wondering which one will be her superior. Just as her eyes settle on this puffy, sort of gnomish looking man, a tall and muscular frame stands directly in front of her, blocking her view.

It's another ensign, given the insignia on his shoulder. Raina grins up at him and tries not to let her mouth drop open. He's actually kind of hot.

"I'm Morven," he says. His voice is deep and a little gravely. He sticks his large and meaty hand out and Raina shakes it lightly. "Science department," he says, looking proud. "And who might you be?"

"I'm Raina, mechanics."

His eyes shoot wide. "A mechanic? Are you serious? A little thing like you?"

She nods and presses her lips together. If she had a nickel….

"I never would have guessed that," he says. His eyes roam up and down her tiny body in a flash and she feels her cheeks flush. "Although, I guess your height comes in handy at times."

A smile creeps onto her lips. "How do you figure that?"

"You know, for crawling into small wall panels, or something. Stuff like that."

She smiles and he grins back. He's even cuter when he smirks.

Did the captain really just say if she fraternizes with the crew she'll be jettisoned into space? That's a shame. This guy is the hottest thing she's seen since she joined the Space Corps and now she's stuck two years without being able to do anything about it. What a disappointment.

"Well, it mostly comes in handy for not being able to reach ceiling panels without a step ladder or having to climb on top of tables to retrieve tools off a shelf."

"I'd love to see how you handle your tools," he says, his face like stone and his eyes ablaze.

For a split second, Raina's unsure if she heard him right. Did he just...?

But then he laughs, his face beaming again. "Don't look so shocked. I'm only teasing you."

"Ha. Right. Teasing," she says, suddenly flustered and hating herself for it.

"Come on, you two," says another ensign, a girl who looks young enough to still be in puberty. She flips her ponytail and winks at Raina. "No time for chitchat. There's plenty of time for that later."

"You got it, Mom," Morven says. He turns back to Raina and rolls his eyes in a melodramatic sort of way. She giggles and he beams at her.

Shit. Did she just giggle?

"Catch you later, Raina," he says, as if tasting her name on his tongue. He turns and follows the tall and skinny ensign with the unibrow to the access shaft leading down.

Raina watches his ass as he climbs.

Oh man. This guy's trouble.

*   *   *

Demeter
1.9.2231 AD
0030 hours

Raina sits in the command chair of the flight deck, her hands shaking with exhaustion, her body chilled to the bone. Freezing drips of water from her hair drench her body, tapping her with frigid droplets. Her muscles ache from her momentary electrocution.

She's in shock but can't move to remedy it. All in good time, she supposes. She wishes she were sorry for what she's done, but she's not. She only did what she had to do.

Tears burn her eyes as she remembers the sight of the greenhouse when she and Pollux looked through the window. The plants shriveled and baked before their very eyes. The leaves twisted and crinkled like burned paper. Two years' worth of research and space exploration, gone in seconds.

Then, there was the Kepler. It smoked and writhed on the floor, just on the other side. Its eyes popped like kernels. Its smoking tongue hung from its burning lips.

The sight was enough to give her nightmares for a lifetime. But she's here. She's alive. And she can't and won't wish it undone.

She looks over at the pilot's chair and eyes Pollux. God almighty, she looks horrendous. Even with the antihistamine Raina gave her from the spare med kit she found on the flight deck, the rash has consumed her entire body, swelling her hands, feet, face, arms, and everything else. And she obviously has a fever. It's maybe driven her mad. But the moment the Kepler and Morven were dead, and the door was closed, her aggression seemed to melt away and she patted Raina on the head.

"Mama says, 'Well done,'" she'd said. As if Raina knew what the hell she was talking about.

Hopefully, a ship will come and give them medical help in time to save Pollux from whatever it is that's infecting her, and maybe even find the source of it, but Raina's honestly not sure that's probable. They're way the fuck out in the middle of nowhere, and given how bad Pollux looks, they may not make it in time.

She reaches across the captain's console and types. When she finishes, she reads what she has written and with a click, posts it. It reads:

DEMETER IN DISTRESS.
FOREIGN BIOLOGICAL ABOARD AND CONTAINED.
CAPTAIN CABANO AND PILOT DAVENPORT, DEAD.

LIEUTENANTS SORREL SPALDING AND VALDA RUIZ, DEAD.

SENIOR AIRMAN OSRIC LAWSON, DEAD.

CORPORAL GAYLA ZENAS, DEAD.

SERGEANT NIALL RIGLEY, DEAD.

ENSIGNS KRIS CUNNINGHAM, AVRAM GERSHOM, TAMSIN NANSEY, AND MORVEN ALPIN, ALL DEAD.

SURVIVORS TECHNICAL SERGEANT POLLUX TATE AND ENSIGN RAINA TEAGUE REQUEST TRANSPORT TO HEADQUARTERS.

COME AND GET US.

When she finishes, Raina leans back in the chair and rests her head.

She supposes she should get to the task of drying off, maybe finding herself and Pollux a change of clothes.

She still has a wound on her leg, but the pain has ebbed to a dull throb. Then there's the chore of disposing of all the bodies, cleaning up the carnage, but she can't quite stomach the idea. She knows they can't wait too long. If they do, things will get disgusting pretty quickly – if Pollux is even able to help.

Maybe tomorrow. It could be days before she gets a response, she'll have time to kill. The thought makes her cringe.

Her eyelids weigh on her. She'd like nothing better than to pass out and drift into oblivion. But images from the past twenty-four hours haunt her every waking thought.

Maybe they'll take a break if she's asleep, but she doubts it.

So tired. So much to do.

The command console beeps once, snapping Raina from her daze. A communiqué has been received.

Dropping her feet to the floor, she leans forward in the chair and clicks it. There's a long paragraph from another cargo vessel, requesting her exact coordinates, and asking the nature and classification of the foreign biological.

She types her response and sends it back.

She's almost afraid to hope. She didn't expect to find a ship so close.

They could force them into quarantine, especially considering Pollux's condition. Perhaps there's hope for her yet.

Even then, they could cure her only to convict Pollux for murdering Morven. And what if Raina's blamed for scorching the payload?

Another communiqué blinks on the command station monitor.

Upon reading the three words, Raina's floodgates erupt, and she's consumed with sobs of relief. Whatever happens, at least the worst of it is over.

The communiqué reads: ON OUR WAY.

ACKNOWLEDGMENTS

I wrote the first draft of this novel back in 2013 and it went through multiple, multiple, oh my god, *SO MANY* revisions, before it reached this version. It was my first agent, Bree Ogden, back in 2014 – maybe 2014? Who honestly knows anymore? – who suggested I use an inverted timeline and pressed me to develop Morven into a full-blooded character, versus a stereotypical walking fragile male ego. Thank you, Bree. For *everything*. Despite her best efforts, it didn't sell then. I can honestly say, I don't think the world was ready for it yet.

My next agent, in 2017, didn't want to touch it with a ten-foot pole, and I didn't blame her, considering how far and wide it had been shopped. So, *Screams* sat for another few years, gathering dust.

In 2019, after the #MeToo movement, I reread the manuscript out of morbid curiosity. All the feminist rage, all the internalized misogyny, all of it was still very much my truth, and maybe (?) I thought, the world was ready for it now? – so I pitched it to my third agent. Bob Diforio shopped it to a few select places and Don D'Auria at Flame Tree bought it. I was equally thrilled and terrified.

Over the years, and the many rewrites and iterations this manuscript has had, I had a plethora of beta readers. At one point, I think between my second and third agent, I threw away the list I was keeping of everyone I needed to thank for this book. I didn't think it would ever be published. I deeply regret tossing that list because a lot has happened since 2013, and I simply don't remember everyone who beta read for me. So, if I miss you, or give you credit where there is none, I'm so very, very deeply sorry. Please forgive my Swiss cheese brain. It means well.

First and foremost I'd like to thank Lupe Diaz Ibarra for reading through my Spanish and making sure I didn't sound too much like a stupid white lady who learned Spanish in high school and on Duolingo, or used Google Translate. Thank you!

Shelli Cornelison, Robin Reul, Emily Suvada, and Lisa Marnell were my early beta readers...that I remember. Thank you! Buckets of love also to Meredith Glickman for her effervescence and tireless support.

My apologies to anyone I've forgotten.

All my thanks and appreciation to Don D'Auria and the crew at Flame Tree, who have been amazing. Thank you!

Bob Diforio is an amazing mentor and a great agent. Thank you!

My father, Robert Snodgrass, dropped out of electrical engineering college after he was in a terrible car accident that broke both his legs in 1967. It changed the course of his life, but he was knowledgeable enough to walk me through how to make a theoretical homemade taser using a soldering iron and spare parts. He didn't live long enough to see this book in print, but I will always cherish that phone conversation when he talked me through it. He was having a ball.

To Daniel, the girls, to Mom, Wendy, Allan, and Erin – I love you all.

This one's for Dad.
Xoxo
– LoriAnne aka 'Anne Tibbets'

FLAME TREE PRESS
FICTION WITHOUT FRONTIERS
Award-Winning Authors & Original Voices

Flame Tree Press is the trade fiction imprint of Flame Tree Publishing, focusing on excellent writing in horror and the supernatural, crime and mystery, science fiction and fantasy. Our aim is to explore beyond the boundaries of the everyday, with tales from both award-winning authors and original voices.

•

•

Join our mailing list for free short stories, new release details, news about our authors and special promotions:

flametreepress.com